SPLITTERS

An Amelia Island Mystery

SPLITTERS

An Amelia Island Mystery

E. Louise Jaques

Jan-Carol
Publishing, Inc

"every story needs a book"

SPLITTERS
E. Louise Jaques

Published February 2014
Little Creek Books
Imprint of Jan-Carol Publishing, Inc

ISBN: 978-1-939289-34-6
Library of Congress Control Number: 2014902528

You may contact the publisher:
Jan-Carol Publishing, Inc
PO Box 701
Johnson City, TN 37605
E-mail: publisher@jancarolpublishing.com
jancarolpublishing.com

To my wonderful husband, Mike. Our life together has been an amazing adventure since 1972, and I'm looking forward to the adventures yet to come. Thank you for being a great partner and father. I love you, heart and soul.

To our incredible children, Matt, Becky, and Tom. I am eternally grateful that you chose me to be your mother. Your love, support, and steadfast belief in me have brought great joy to my life. You inspire me every day with your intelligence, passion, achievements, and loving hearts.

ACKNOWLEDGMENTS

I would like to thank my editors—Amanda Cook, my niece and friend; Amy Frazier, with Little Creek Books; and Mike, Matt, Becky, and Tom Jaques—for their assistance and insight.

A special thank you to the creative Kristen Chumley for the cover design and for being the lovely model in the cover photo of my first novel, *Dreams of Amelia.*

I am grateful for the encouragement and support of my siblings: Mary, Virginia, Maddie, Anita, Tony, Brian, and Veronica. I love you all.

CHAPTER 1

THANKSGIVING SURPRISE

*N*ow *that my dream has come true, is it really what I want?* Laura thought as she wrapped her sweater tight against the cool ocean breeze and gazed at the stars in the evening sky. It was a dream born of a burning desire to find purpose in the next chapter of her life, coming together with a vacation to Amelia Island, Florida, for her 55th birthday the previous May.

"This is the strangest Thanksgiving ever!" she called to her husband, John, who was intently watching the television in the great room. "Our children are far away, we're in a condo on the beach, and we're moving into a second home tomorrow."

"I really miss having the kids with us, too," John said. "Next year we'll all be together again. TOUCHDOWN!"

Laura usually enjoyed watching football, but tonight she wasn't in the mood. She closed the glass door to silence the noise of the cheering Dallas fans on TV and listened to the calming sound of the waves. She took a sip of wine as she settled into a comfy chair on the deck of the rented townhouse and thought back to their first visit to the area. Within hours of her and John's arrival, there was a magical feeling that this beautiful, tranquil island was calling her home, and by Labor Day weekend they were buying a lovely home within walking distance to the beach. Her dream now included writing a novel set on Amelia Island.

After watching the moonlight dance on the water for a while, Laura turned on her laptop, went to Google Earth, and typed in the address of their oldest son, Steven's apartment in Paris. The image zoomed over the Atlantic Ocean to the City of Light. Then she traveled across Asia to their daughter's place in Sydney, Australia, where Jenny was working for six months.

The next trip around the globe brought her to Kate's house in Seattle. Their youngest son, Jack, was spending the weekend with his college girlfriend's family. Her heart was filled with love and pride for her amazing children. And finally she zipped over the US to their new house that was located near Jacksonville, in the northeast part of Florida.

"It's like our family's scattered to the far ends of the earth," she whispered to the night sky while blinking back tears. *The hardest part of being a mother is letting your children go.* As she turned off the computer and opened the sliding door, a shot rang out.

"John, did you hear that? It sounded like a gunshot!"

"No, I didn't hear anything. It's probably an old car backfiring."

Laura rushed into the kitchen and opened several drawers before finding a working flashlight. "Honey, I'm going outside to check it out. I won't be long."

"The game's almost over; I'll be out in a minute. Be careful."

Laura walked around to the back of the condo and across the wooden boardwalk, straining to hear any unusual sounds in the night. Carefully stepping down on the sand she turned off the light, held her breath, and listened. The endless waves washing on the shore were all that she could hear. Breathing deeply to calm her jangled nerves, she walked north along the beach.

The flashlight shook in her hand as the light danced in front of her. She aimed it right toward the water and then left toward the sea oats and dunes. At the second boardwalk, she noticed something on the far side of the steps. Laura gasped as the beam of light landed on a pair of men's shoes and pants with the owner still inside of them.

"Oh my God!" she cried. She was frozen in place until she felt a hand on her shoulder. She jumped, screamed, and dropped the flashlight. John put his arms around his wife and laughed. "Sweetie, it's just me."

Laura hugged her husband before retrieving the flashlight and whispered, "John, over there." She pointed the light toward the boardwalk. "I can't bear to look!"

John took the flashlight and walked over to the body. He carefully leaned over and checked for a pulse, then took out his cell phone and dialed 911.

CHAPTER 2

FERNANDINA BEACH

"I'm such a coward."

"Who are you talking to?" John asked as he brought more empty moving boxes into the garage on Friday morning.

"Just talking to myself—again. I seem to be doing that a lot lately," answered Laura as she slit the tape on the bottom of a box and flattened it under her foot. John walked over to his wife and put his arms around her, pulling her close. He was almost a foot taller, and she felt safe in his embrace. He gently stroked her short, chestnut-colored hair and rested his chin on the top of her head.

"You're not a coward. No one wants to see a dead body. I'm glad I was there to check if the man was alive and to talk to the police. They sure arrived quickly last night."

"I'm happy you were there, too, John. But what if I could have done something to save him and I wasted time by not seeing if he was still breathing?"

"The police said it looked like he died instantly from a single shot to the heart and there wasn't anything you could have done."

"I can't get the picture of his shoes out of my mind, and I didn't want the image of his face burned into my brain."

John released his wife and asked, "Wasn't one of your ideas for a novel about a murder mystery?"

"Yes, I wrote an outline about a 50-something woman who solves a murder on the Island. How strange is it, that life's imitating art? I also had an idea about a teenage girl moving to Amelia who remembers a past life on the Island. At this point, I think that's a better idea. But I want to get unpacked and settled in before I start writing."

"Why don't we take a break from unpacking and drive into town for lunch?"

"And after we eat, let's stop at the hardware store. I need a hammer and picture hooks, and I noticed there was a wasp nest by the front door," added Laura.

"It's amazing that we both felt so at home here the first time we visited," said Laura as they drove up Amelia Island Parkway under a canopy of live oaks heavy with Spanish moss. "I hope the Island inspires me to write. I used to believe in the saying 'bloom where you're planted,' but now I feel it's time to 'find a place where your soul feels at home.' So far my soul is enjoying this place—even after finding a body on the beach!"

They drove north on Fletcher Avenue past an eclectic group of homes including new mini-mansions, old Florida-style houses, and weathered cottages. Several hotels, condos, and restaurants also dotted the shoreline. Heading west on Atlantic Avenue they passed modest, well-kept homes. *I wonder if the people who live in these houses are descendants of the shrimpers and harbor masters, or maybe the pirates or ladies of the night who populated this sea port in its heyday in the 1800s,* Laura thought. She'd read a book about the colorful history of Amelia Island, the 13-mile-long island that had been ruled under eight different flags including the Spanish, French, English, Confederate, and Union banners, among others.

As they entered the historic city of Fernandina Beach, with lovely Victorian houses and 19th century brick buildings, she felt an air of peacefulness in the town, and she wondered how the locals were reacting to a murder on their idyllic island. Parking near the riverfront harbor, they strolled down the tree-lined Centre Street and admired the holiday displays in the shop windows.

After a delightful lunch at Kelley's Courtyard Café on South 3rd Street, and a stop at Ace Hardware, they returned to their home on Hopeful Court near Summer Beach. The Ritz-Carlton Hotel was a short walk away and so was the beach access at Scotts Road. It was a perfect location on an almost perfect Atlantic barrier island.

John kissed his wife and went in the house. *He's still tall, dark, and handsome,* she thought as she watched him walk away. *And I'm still short, and perimenopause is making me more round all the time.* Laura was about to break down another carton when the mail carrier placed something in their box at the end of the driveway. *Maybe it's the package Jenny sent from Australia!* She opened the mailbox and was disappointed to see nothing but holiday flyers. Turning to go inside she was surprised to hear her name being called.

"Laura? Laura Bennett, is that you?" a voice called from across the street. There were only four houses on the cul de sac, and she hadn't met any of the neighbors yet. She looked at the tall, slender, impeccably dressed woman walking toward her. Reaching back into her memory, she was shocked to see her one-time best friend approaching.

"Oh my God! Cassandra Harcourt! Do you live here?"

Cassandra hugged Laura, and the two women stared at each other for several moments. "Yes, yes, we bought the house last summer. I thought I'd never see you again. You look great! Are you still living in St. Louis?"

It took Laura time to recover her composure. She was shocked to see someone she'd met her first year of high school, when she moved to Andover, Massachusetts, from Toronto, Ontario, Canada. For two years Cassie had been her best friend. *She's just as beautiful at 55 as she was at 15,* Laura thought.

"Yes, we have a house there, and this is our second home. Now that the kids are gone, we decided to invest in a place in Florida. John will probably be working for another decade, but we thought we'd get a house near the ocean where we could all be together for vacations and the holidays. Did you move here with Justin?"

Cassandra sighed, "Justin was two husbands ago. I'm married to Robert Armstrong now, and he's still in Boston for the next two years until he retires. I just dropped him off at the airport, because even on a holiday weekend, nothing's more important than his career. I know I shouldn't complain; he's one of the top defense attorneys in New England."

"How often does he come down?"

"Once or twice a month. We decided our daughter, Allison, should go to one high school instead of making her move here in her junior year. We bought this place last June so she could start at Fernandina High."

"Mom, I'm ready to go!" called a pretty, blond girl as she ran across the street toward the women.

"This is my daughter, Allison. This is Mrs.—sorry, Laura, I don't know your married name."

"It's Beck. Nice to meet you, Allison. How do you like high school?"

"It's okay. It's a pretty good school, and I'm starting to make friends. I love hanging out at the beach, and it's awesome that we can walk there from the house."

"That's one of the reasons we bought this house too," Laura added. "It's great to have the ocean so close."

"We'd better go or we'll be late for Allison's piano lesson. It was so nice to see you again, Laura. We'll have to get together soon," said Cassie.

At that moment, a car drove up, and Laura's real estate agent, Janice Blackwell, got out along with a young girl. "Laura, how was the move? Are you getting settled in?"

"Hi, Janice, and this must be Lexi," Laura said, then she introduced Cassie and Allison.

"Hello, it's a pleasure," Janice said. "Are you a 'splitter' too?"

"I'm sorry, what's a splitter?" Cassandra questioned.

"It's what some of us in real estate call people who 'split' their time between two homes and aren't near retirement. It's usually couples with grown children who want to spend time in a vacation home on a regular basis. It creates a lot of business for realtors and the airlines. Your neighbor, Faith Proctor, splits her time between Atlanta and Amelia. I sold her the house three years ago."

"My daughter and I live here full-time, and my husband comes down from Boston when he can."

"Mom! We're late for my lesson," pleaded Allison.

As they started to leave Janice said, "Oh, did you hear about the man who was murdered last night? I couldn't believe it! Right here on Amelia Island! What's this world coming to? His name is—I guess I should say was—Eduardo Conti, and he was shot on the beach just outside his house. My cousin, Sheila, works at the police station, and she called me this morning to fill me in."

Cassandra stopped walking and turned around as all the color drained from her face. She stared at Janice.

"Cassie, what is it? You're white as a sheet," said Laura.

"I, um, we bought on this Island because we thought it was a safe place for Allison and me. We wanted to leave the big city, especially after the bombing at the Boston Marathon. It's unnerving to think there was a murder so close to our house. Ah, I've got to go. Great to see you, Laura. Nice to meet you, Janice," she said as she rushed to join her daughter.

It's amazing that Cassie lives here, thought Laura. *But she looked like she'd seen a ghost. I wonder how much more upset she'd be if she was the one that found the body. And I don't blame her for wanting to find a safe small town to raise her daughter.*

"Janice, please come in. All we have is iced tea, if that's okay. I think I have some cookies that Lexi would like."

CHAPTER 3

THE CRASH

Amy Temple drove past the shopping mall in the drenching autumn rain. She was grateful that she wasn't among the day-after-Thanksgiving shoppers trying to juggle their umbrellas and overstuffed packages. Arriving at her friend Faith's home in Buckhead, she tried to ignore the ache in her heart from the fact that her husband, Doug, wasn't with her today and would never be sharing the holidays with her again. She'd moved to Atlanta to be with him and now he'd broken her heart and left her in a strange city on her own.

Thank goodness Faith is in my life. I don't know how I would have survived the past few months without her, Amy thought as she rang the doorbell. Austin Proctor opened the door with a big smile and gave her a hug.

"Mom's in the kitchen, Miss Amy. Sorry to hear about your split from Mr. Masterson."

"Thanks, Austin. It's been hard but I'll get through it. Doug moved out last month."

"Didn't you see it coming?" he asked.

"Austin!" admonished Faith as she walked in the front hall. "How could you ask such a thing, young man? Did you learn how to be rude in your first semester of college?"

"It's alright, Faith," Amy said as the color rose in her cheeks. "Just because I'm a psychic medium, Austin, it doesn't mean I can see my own future. Many psychics don't see what's going to happen to them or their loved ones."

"Sorry, Miss Amy. I didn't mean to offend you."

"That's okay. Love is mysterious. Who knows why it lasts or why it ends. No one has all the answers."

"It's lust that never ends," said Miles with a mischievous grin as he walked down the stairs into the hallway.

"Honestly! You boys have forgotten your manners! I didn't raise my sons to be so coarse. And where is your father? He was supposed to be home an hour ago. That man would be late for his own funeral. I don't know what was so pressing that he had to go into his office today."

Austin and Amy began setting the dining room table. "Isn't this new china amazing? I love the gold rim and delicate flowers. I talked Mom into buying this pattern. It looks perfect with the crystal stemware."

How could they not have known that Austin was gay? Amy thought as she placed a vase of flowers in the center of the table. *I'm surprised Faith and Charles took it so hard when he came out.* "It's lovely, Austin. Your mother is lucky to have you help her."

The doorbell chimed. "I'll get it," called Miles as he passed through the dining room giving his brother a punch in the arm as he walked by.

"Miles, you jerk!"

Miles was still laughing as he opened the door but stopped when he saw two police officers standing on the front porch. "Mother, you'd better come here."

"Now what?" Faith said as she walked into the hall then stopped as she saw the officers' grim faces. "What is it? What's happened?"

Amy came out and placed her arm around her friend as the policeman told them that Charles had been in a car accident and was taken to St. Magdalene Hospital. Faith began to waver and Miles rushed over to catch his mother as she fainted. He carried her to the sofa and gently placed her down. By the time Faith recovered, Amy had gotten the details of the accident and told the officers they'd drive to the hospital immediately.

The emergency room was in chaos as they rushed in and inquired about Charles. A rotund nurse led them to a crowded waiting room and said the doctor would see them shortly. Miles paced, Austin prayed and Faith sobbed as they waited. Twenty minutes later, Amy looked up and saw Charles standing in front of her with an unbearably sad look on his face. But it wasn't her friend's husband in the flesh and she knew he had crossed over.

"Tell them I love them and I'm sorry. It was a mistake, a terrible mistake," said Charles' spirit.

"What mistake, Charles?" Amy silently asked but he disappeared before he could answer.

A young, haggard-looking doctor walked into the room. "Mrs. Proctor?"

Faith stood slowly as her sons came and held her on each side. "How is my husband?"

"I'm so sorry, but he didn't make it. We did everything we could. He wasn't wearing a seat belt and sustained severe head injuries. Please accept my condolences."

An unearthly cry escaped from Faith's lips and Amy knew she would never forget the heartbreaking sound. Amy's distress about the end of her marriage was nothing compared to the agony her friend was experiencing at this moment.

CHAPTER 4

SEA GLASS

B illowing clouds drifted across the clear blue sky on Monday afternoon as Laura returned to the seashore near the condo they had rented for Thanksgiving. It was low tide, and the beautiful, wide beach was almost deserted. Off in the distance she could see three horses and their riders sauntering near the shallow waves and thought it might be fun to arrange a time to ride horses when all their children were there next summer.

She'd planned on going home and unpacking after dropping off John at the airport to return to St. Louis, but she found herself being drawn to the beach instead. Looking down she noticed a small piece of milky-white sea glass, and as she retrieved it from the sand, a funny thought ran through her mind. *I used to be as clear and sharp as a shard of crystal but now I'm like this sea glass—cloudy with soft edges.* The idea made her smile but also contributed to her ever-present concern about getting older.

Walking north along the shore, Laura could see the police tape surrounding the boardwalk where she'd discovered the body, and a small group of curious bystanders was milling around the area. A part of her wanted to turn around and run in the opposite direction but her legs kept moving her closer.

"Did you know he was in the Mafia?"

"I heard the FBI was keeping tabs on him."

"My brother-in-law said the IRS had questioned him, too."

Laura listened to the small group standing near the boardwalk. A chalk outline wasn't possible in the sand but she knew exactly where Mr. Conti took his last breath.

"The young man who cares for my lawn also worked for Eduardo. He's told me interesting stories about the Italian. You wouldn't believe the things I've heard!" said an older woman.

"Do they have any suspects?" asked a bearded young man.

"I don't know, but I bet he pissed off some husband. I heard the cops are going to question some of his 'lady friends,' and they want to talk to the couple who found the body," another bystander commented.

Laura gasped at this last remark causing everyone to turn around and stare. Laura spun on her heals and quickly walked back toward her car. *If life isn't random then there's a reason why I found Mr. Conti. I need to find out more about the dead man.* Her ringing cell phone startled her, and she jumped at the sound.

"Hey, Momma, what's up? Are you still unpacking?" asked her son, Jack, calling from the University of Missouri, or Mizzou as the locals called it.

"Hi, Jack. No, I'm leaving the beach and heading home right now. Something 'drew me back to the scene of the crime,' as they say. I feel connected to the man that was murdered, but I don't know why or what I'm supposed to do next."

"Be careful, Mom. Dad isn't there to protect you, and I don't want you to get hurt. There's a killer out there. Let the police handle it."

"I'll be careful, honey," said Laura. Wanting to change the subject she continued, "It's hard to believe you're going to be finished the semester soon and then just one more until you graduate and move to Boston. It's great that you have a job lined up, but we're going to miss you so much. I'm glad you'll be here with Dad and me for Christmas. It'll be strange not being with Steven and Jenny over the holidays."

"More presents for me!"

"Definitely. Have a good week, Jack. I'll talk to you soon."

Arriving at her new part-time home, Laura felt overwhelmed by everything in her life that had led to this moment. Instead of opening another moving box, she poured a glass of iced tea and walked into the screened-in lanai. She dropped onto the chaise lounge and closed her eyes. Breathing deeply, she let the emotions flow.

The trials Laura had faced over the past few years began with her husband's battle with cancer. Less than a year later came the unexpected death of her mother, followed by her older brother, Arthur's, fatal heart attack two months later. All of this, on top of the empty-nest syndrome and her inability to find a decent job, made for tearful nights and anxious days. She felt she was meant to do something meaningful once her children were gone, but she had no idea what that something was.

Then the impulse came to buy a second home in Florida, something Laura and John had talked about since they were married 33 years earlier, after graduating from college. Now she was completely alone for the first time in her life. John would be back in three weeks for the holidays, but she'd never been by herself for this long.

Was buying this house a good decision? Will I be too lonely and get tired of my own company? she wondered. *What will I find out about myself when I'm left with only my thoughts for days on end? I'm such a cliché—a middle-aged woman trying to find herself. How lost am I? Who am I when I'm not a full-time mother anymore? And how do I write a novel? Until John suggested that I write a book about Amelia Island, a novel hadn't crossed my mind. I've enjoyed reading about the fascinating history of the Island, but how do I translate that into a work of fiction?*

The doorbell rang bringing Laura back to the present. A smiling Allison was standing on the front porch with a note in her hand.

"Hi, Mrs. Beck. My mom asked me to give this to you. She hopes you can come."

"Thanks, Allison. Tell her I'll call her later. Are you excited about Christmas?"

"My stepdad doesn't like the holidays very much, so my mom and I have our own special traditions. We decorate the tree and make a gingerbread house, and we used to go on a sleigh ride when we lived up north."

"We make a gingerbread house too. Maybe they'll have horse-drawn carriage rides in Fernandina Beach at Christmas time, and you can start a new tradition."

"That would be wicked cool!" Allison said with her eyes brightening. "It's hard to move away from your friends. I miss our old house and my big bedroom in the attic. Things here sure are different."

"You're right; change is difficult at any age. Thanks for bringing this over." Laura smiled as she closed the door and remembered that she had stopped saying 'eh' when she moved away from Canada and began using 'wicked cool' when she lived in Massachusetts as a teenager. Then she stopped saying 'wicked' when she moved to the Midwest and for a short time started adding 'at' to the end of a sentence, as in "where's the party at?" She discontinued that too once her parents teased her about it.

Laura looked at the note which read, "Join me for a Wining Wednesday at 8 pm. I'm looking forward to catching up on the past few decades. Cassandra." *It's so strange that the person who made me fearful of friendship is back in my life. Will she hurt me again like she did when we were teens?*

CHAPTER 5

CHARLES

" Georgia, Georgia, the whole day through. Just an old sweet song keeps
Georgia on my mind . . ."

Amy held Faith's hand as the choir sang Charles' favorite song at his
funeral on Tuesday morning. The Baptist church was filled to overflowing,
and the sadness was like a physical presence in the room. Faith's parents
and her younger sister, Amanda, had flown in from San Francisco and
were now seated with her in the front row. Her mother and father had
spent Thanksgiving with Amanda before their planned month-long vacation in Hawaii.

Edgar Tomlinson, Charles' boss, gave the first eulogy, which was followed by heart-felt speeches from Miles and Austin. The older boy talked
about his pride in his father's accomplishments and Charles' contribu-
tions to their family and the community. Austin recalled the good times
with his dad and the fact that Charles was starting to accept him for who
he really is.

There was an audible gasp at Austin's last comment, and Amy turned
around and stared at the congregation behind her. *How can people be so
homophobic in the 21ˢᵗ century? What difference does it make to them who Austin
likes?* Faith was lost in her own world and hadn't noticed the reaction to

her son's remark. She was struggling to keep her composure and make it through the service.

At the gravesite, while the family and close friends were huddled under black umbrellas in the drizzling rain, Amy caught a glimpse of Charles' spirit standing beside his wife, but once again he disappeared before she could connect with him.

"I've decided to go to our Florida home tomorrow. I can't be alone in this house right now," Faith said after everyone had left that night and the boys had gone to bed. "Amy, would you please come with me? I told my parents not to cancel their trip to Hawaii, since there's nothing they can do. They've been planning this vacation for two years. Miles and Austin will be going back to school in the morning, and I need to leave too."

"Of course, Faith. I can cancel my appointments for the next few days. We can drive down in the morning and be there for a late lunch. A walk on the beach will do us good."

***

Faith slept for most of the five-hour drive on Wednesday morning and awoke just before they crossed the border into Florida. They got off Highway 95 at the second exit and drove east toward Amelia Island. Crossing the bridge, Faith felt a sense of relief, and the crushing sorrow lifted just a little. As they turned down Hopeful Lane to Hopeful Court, they passed a police cruiser.

"I wonder what that's all about," Faith said. "This is such a boring little subdivision, I can't imagine why the police would be at Mrs. Biddle's house."

"Isn't she that meddling neighbor; the one who keeps poking her nose into other people's business? The bionic busy-body Mrs. Biddle!"

Faith giggled, "That describes her perfectly."

I'm glad Faith has something to take her mind off her terrible loss. I wonder why Charles won't communicate with me. It's so frustrating, and something feels wrong about this whole situation, Amy thought as she pulled into the driveway. They barely had time to get their luggage out of the car when Betsy Biddle waddled over.

"Faith! Did you hear about the murder? Right here on our beach! His name was Eduardo Conti. Quite the Italian lover so I hear. Is Charles coming down this weekend? He's such a lovely man. And who is this? I'm Betsy Biddle. Haven't I seen you here before?" she said without stopping to take a breath.

Amy walked over and held out her hand. "Hello, I'm Amy Temple, a friend of Faith's from Atlanta. I'm sorry to say that Charles was in a car accident last week and passed away."

There was a look of shock on Betsy's face and a look of gratitude on Faith's face.

"Oh my! Faith, I'm so sorry. Why didn't you call me? If there's anything you need just let me know. Any time, day or night."

"Thank you, Betsy, but right now I want to get settled in. I'll talk to you soon," Faith said as she picked up her luggage and unlocked the front door.

"It was a pleasure to meet you, Betsy," Amy said as she followed her friend into the house and shut the door on the meddlesome neighbor. *Faith doesn't need to hear about another death right now. I'm sure Mrs. Biddle will be back to give her all the gory details soon enough.*

They made a pot of coffee, walked out to the lanai, then sat in silence for a long while. "Oh my goodness, Amy, it just crossed my mind that you can see Charles! Have you seen his spirit? Have you talked to him?"

Amy knew this conversation was coming but wasn't happy it came so soon. "I saw him in the hospital when he crossed over. He said to tell you and the boys that he loves you and he's sorry; it was a mistake, a terrible mistake. I saw him again standing beside you at the gravesite but only for an instant. I haven't seen him since."

"What mistake? What in heaven's name was he talking about? The fact that he was speeding and wasn't wearing a seat belt? The fact that he'd been cheating on me—again?"

Faith began to sob, and Amy sat beside her held her close. Charles' infidelity was news to Amy, especially the "again" part.

"Again?"

Several minutes went by before Faith was able to speak. "It happened in the second year of our marriage. She was his high-school sweetheart. What a cliché! A woman, who I thought was my friend, told me about it, and she delighted in giving me the news. Charles ended the affair and promised it would never happen again. It wasn't completely his fault, though. I was going through a difficult time and was despondent and withdrawn. In a way I can't blame him for looking elsewhere for affection."

Amy was silent. She didn't want to press her friend for details if Faith wasn't prepared to say more. She was confident the facts would reveal themselves at the proper time.

"But he'd changed over the past few years," Faith continued. "I know he was concerned about work, and he seemed restless and sometimes even depressed. I think he was trying to recapture his youth with the sports car and the little tramp."

"Faith, I'm so sorry. Charles seemed preoccupied lately, but I thought he was just worried about his job. I had no idea he was cheating on you. Betrayal, secrets, and lies. Is that what so many relationships are all about these days? Let's go for a walk on the beach. We need some fresh air."

Faith and Amy walked north along the shoreline as the wind blew in from the ocean. Faith didn't mind the cool breeze in her face. The chill in the air made her focus on the physical world, taking her mind off her inner turmoil. Up ahead, they could see a small crowd standing near a boardwalk. As they drew closer, they could hear the comments about the man who'd been murdered on Thanksgiving night. A bystander mentioned the dead man's name, and hearing it for a second time, Amy was certain it was familiar but she couldn't place from where or when.

"Do the police have any suspects?" asked Faith.

An elderly man nodded. "I think they suspect his Italian son who's been visiting. From what I hear, there wasn't any love lost between father and son, and several times they were heard arguing in restaurants. This is a small town and word travels fast. But then again it could have been a jilted lover or a jealous husband. Conti was quite the ladies' man—a lothario, as they say."

"There's still a murderer out there, and we don't know if the man knew his killer. I'm having a home security system put in this week. I simply don't feel safe anymore, especially when my husband isn't here," commented a woman who was standing back from the group. "I left the big city to find a safe place, but I guess there are no guarantees."

"Faith, are you hungry? I just realized we didn't have lunch!" Amy said as they left the group and walked south on the beach toward home. "How about an early dinner? What's your favorite restaurant? It's my treat."

Faith didn't answer right away. Every place she thought of reminded her of Charles, and her heart ached knowing they'd never sit in a restaurant again enjoying dinner and discussing their boys.

"There's a place in town called Ciao Italian Bistro that we enjoy. I suppose 'Italy' is on my mind with that man's murder." Faith realized that she'd said 'we.' After twenty-six years as a married woman, she was going to have to learn to say 'I' and 'me' instead of 'us' and 'we.'

When they returned home from dinner, they saw Cassandra standing in her front yard staring at the glorious colors of the sunset in the darkening sky. "Oh, Faith!" she said walking over to her neighbor as she got out of the car. "I'm so sorry. Betsy told me about Charles. You must be devastated. I didn't know him very well, but he seemed like a wonderful man."

Tears came to Faith's eyes once again as she struggled to talk. "Thank you. It's been a terrible shock. I don't know how I'll manage on my own. If you'll excuse me, I think I'll take one of those pills the doctor gave me and go to bed. You don't mind do you, Amy?"

"Not at all. Get some rest."

Faith walked into the house as Amy introduced herself to the tall, raven-haired woman with deep-set eyes and an aquiline nose.

"It's nice to meet you. I'm glad Faith isn't alone at a time like this."

"You sound like you're from Boston."

"I can't hide where I'm from, like Matt Damon. Certain words always give me away. Poor Faith. Charles' death is a tragedy."

Both women looked up into the evening sky wondering why he had died in the prime of his life and in such a terrible way. The sky didn't provide them with an answer.

"Oh," said Cassie, "tomorrow night I've invited a new neighbor over for a glass of wine—actually she's an old friend from high school who just moved into the house across the street. It would be great if you and Faith would join us around eight. Let me know if Faith is interested, but it might be a good distraction for her. I hope to see you both tomorrow."

"Thanks, Cassandra, I'll let her know, and we'll call if she feels up to some company."

CHAPTER 6

EDDIE CONNER

Nightmares invaded Laura's dreams on Tuesday night. Shortly after falling asleep, she dreamed that she was walking along the shore at dusk. Heavy black clouds swept across the sky, and thunder rumbled in the distance. She was drawn to the water's edge, as the waves grew higher. There was a loud bang behind her, and as she turned toward the sound, a gigantic wave crashed over her, throwing her to the sand. She felt a heavy object strike her; when the water receded she saw men's pants and shoes with half a body in them.

Laura screamed in her dream and awoke screaming as well. She was shaking and perspiring as she tried to catch her breath. *Great,* she thought, *the night sweats are back along with the nightmares!* She reached over for John and realized she was alone. She rose out of bed and wandered around the house for the next hour, wondering once again if they'd made the right decision to move to the Island at this time. She was alone and lonely.

Eventually she was able to sleep again, and this time she dreamed she was 15 years old, sitting at her desk in her old bedroom and writing in her diary. Tears splashed on the page as she recounted the betrayal by her best friend on the first day of her junior year of high school. 'How can Cassie be so cruel? How could she embarrass me in front of everyone? I'll never forgive her!' she wrote.

Once again Laura awoke from her dream in a sweat. The sun was rising behind the vertical blinds, so she went into the kitchen to make coffee instead of risking another nightmare. She wished John were there to talk to. He often travelled on business, but this time it would be weeks instead of days until they were together again. With a mug of coffee in hand, she walked into the room Jenny would use when she returned from Australia and started to unpack the moving boxes. In the second box, she noticed a copy of the letter Laura's mother had given to her the night before her wedding. She felt a pang of sadness and loss recalling her mom's joy when she'd handed Laura the note that was rolled up tightly and tied with a white silk ribbon.

AFTER THE WEDDING

If you LOVE unconditionally and show that love in words and actions every day,

If you treat each other with the utmost RESPECT and listen to each other with an open heart,

If you have GRATITUDE for your similarities and APPRECIATE your differences,

If you NURTURE and CHERISH your children but recognize the unique character of their souls,

If you CELEBRATE special moments, both large and small,

Then your marriage will be as wonderful as your wedding.

Congratulations, my beautiful Laura!

I didn't realize that Jenny had a copy of this note. Thanks for your wisdom, Mom. You were right about everything, and I miss you every day.

At the bottom of the third carton, she found some of her daughter's books and among them she spied an old diary. But it wasn't Jenny's diary, it was Laura's—the one she had dreamed about. Picking it up like it was a precious object, she brought it to the kitchen and placed it on the granite countertop. Laura decided she wasn't ready to revisit that chapter of her life quite yet, and she placed it in a drawer. *Why was my old diary with Jenny's things? Did she find it in the basement and read it?*

The ringing phone startled her. "Hi, Laura," Janice said in a chipper voice. "I made the appointment with my hair dresser that I promised you. Her name's Andrea, and she works at the Amelia Island Plantation salon. You're all set for 1:00."

"Thanks, Janice. It was nice of you to do that. I didn't have a chance to get my hair cut before we moved."

"Glad I could help. If you need anything else, let me know."

Just before 1 o'clock, Laura drove south on Highway A1A to the first roundabout at the Plantation. She parked under a massive live oak tree dripping with moss and was captivated by the lovely grounds, boardwalks, and quaint Florida-style market that overlooked a large pond and fountain. Entering the upscale salon, she heard a boisterous woman talking about the drama of the hour. Laura was seated next to the buxom, red-haired woman and couldn't help but overhear the conversation.

"Sheila, what do know about the man who was murdered?" asked a stylist.

"As you know, I hear everything that goes on at the station. I'd seen Eduardo Conti many times in town, and he always gave me the creeps. I was shocked when I read that wasn't his real name. Mr. Conti was actually Eddie Conner from Toledo, Ohio! I thought that Italian accent was phony."

This must be Janice's cousin, Sheila, who works at the police station, Laura thought as her stylist, Andrea, washed her hair. *I wonder what else she knows.*

"I heard he was into money laundering and used his import–export business as a front for criminal activities," said a manicurist. "One of my clients dated him a few times but broke it off when some scary-looking men came to his house one night. She was terrified of getting involved with something illegal. I hear she wasn't the only woman on the Island he was sleeping with."

Laura listened closely as her hair was being cut. *I've got to find out more about Mr. Conti. If I figure out why I found the body, maybe I'll stop having nightmares about him. This is not what I expected my first week on the Island. I was hoping to be inspired to write a novel—not solve a real-life murder.*

Driving back to Summer Beach, Laura thought about the quote from the author Virginia Wolf she had framed on her desk back home: "A woman needs money and a room of her own if she is to write fiction." Laura had more than a room—she had a whole house to herself for a while—and the money came from an unexpected inheritance from her mother. Now there was no excuse for not fulfilling her dream of writing a book and having it published, even though she'd only considered writing a self-help book before. Since they bought the house on Labor Day weekend and John had suggested she write a novel, characters had been roaming around in her mind. But actually sitting down and writing was more difficult than she thought.

The phone rang as she entered the house, and she was grateful to hear John's voice. "How's my best-selling author today?"

"Hi, love. Well, I have a working title for my book," Laura said with a laughed, "I guess that's a start. Even though I've read two books on how to write a novel, I'm still finding it hard to begin. The story about the teenage girl who moves to the island and meets the young man of her dreams—again—is the one I'm going with, but I'm still trying to figure when they had a past life together. Maybe the Roaring 20s would be good."

"Sounds promising. Anything new on the guy we found?"

"I'm starting to get bits and pieces of information. I'll send you an email when I know more. I wish you were here with me and not just because there's still a killer out there. I miss you."

"I miss you too, honey. A few more weeks then we'll be together for the holidays. Have a good afternoon. Love you."

Laura had just hung up when the phone rang again.

"Hi, Mumma. How was the move? Dad emailed me about the body you found on the beach. What's up with that?"

"Oh, Jenny! It's so good to hear your voice. It's still hard to believe you're half a world away. The move went fine, and we still don't know too much about the man who was killed. But how are you? How's the job? Have you made friends? Are you eating well?"

"You're such a mom!"

"It's hard to let go, sweetie. You'll always be my baby, and I'll worry about you until the day I leave this planet."

Jenny laughed. "I guess I wouldn't want it any other way. The job's going well, and I've met some really nice girls that work in another department. We're going out for Thai food and drinks on Friday night. It's fantastic being so close to the beach even though its summer here and pretty hot. It's great being able to walk on the shore every day."

Mother and daughter chatted for the next half hour as Jenny described her interesting life in Australia and the delights of being in a new environment with low-key, multinational people. *This is my greatest achievement. Raising three happy, healthy, independent young adults,* Laura thought. Silently, she sent all the love in her heart to her daughter and then to each of her sons and thanked them for making her a mother.

Only after the conversation ended did Laura remember that her old diary was among Jenny's books. *I'll ask her next time we talk. What else was I supposed to do today? My memory isn't what it used to be. Wine—I wanted to bring a bottle of wine to Cassie's tonight. I'm nervous about being with her after so many years. I hope we can talk about what happened in the past between us. Too many questions have been left unanswered for too long.*

CHAPTER 7

NEW FRIENDS

Walking into Cassandra's family room, Laura was surprised to see two women sitting on a cream-colored leather sofa. The first woman was slim and immaculately dressed, with bobbed, blond hair. *The epitome of a Southern belle,* Laura thought. Even though she'd lived in the US for decades, she still felt different from Americans in many ways. Laura shook the perfectly manicured hand but noticed sadness in the lovely blue eyes.

"Welcome to Amelia Island, I'm Faith Proctor. It's a pleasure to meet you. And this is my friend, Amy Temple." Laura shook Amy's hand thinking she looked familiar.

"I'm afraid I may not be very good company this evening," Faith said softly. "My husband just passed away, and I'm not quite myself."

"I'm so sorry for your loss, Faith. It's wonderful you've even come here tonight," Laura said. Turning toward the petite woman with dark, curly hair and a button nose, Laura saw something reassuring in her deep brown eyes. "Have we met before?"

"You may have seen Amy on television. She's a famous psychic medium, and she helped the Atlanta police find a missing toddler last year," added Faith.

"Of course. That story had a happy ending as I recall."

"Yes, they found the little boy in an abandoned mobile home about a half mile from his house. He was a curious three-year-old who went exploring and got lost. He crawled through a doggy door and had fallen asleep on an old mattress. I wish all the cases I've worked on turned out so well. Cassandra said that you're living here part-time. Where's your other home?" Amy asked.

"St. Louis. My husband, John, travels a lot for business, and he'll come here as often as possible, flying into Jacksonville instead of Missouri for the weekends. We hope the kids will use the house when they can, but right now two of our children are living far away." Laura explained where her children were living and what they were doing. "It's hard having an empty nest."

"My boys, Miles and Austin, are away at college too. I miss them so much," said Faith.

Cassie checked on Allison, who was watching a movie in her bedroom, then carried a tray of filled wine glasses into the great room and handed them out. "To the women of Hopeful Court on this Wining Wednesday. To Faith, who faces life's challenges with grace and dignity. To Amy, who sees beyond the five senses and helps those in need. To my old friend, Laura, who with any luck will become my friend once more. And to Charles, who's watching over us tonight. Cheers!"

The ladies tapped their glasses together, and each felt electricity in the air. Amy could sense Charles' spirit in the room, but she didn't see him. They all took a seat around the attractively decorated room and sipped the wine. They were lost in thought, and no one spoke for several minutes.

"Are you all unpacked, Laura?" Amy asked.

"Most of the boxes are empty, and I still have a few pictures to hang. I was thinking today that I'm going to have to find someone to cut the lawn when we're not here."

"I have a service that takes care of the yard and cleans the house. It's a brother-and-sister team. Although the girl is mentally a little 'slow,' she does a good job. I contacted several of their references before I hired them. I'll get their card for you before you leave," added Cassie.

"That would be great, thanks."

"Betsy told me that the Fergusons next door are moving back to Vermont for a year or so to help their daughter. Their oldest grandchild is autistic, and the youngest is having medical problems. They're thinking about renting out their house for a while," Cassie said.

"Oh my goodness. Amy, why don't you look into renting their house?" asked Faith. "I'm planning on spending a lot of time down here during the winter, and you could live next door. Most of your work is done over the phone or the Internet, isn't it?"

"Yes, and I guess it's a possibility," Amy said then looked over at Cassie and Laura. "My husband and I recently separated, and the lease is up on our apartment at the end of the year. Maybe a change of scenery would be good."

"It's remarkable," commented Cassie "We're all going through major changes in our lives."

"When did you and Laura meet, Cassandra?" Amy asked.

"It was on the first day of high school. Laura had just moved to Andover, Mass. from Toronto and looked like a lost puppy," Cassie began. "I had to rescue her."

"I can't tell you how grateful I was that Cassie became my friend that year. She was my best friend through our freshmen and sophomore years."

"Then what happened?" asked Amy, sensing there was more to the story.

"Oh, I don't know," said Cassie, "I think we just grew apart and started hanging out with other people. You know how fickle teenage girls can be."

Laura smiled and looked away. She knew Cassie didn't believe what she said was true, but now wasn't the time to open old wounds. Laura continued, "I went to St. Louis University, met my husband, and I've lived there ever since. My parents and brother moved back to Toronto when I was 23, so I didn't return to the Boston area."

The doorbell rang. "Who in the world could that be?" Cassie asked as she got up to answer the door.

"Hello, Cassandra. I hope it's not too late, but I got this letter in my mailbox and it belongs to you. Oh, I see you have company. Is it a party?" asked Betsy Biddle as she strutted past Cassie into the family room.

"We were just welcoming Laura Beck to the Court. Please do come in Betsy, can I get you a glass of wine?"

"Just a little, dear. Hello, Laura. You bought the McCreary's house didn't you? How are you holding up, Faith? Are the boys devastated that they lost their father? Are the police sure it was an accident?"

"The boys are doing as well as can be expected. It's a difficult time."

Laura looked at Mrs. Biddle, and she was stunned by the older woman's insensitivity. Cassie walked in and handed the wine glass to her heavy-set neighbor.

"Why were the police at your house, Mrs. Biddle?" asked Amy, turning the conversation away from her friend's tragedy.

"It was about the murder. You know, the man who was shot on Thanksgiving. When I saw his photograph in the newspaper standing next to his expensive sports car, I knew I'd seen it before leaving our neighborhood. It was about a week ago, at one o'clock in the morning. Millie, my cocker spaniel, was barking, and I went to check on her. That's when I saw that Italian man's car driving past my house. In the middle of the night! I can't imagine what he was doing here. So I called the police to tell them what I saw."

"Do they know whose house he was at?" asked Faith.

"They have no idea—yet, but I'm sure they'll find out."

Laura looked over at Cassie and saw the color drain from her face once again at the mention of the murder. Amy noticed Cassie's reaction too. Amy hadn't picked up any psychic information on the death of Mr. Conti, but she'd only been on the Island for a short time and was focused on helping her friend cope with her loss, not on solving a local crime.

Betsy drained her glass and said she had to get back to Millie. Cassandra showed her out and was relieved that her nosy neighbor was gone. "I wonder if Betsy took the letter from my mailbox so she'd have an excuse to come over. I wouldn't put it past her."

"Why did you decide to buy a house on the Island right now?" Amy asked Laura.

"It's funny, I've been through a lot of big things in the past few years. My husband had cancer, my mother passed away, and then my brother suddenly died of a heart attack two months later. But it was a small thing that triggered my longing to try something new.

"It was this time last year when John and I were decorating our Christmas tree, and I picked up a Jiminy Cricket ornament and hung it

29

on the tree. The song *When You Wish Upon a Star* from the Disney movie *Pinocchio* came to mind, and then I reached the line, '*If your heart is in your dream, no request is too extreme.*' I almost started to cry when I realized that I didn't know what my dreams were any more."

"It's something many of us face at some point," said Amy.

"I'd been a full-time mom—exactly what I'd wanted to be—but our youngest child is almost grown. I had no idea what I wanted for the rest of my life. There was a deep pain in my heart that night, and I knew I needed a change. Then we came to the Island last spring on vacation, and I fell in love with the Island. Moving here part-time just felt right."

"I know exactly how you feel about the children growing up," added Faith. "The boys are so independent these days, and heaven knows where they'll find jobs after graduation. I'll be devastated if they don't stay in the South. I have my charity work, but at times I feel I need something more too. And now . . .," she added, fighting back tears.

The three women lowered their eyes, feeling the anguish in Faith's words. At this point—beyond middle age—each had experienced sorrow and loss. They were all past the halfway mark of their lives and had to make decisions about the remainder of their time on earth.

Cassie walked into the kitchen and opened another bottle of white wine. Refilling the glasses, she said, "I knew I wanted to spend more time with Allison. She was growing up so fast, and you know how much trouble teenagers can get into, so I decided to leave the law firm. This jury-consulting job is perfect even though I have to travel occasionally. A young teacher from a local nursery school stays with Allison when I'm away. I'm so fortunate to be able to work on my terms."

"I worked as a proofreader at a direct-mail company when the kids were in college," said Laura. "The women in my department were great, but the job itself was awful, and I finally quit. Finding another decent job at my age was impossible. I felt stuck and sad and longed for something new."

"Unfortunately, I never had children," added Amy. "And my job's so flexible it would have been easy to work around a child's schedule. Life doesn't always turn out the way you thought it would. Twice divorced and childless is not the life I'd imagined."

Allison walked into the room and plopped down on the sofa beside her mother. "Can I have sip of wine?" she asked.

"Absolutely not, young lady! There's chocolate-chip ice cream in the freezer if you'd like some before bed," Cassie replied giving her daughter a hug before the young girl left for the kitchen.

"Does she look like her father, Cassie?" asked Amy.

"My second husband and I adopted Allison. I'm not able to have children."

"I'm very sorry," replied Amy.

"Oh, don't worry. I'm grateful I have my wonderful daughter."

The ladies chatted about their lives before they landed on Amelia Island. Cassie talked about wanting to leave the big city, especially after the tragedy at the Boston Marathon. Everyone in the city had been traumatized by what had happened on that April afternoon, and Cassie had known several people who were injured. The images were seared in her mind, and she knew it had affected Allison too.

After another two hours of conversation, Laura was amazed at the comfort level they had with one another in such a short time together. She was even more surprised how at ease she felt being around Cassandra again after all these years and the ordeal she'd experienced with her one-time confidant.

"Well, ladies," Cassandra said with a muffled yawn. "I've enjoyed your company tonight. I hope we can do this again next Wednesday."

CHAPTER 8

PAOLO

The following morning, Laura drove west on Lime Street past the hospital and turned into the whitewashed, single-story police station with the cobalt blue awning. Fernandina Beach was a small city and it was easy to find whatever you needed. Against the advice of her family to let the matter go, she'd contacted the police to get more information on the victim. As she entered the building to speak with Detective Davis, whom she first met at the crime scene on Thanksgiving night, a booming voice assaulted her.

"Persone sono idioti! Si sta sprecando il mio tempo," a voice shouted. A slim, dark-haired, handsome young man stopped and stared at Laura before charging through the front door. She physically felt the wave of anger he left behind. The tall, stout Detective Patricia Davis walked over and shook her hand. "Please have a seat in the conference room, Mrs. Beck, and I'll tell you what I can."

"Was that Mr. Conti's son?"

"Yes, and he's quite a piece of work. We've asked him to stay in town during the investigation and he's not too happy about it. High strung is an understatement for that guy."

"Detective Davis, I'd heard that Mr. Conti wasn't Italian but his son seems to be."

"That's right. I can't release classified information on the investigation into the murder but I can tell you about the Conti's background since it's on the Internet. Eduardo Conti was born Edward Alvin Conner in Toledo, Ohio. His mother was from Italy and he learned to speak Italian as a child but she died when he was ten, and from what we understand he had a troubled relationship with his father.

"After graduating from Ohio State in 1970, Conner moved to Milan and changed his name. He started an apparel business and eventually moved back to the US, leaving behind an ex-girlfriend and an infant boy named Paolo. He supported them financially but rarely visited. Conti led people to believe he was from Milan and he was often described as a narcissistic con man. He's been on the FBI's watch list for many years."

"Is Paolo a suspect in his father's death?"

"There have been rumors of conflict between the two men and that's what we're investigating. People in town have heard them arguing in public places."

"Are there any other suspects?"

"I can't be specific, but there have been questions about money laundering up North and illegal business dealings. Then again, it might have been an angry husband. There's talk about several married women who were charmed by the man."

Laura decided that Detective Davis would never allow a slick, smooth-talking Italian to tempt her.

"That's about all I can tell you at this point. And if you remember anything else about the night you and your husband found the body, please give me a call."

Laura thanked the detective and walked out into the mild, late-fall afternoon. She turned her face toward the warm sunshine that caressed her face. While absorbing what the detective told her, she decided to go to the beach again. It was the perfect place for her walking meditation. Laura drove to Peter's Point Beach Park, which was one of the several public parks on the eastern shore of Amelia Island. Someday she hoped to walk the entire length of the beach from Fort Clinch on the northern tip to the state park on the south end. She headed north on the nearly deserted shore and pulled out her cell phone to take a photo of a flock of birds. Then she noticed a lone figure standing beside the police-taped boardwalk.

"Amy, I'm surprised to see you here."

"Laura, it's nice to see you again. I had a dream last night about a body washing on shore even though I know the victim was found near the boardwalk. I felt drawn here. I'm surprised the police haven't taken down the tape yet."

"I didn't want to say anything when we were at Cassie's but I'm the one who discovered the body. John and I were renting a condo near Conti's house. And the other night I had a dream that I was standing on the shore and half a body was swept on top of me! Maybe you saw my nightmare."

The two women stared at the site where the body was found. Amy closed her eyes and let impressions flow over her. Mental images flooded her mind as they often did when she was investigating a crime. Laura knew enough to remain silent as she watched several emotions cross Amy's face. At last, her eyes opened and Amy took a deep breath and looked up at the multi-million dollar house that had belonged to Conti.

"He knew his killer. Conti let the person in the front door then they both walked out to the patio then down the boardwalk to the beach, but I'm not sure why," Amy said.

"Did you see who the shooter was?"

"No, but I think it was a man. There was an argument and a single shot. I wish I could get an image of the killer but it's not clear."

"It must be awful seeing murders in your mind. How do you handle the emotional toll it must take on you?"

"I try and compartmentalize my work like anyone who deals with death, the way doctors and undertakers do. I want to use my abilities to help people find justice or closure and solving a mystery makes the stress worthwhile. Would you like to get a cup of coffee? Maybe we could figure out if I was tuning into your dream."

The women walked to the closest beach access and across Fletcher Avenue to The Surf restaurant. They both decided on a glass of pinot grigio instead of coffee and when the waiter left, Amy decided to ask Laura a question that had been on her mind.

"I don't mean to pry but why did you and Cassandra stop being friends in high school? I felt like there was a lot more to the story."

Laura took a deep breath and sighed. "To be honest, Amy, I still don't have an answer. We'd been great friends until she went to Maine for the summer after our sophomore year. She was working as a nanny for a wealthy family and we wrote to each other until the beginning of August. Then her letters stopped and when she got back to Andover on Labor Day weekend, she kept making excuses why we couldn't get together. On the first day of the school year she embarrassed me in front of the entire lunchroom and that was it.

"Cassie changed that summer. She went from being fun-loving and friendly to sarcastic and unhappy. A couple of times I wrote to her and asked her what had happened but she blew me off. Eventually I gave up and when I went to St. Louis University we lost touch. It was a shock to see her the other day."

"She seems friendly but I feel she has a lot of secrets. It was strange—I got the sense that she knows something about the murdered man."

"Oh my gosh, Amy, I thought so too! Both times that Conti was mentioned she turned pale. I thought it was because there was a violent crime so close to our homes but now that I think about it, there's probably more. But we're just getting to know each other again and I don't want to question Cassie about it."

"That's understandable, but I wonder what the connection is. Maybe Faith can give me some insight into what's going on. Poor Faith. I gave her some privacy today to grieve. She's still in shock and needs to process everything. I'm glad I can be here for her and I've been thinking about renting the Ferguson's house."

The anguish on Amy's face was obvious as she thought about the end of her marriage and the death of her friend's husband. *No one is immune to tragedy and pain,* Laura thought. To change the subject Laura asked, "When did you know you had psychic abilities?"

"My mom said I was still in my crib when I started talking to people only I could see. It seemed natural to communicate with them and it took me a while to realize I was actually speaking to spirits. My mom was psychic too and it was hard on my dad, but at least he didn't think I was mentally ill. That happens all too often to psychically sensitive kids."

"What do you do when you're contacted about a case?"

"Well, if someone is missing, which is the most common case I work on, I try and connect on a vibrational level to the person I'm trying to find. I don't look through anyone's eyes as some psychics do. I'm more of a reporter of what I see so I can keep any negative emotions from overwhelming me. In the beginning I tried to feel what the missing person was feeling and see if they were alive or on the other side, but it was too draining and painful."

"So you learned to detach emotionally?"

"Yes. I send positive energy to the person and ask them to communicate with me any way they can, but there are no guarantees. I get visual and auditory impressions and sometimes use remote viewing where I can mentally receive information about specific locations."

"Are you ever afraid for you own safety when you're investigating a murder?"

"Sometimes. That's why I liked having Doug around. He's a tough guy and I felt safe. But the downside of our relationship became too great and I became fearful of his anger. It was the exact opposite of why I married him! Be careful what you wish for."

The women sat in silence for several minutes. "I guess in a way I have some psychic abilities," said Laura. "Since I was a child I've been remembering past lives and I've been doing past life readings for friends and family for twenty years. I've decided to write a novel about a 17-year-old girl who moves to Amelia Island and falls in love with a boy she's loved in a past life. It's one way I hope to open young people's minds to the possibility that a part of our souls return to the earth many times. I'm doing historical research so I can be accurate when I'm writing about the Island's past."

"I'd definitely consider you to have paranormal abilities. It always amazes me how many people do but rarely admit it."

"A while ago, I went to an Afterlife Awareness Conference and it was incredible to meet people who believe in life after death and reincarnation. Many of the attendees had lost children and it was heartbreaking to hear their stories," said Laura.

"I've heard of that conference but haven't gone. Was it mostly people who wanted to contact their loved ones who'd crossed over?"

"It was a real mixture of people—those dealing with their grief as well as ER doctors and nurses, hospice workers, mediums like you, and people who were simply exploring their spirituality. I was in last category."

"That sounds interesting. If you plan on attending again, let me know."

"I will. It was amazing at the dinners that were included in the Conference, when people at the table were taking about their near-death experiences or out-of-body travels, their contacts with ghosts, or communicating with the other side. There's never been another time when I felt so connected with a group of strangers who understood my beliefs."

"It's great when you find individuals of a like mind, but sometimes it can be difficult too. My first husband was a gifted psychic but he was too lost in the spirit world to pay attention to what was going on in the physical world. I loved him and I learned so much from him but in the end, his failure to take care of the simplest things drove me crazy. I left after four years."

"Do you see your own future?"

"No, not usually. Many psychics do see their own futures but I normally don't. I guess that's why I'm going through another divorce. Doug was everything that my first husband wasn't. Stable, secure, in charge of his life and his emotions and when we first met he was fascinated by what I did. He made me feel special and protected. He said all the right things to make me believe he was interested in my ability to help people.

"Yet, in the end, it became obvious that he wanted to use my psychic gifts for financial gain, thinking that if I tried hard enough I could make predictions about his business dealings and spy on his competitors. When I called him on it he became verbally abusive. He didn't physically hurt me but his anger scared me. That's when I knew it was over."

"It must have been hard to take."

"It broke my heart to be fooled by such a chameleon. He had a chip on his shoulder because the Marines rejected him and making money working for a private security company was his way to prove himself. Wait! That's where I've heard Conti's name. I'm sure Doug talked about a business deal with Conti that went bad. I don't really want to, but maybe I should call him and find out what happened. It might give us some clues into why Conti was killed."

Laura looked at Amy and again, she was amazed at how comfortable she felt with this stranger. It was liked they'd known each other forever. *Maybe we have known each other before in a past life and came back together for a reason.*

"This may be not be unusual for you, Amy, but being involved in a crime is something new for me. And I'm not sure I like it! John and the kids are worried I'll get in over my head and they may be right."

"I guess we'll have to protect each other." Amy sat in silence for a long moment. "I've just decided to rent the Ferguson's house. I think I'm needed here and not only by Faith, although that would be reason enough."

"I'm so glad you'll be here for the winter. It's incredible that more has happened to me in the past week than in the past two years. I wanted some excitement in my life and I'm certainly getting it."

"We'll work on this together, Laura. There's someone dangerous out there and he—or she—could still be on the Island."

CHAPTER 9

THE NOTE

Charles is now in heaven with the others I have loved and lost, Faith thought as she walked to the mailbox after the carrier drove by. Among several pieces of junk mail, there was a letter addressed to her in Charles' hand-writing. She caught her breath and held the envelope to her chest. Tears flowed down her face as she slowly walked back into the house. *He must have mailed this from his office last Friday. I'm not sure if I can read his final words.* She placed the letter on the coffee table and stared at it for half an hour before picking it up again.

Amy entered the house and saw the distress on her friend's face. "Faith! What is it? What's happened?"

Faith handed her the envelope. "I can't open it. I can't bear any more unpleasant surprises. It's too much, it's all too much," she said as she walked into her bedroom and closed the door. Amy knew she needed to leave her friend alone. There would be plenty of time later to face what Charles had to say to his wife.

Scrolling down the contacts list in her phone, Amy hesitated before pressing Doug's number. "What do you want?" said her almost ex-hus-band gruffly.

Why does he treat me this way? "Doug, I just wanted to let you know that I'll be moving my things out of the apartment before Christmas. I'm planning on renting a house beside Faith's on Amelia Island. That way you won't have to worry about bumping into me in the city."

"Sorry, Amy. I'm having a bad day. Give Faith my condolences. Charles was a decent guy. It's a good thing you're with her."

"I also wanted to ask you about a man who was murdered last week, and I think I remember you mentioning his name—Eduardo Conti. Didn't you talk about him a while ago?"

"Yeah, the bastard screwed us over in a deal, and I almost lost my job. I wanted to kill the guy. I guess I don't have to think about that now," he said with a laugh. "Asshole got what he deserved."

"What was the deal about?"

"I negotiated the purchase of a new type of ammunition he was bringing into the country under the Fed's radar. But he sold it out from under us to one of those private military companies. Those bloody guys get all the good government contracts. I was trying to contact Conti last week, but then I heard that he was offed," he said.

"What type of ammunition?"

"None of your business. The less you know the better. The screwed-up deal is partly your fault."

Amy could feel the intensity in Doug's voice. She automatically cringed, knowing a verbal attack was coming her way.

"You help people you don't even know, but you wouldn't lift a finger to help your own husband. You could have told me what Conti was up to if you'd wanted to with that remote viewing stuff you do. You're a miserable excuse of a wife!"

Amy pushed 'end' on her smart phone. She couldn't stand any more insults for maintaining her integrity. Sadness flowed through her body, and her heart ached.

***

At dinner that evening, Amy told Faith about her conversation with Doug. Faith looked aghast, and asked, "Heavens! He actually said that to you?" She started to giggle, then they both began to laugh and couldn't stop.

"I guess if we don't laugh, we'll lose our minds," said Amy. "What is wrong with these men? Yours has a mid-life crisis, buys a flashy sports car, and has an affair. Sorry, Faith, I know you're still in shock."

"Don't worry, Amy."

"And mine has work-related problems and blames me! I'll never understand the male mind."

Faith took a few deep breaths and calmed down. "You don't think Doug or anyone in his company could have harmed Conti, do you?"

"No, but if Conti had double-crossed someone else in the private military or private security business, who knows. So many of those ex-military types think the rules don't apply to them."

Faith walked over to the coffee table and picked up the letter from Charles. "I'm ready to open this now."

"You're a steel magnolia, Faith. Do you want me to read it to you?"

"Would you mind?"

Amy opened the envelope and took out a copy of an insurance policy. There was a note attached to the front page, and Amy read, "My darling Faith, I have always loved you, and I always will. I have enclosed insurance information that you should be aware of. Charles." On the second page of the policy, a paragraph was highlighted describing a clause that stated Charles would receive an additional two years' salary if his death occurred at work, traveling to or from work, or at a company-related event. *Was the accident not an accident?* Amy wondered as she handed the document to her friend.

The look on Faith's face gave no doubt that this same idea crossed her mind too. "He wouldn't have sacrificed his life for money, would he?"

"Maybe you should call Edgar and find out what's going on with the company. I know they were in tough shape, but it couldn't be that bad. But why would Charles send this letter here?"

"After I found out about his affair, I told him I was coming here after Thanksgiving for a while. I suppose that's why he sent it to Amelia. But Amy, I can't talk to anyone at his company, and please keep this between us. I'm certain the insurance won't be paid if they suspect he intentionally caused the accident. And I can't survive without his insurance!"

41

Amy sighed and answered, "I won't say anything. In this case, even the suggestion that it may have been intentional would only hurt, not help, and we may never know what really happened." *I wish Charles would contact me and let me know what really happened and why he sent Faith a copy of the insurance policy when he did.*

CHAPTER 10

PARISIAN LIFE

Torrential rains pounded the Island on Saturday morning, and the crashing thunder woke Laura from a sound sleep. She was disoriented when she opened her eyes, not yet accustomed to her new bedroom. Opening the plantation shutters she thought, *A perfect day to start my novel. I've no excuse with weather like this.* She called John while making coffee and chatted about what he was going to do with his weekend. Then she checked her email to see if her kids had sent her a message. Steven had written her from Paris, so she emailed back and set up a time to connect with him on Skype an hour later.

"I know what I want to write about, so why is it so hard getting started?" she asked the chameleon scurrying across the screen door in the lanai. Not surprisingly, he didn't have an answer. Then Laura remembered the diary that she'd dropped in the kitchen drawer. In an instant, she was back in high school, walking with her lunch tray toward the table where Cassie was talking to a group of their friends. As she approached, she heard Cassie say, "Of course she's a virgin. There isn't a single guy at this school who'd want to be with her. She's flat as a board and talks with that stupid accent. She's probably a frigid Canadian." The laughter assaulted Laura, and she'd quickly turned, dumped her lunch in the trash, and ran out of the room.

Laura didn't have to read the diary to remember how her life had changed that day. She knew the friendship was over, and several comments she heard Cassie make about her in the next few months only confirmed it. Eventually she'd made other friends, but when she left Andover, she didn't care if she ever returned. Hurt and betrayal were all she felt when she thought about high school. She never learned what happened that summer to make Cassie destroy their friendship, even though she'd asked a couple of her classmates who had also spent that summer in the same Maine town.

In their junior year, Cassandra started to hang around with kids who liked to party on the weekends, but she was an excellent student and straightened out her life. Laura had heard that Cassie had gone to law school after graduating from Boston College. The kitchen timer beeped, and Laura was glad she'd set it to remind her to turn on her computer to talk to Steven. These days, her memory was not always reliable.

"Mom, Paris is amazing! It's hard to believe I've been here for three months already."

"I can't wait for our visit in March. By then, you'll be an old pro and know the city well. I miss you so much, love."

"Me too, Mom. My first days in Paris were filled with excitement and wonder but also stress and loneliness. It was a totally new experience living on my own in a foreign country, without much knowledge of the people or culture and no ability to speak their language. Emotionally I was up and down, excited at the opportunity to explore such a beautiful and historic city, yet often feeling isolated and alone, as I couldn't communicate with the people I encountered on a daily basis. At times it felt as if I was not actually here in person, instead feeling like I was watching a documentary or live footage of life in Paris."

"That's exactly how I feel here, Steven, like I'm in a movie."

"My inability to interact with people stopped me from enjoying it in the beginning, and I was afraid I'd made a mistake. I missed you guys and my friends, and the comforts of daily life I'd never fully appreciated. In the States, stores are open every day and for long hours, customer service works to ensure your satisfaction, and I always had endless options for news and entertainment, on TV, the radio, or through newspapers."

"We never appreciate how easy our lives are until we don't have all the conveniences," added Laura.

"You're right, Mom. They're the daily experiences that you can't see or understand before moving to a new country. It can consume you because it can feel as if your entire support system is gone and your ability to help yourself has been taken away. But as more time goes by, the nuances of life in the city reveal themselves. You come to understand the people and their values, and the frustrations and pain points begin to fade away and appreciation takes hold."

"I'm so proud of you, Steven, to take a chance and work so far from home. And I can't wait to visit!"

***

A knock on the front door made Laura jump after she turned off the computer. Standing in the pouring rain was a handsome, well-built young man with short, wavy hair and a lovely girl with a dark brown braid that almost touched her waist.

"Mrs. Beck? I'm Ronnie Gordon, and this is my sister, Shirley. Ms. Harcourt said you were lookin' for help with the house."

"Oh, yes. Please come in out of the rain. Cassandra gave me your card, but I haven't had a chance to call you. I guess you're not too busy this time of years since the lawns don't need cutting. And Shirley, you take care of the house cleaning?"

The young woman smiled and looked away. "Yeah, Shirley's shy, but she's great at cleanin'. And she's real careful too. She won't be breakin' things. Our parents died in a car crash a couple years ago and I took over my dad's lawn service business. I'm tryin' to raise Shirley in a God-fearin' way like our folks wanted. I know the grass doesn't need cuttin', but your trees and bushes could use a trim. Here's a list of our services and references."

Laura noted intensity in the young man's demeanor, and he seemed sincere, but he made her a little uncomfortable. *I must be getting old and paranoid,* she thought as she opened the folder. *Cassie trusts them so I guess I should too.* "Ronnie, why don't you start the yard work when you can, and Shirley can clean every other week when I'm in town. Next Friday would be a good time to start if that works for you. Here's my cell number in case there's a problem."

"Thanks, Mrs. Beck. I'll drop Shirley off next Friday mornin' at 9:00."

Laura took the folder into the kitchen once they had left and read through the list of references Ronny had included. She saw Cassie's letter, one from Mrs. Biddle, and then several pages later she read one from Eduardo Conti. She was surprised that Ronnie hadn't taken this one out under the circumstances. Turning on her computer, she Googled the late Mr. Conti, hoping to understand the man's life and what may have led to his untimely demise.

Laura clicked on an entry, an article about the sale of Conti's Italian line of men's clothing to a New Jersey company in the early 1990s. He'd started the business with a partner in Milan who had died in a hit-and-run accident shortly before the sale. It stated that Conti was questioned about his partner's death, but no charges were ever filed. The next article was about his involvement in real-estate deals in New York and New Jersey with wealthy members of Orthodox Jewish communities.

Laura remembered reading about several New York businessmen, rabbis, and New Jersey politicians who were arrested for money laundering, Ponzi schemes, and tax evasion in the mid-2000s. She wondered if Conti was involved somehow or had learned from these men how to evade arrest for illegal activities. There was no mention of the Mafia in connection with Conti, and she speculated that he deliberately kept his distance from the organization. Laura decided to delve deeper into Conti's past later in the week. She needed to start writing her book, and doing research on the murder victim was just another way of procrastinating.

She wanted to include descriptions of the Island in her novel: the beautiful marshlands like the Low Country described in Pat Conroy's novels; the fascinating history of the pirates who smuggled restricted goods from Europe and African slaves across the St. Mary's river into Georgia after the War of Independence; and the ghosts who inhabited many of the Victorian homes in the historic district of Fernandina. There was a lot to write about—now Laura just had to begin.

CHAPTER 11

JUST THE WAY YOU ARE

As the rain cleared on Saturday afternoon, Faith heard someone opening her front door. *It's the Island killer! Don't be ridiculous, Faith.* She went into the front hall and squealed when she saw Austin standing there. "Darling! What are you doing here? You should be at school studying for exams."

"I needed to see you, Mom," he answered as he held his mother tight. "Miles and I were talking last night, and we're worried about you. I had to make sure you're okay."

"Oh, my love, I'm fine. Amy, look who's here."

Amy walked in the room and hugged the young man. "You've made your mother smile. I'm so glad you came."

They talked for an hour about everything except Charles. Finally, Austin said, "Mom, do you ever wonder if Dad hit that wall on purpose?"

Faith gasped and wondered if her son knew about his father's recent affair or financial difficulties. "Why would you ask such a thing?"

"I know that Dad was devastated when I told him I was gay. Do you think he was so ashamed that he didn't want to be around me anymore?"

"Absolutely not! He was proud of you and loved you dearly. He was coming to terms with who you are and in time would have accepted it. Please don't ever think that you're the reason he died. It was an accident."

"I just . . . I don't know. The Bible says I'm an abomination . . ."

"Austin, let me show you something that was supposedly written by a professor at the University of Virginia about what the Bible says," added Amy as she walked to the kitchen island and turned on her laptop. "Here, read this. It was allegedly written to a radio talk-show host, but its origins are unclear. The host did say on the program that homosexuals are a 'biological error'." Amy showed Austin and Faith a letter that had been circulating on the Internet.

> *Dear Doctor,*
>
> *Thank you for doing so much to educate people regarding God's Law. I have learned a great deal from your show and try to share that knowledge with as many people as I can. When someone tries to defend the homosexual lifestyle, for example, I simply remind them that Leviticus 18:22 clearly states it to be an abomination— end of debate.*
>
> *I do need some advice from you, however, regarding some other elements of God's Laws and how to follow them.*
>
> 1. *Leviticus 25:44 states that I may possess slaves, both male and female, provided they are purchased from neighboring nations. A friend of mine claims that this applies to Mexicans but not Canadians. Can you clarify? Why can't I own Canadians?*
> 2. *I would like to sell my daughter into slavery, as sanctioned in Exodus 21:7. In this day and age, what do you think would be a fair price for her?*
> 3. *I know that I am allowed no contact with a woman while she is in her period of menstrual unseemliness (Lev. 15: 19–24). The problem is how do I tell? I have tried asking, but most women take offence.*
> 4. *When I burn a bull on the altar as a sacrifice, I know it creates a pleasing odor for the Lord (Lev. 1:9). The problem is my neighbors. They claim the odor is not pleasing to them. Should I smite them?*

5. I have a neighbor who insists on working on the Sabbath. Exodus 35:2 clearly states he should be put to death. Am I morally obligated to kill him myself, or should I ask the police to do it?

6. A friend of mine feels that even though eating shellfish is an abomination (Lev. 11:10), it is a lesser abomination than homosexuality. I don't agree. Can you settle this? Are there 'degrees' of abomination?

7. Lev. 21:20 states that I may not approach the altar of God if I have a defect in my sight. I have to admit that I wear reading glasses. Does my vision have to be 20/20, or is there some wiggle-room here?

8. Most of my male friends get their hair trimmed, including the hair around their temples, even though this is expressly forbidden by Lev. 19:27. How should they die?

9. I know from Lev. 11:6–8 that touching the skin of a dead pig makes me unclean, but may I still play football if I wear gloves?

10. My uncle has a farm. He violates Lev. 19:19 by planting two different crops in the same field, as does his wife by wearing garments made of two different kinds of thread (cotton–polyester blend). He also tends to curse and blaspheme a lot. Is it really necessary that we go to all the trouble of getting the whole town together to stone them (Lev. 24:10–16)? Couldn't we just burn them to death at a private family affair, like we do with people who sleep with their in-laws (Lev. 20:14)?

I know you have studied these things extensively and thus enjoy considerable expertise in such matters, so I am confident you can help.

Thank you again for reminding us that God's word is eternal and unchanging.

"Wow, they never talk about those Bible passages in church," said Austin. "I guess they pick and choose what they want us to know and believe."

"I've never questioned what the Baptist church taught us," added Faith. "That letter has opened my eyes about taking the Bible literally." She walked over and hugged her son. "Austin, you are perfect just the way you are. I'm certain that God loves you the same way He loves all His children."

"My belief is that humans create religions," said Amy, "and we give God human qualities. That's why the Old Testament describes a demanding, vengeful God, so the priests could control the uneducated masses through fear. Jesus talked about a God of love, and I believe God is only love. He would never condone any acts of violence in His name."

"But doesn't He condemn evil people to hell when they die?" asked Faith.

"I've studied spirituality for many years, and I agree with the teachings that say we are all a part of the Divine, and hell is the absence of God's Light. Each person's soul is the judge and jury when we cross over, and we review our lives and experience once again—all our positive and negative actions. If a person has done terrible things, he may not be able to face them and turns away from God, creating his own private hell."

"So we judge ourselves?" asked Austin.

"Yes, and since we're all sparks of God, everyone can eventually return to the Light. There are loved ones and advanced souls that help us on the other side. There's forgiveness when a soul faces his or her actions and atones for the harm done to other people and Mother Earth."

"That makes sense. But it makes us responsible for what happens to us instead of God being responsible."

"That's right, Austin. Our souls choose when we're born, what our lessons will be, and when we'll leave this earth. God's will is actually our soul's will with divine guidance."

"Man, that's a lot to think about. I only know that being gay wasn't a choice. It's just who I am and always have been. So, I guess my soul made that decision before I was born?"

"That's what I believe," added Amy. "For whatever reason, your soul decided to live this particular lifetime as a gay man."

Austin was lost in thought for several minutes. "Oh, wow! Miss Amy, you can see spirits. Have you seen my dad?"

"Just briefly after he passed, and he told me to tell you, your brother, and mom that he loved you and he was sorry."

"Do you think he meant he was sorry about leaving us?" Austin asked softly.

"Yes, that's probably what he meant," answered Amy. She walked to the window, gazed outside, and watched the final drops of rain drip from the palm leaves. She turned around in time to see Austin take his mother's hand in his, and Amy was touched by this kind gesture.

"Why don't we go to the restaurant near the harbor and get some dinner?" said Faith as she hugged her youngest child. "We can celebrate life and love and excellent seafood."

CHAPTER 12

THE BEST SURPRISE

The doorbell rang as Laura put away her notes on the locations she wanted to include in her novel and turned off her laptop. She was surprised to have someone at her door again and was glad the rain had stopped. She let out a cry of joy when she saw John standing on the front porch, holding a Christmas tree.

"What are you doing here? And you bought a tree!"

"I rescheduled my meeting on Monday, and I got a reasonably priced last-minute flight. I rented a car so I wouldn't ruin the surprise. The tree was an impulse buy when I passed a nursery in Yulee. I hope it doesn't drop all its needles before Christmas," John said as he leaned the Fraser fir against the wall in the family room. Laura wrapped her arms around his neck and gave him a long kiss.

"I missed you, and this is the best surprise ever!"

"Do we have a tree stand here?"

"Yes, it's in the garage next to the decorations. We don't have any eggnog to drink while we decorate the tree, but I do have champagne in the fridge. I guess we can start a new tradition since we're in a new house, in a new state, and without the kids. I'll get the wine if you get the stand and ornaments."

They chatted while decorating the tree. Laura picked up the Jiminy Cricket ornament and laughed. "This little guy is one of the reasons we have a house in Florida," she said and reminded John of the story she had told the ladies. "But he didn't tell me what an adventure this move would be! Oh, I hired a brother and sister to take care of the yard and clean the house. Cassie recommended them, and they seem trustworthy."

"Did you check their references?"

"No, but Cassie did. Actually, Eduardo Conti was one of them. This man keeps popping into my life."

"Time to turn on the tree lights!" John said as he plugged in the cord. "It looks great, as usual."

"I'm going to the walk the beach next week and look for shells that I can turn into ornaments. We need a few Florida decorations on the tree this year." Laura and John sat on the sofa looking at the tree covered in three decades' worth of ornaments that were collected from all of their vacations and the children's activities. There were several hockey, soccer, and lacrosse ornaments among the more traditional ones.

"I know that I've always traveled a lot, but I'm used to you being there when I get home. I don't like the house when you're not there," John said.

"Does that truly make me a 'housewife'?" Laura said with a laugh.

"It makes you a part of my life that I never want to let go. I can't imagine my life without you, honey."

"You don't have to worry. Nothing will ever keep us apart—for more than a few weeks anyway. It'll be an adjustment for both of us now that we're splitters, as Janice called us. I need to find a purpose for the next part of my life, and I hope being a writer will be my inspired path."

"You're right. It's time for you to try and pursue your dream. It's just that I'm going to miss you, especially on the weekends."

"But it'll be great when we're here together and amazing when the kids are with us. And someday we'll have grandchildren to take to the beach!"

***

The weather was unusually warm as Laura and John strolled down the tree-lined main street in Fernandina Beach on Sunday morning. The Christmas decorations were lovely, and Laura was looking forward to touring some of the decorated Victorian homes that were open to the public the following weekend. She was sorry she'd missed the open houses at the local bed-and-breakfast houses that offered tours and homemade cookies. As they entered a small café, Laura noticed Paolo Conti sitting in a corner intensely focused on a newspaper article. After they were seated at the table next to him and ordered coffee, she decided to introduce herself.

"Excuse me, Mr. Conti. We met at the police station last week," she said offering her hand. "I'm sorry about the loss of your father."

"*Grazie*, thank you for your concern."

"My name is Laura Beck, and my husband, John, and I found your father on the beach."

Paolo looked shocked but said nothing.

"Do you have any other family members here with you?" questioned John.

"No, I am alone. There is only my mother and myself in my immediate family."

"We'll she be joining you here?" asked Laura.

"My mother is why I am in America. She has lymphoblastic leukemia. She has had many treatments but is still very ill."

"That must be so difficult. Is there anything else you can do for her?" asked John.

"We found an experimental drug given at a university in Germany, but it is expensive and not covered by the insurance. My father has provided us with very little over the years, and I requested the money from him. But he did not agree. He insisted that the treatment was not proven to work and would not pay for it. I was so angry with the man."

"That's understandable. Is that what you were arguing about?" added Laura.

"*Si*, I suppose our voices were raised at times. And now the police suspect that I am the murderer of my father! *Ridicolo!* I am to inherit his estate, but not if I am in prison for his murder. I would never do that to my mother. Those police, they are incompetent, and I do not trust them to solve this crime. I am afraid my mother will run out of time before this matter is settled and I receive my inheritance."

The waitress interrupted their conversation and asked what they would like to order. After making their decisions, John commented, "It makes sense that you wouldn't jeopardize your mother's health. I hope they find whoever it was that shot your father."

"Wait! I just read an article about leukemia, and I think it was the type you mentioned. There was a doctor at Washington University in St. Louis, Missouri, that was studying the disease then got it himself. His team of doctors put everything else aside for months and tried to figure out possible cures for their coworker, and they did save him. Maybe they'd be able to help your mother."

"You said this university is in Meezouri?"

"Yes, Washington University in St. Louis, Missouri." Laura took a personal calling card out of her purse and wrote down the information on the back. "I'm sure there's something on the Internet about the case," answered Laura.

"*Grazie, grazie!* I will investigate this situation. I must be going," Paolo said as he placed money on the table, picked up his newspaper, and left.

"He sure is a passionate guy," said Laura. "Do you believe that he would hurt his father?"

"Maybe he argued with Eduardo and just lost it," said John.

"I'll have to ask Detective Davis if they have any more leads. I don't think Paolo killed his father."

"Just be careful, honey. I won't be around to help," answered John.

CHAPTER 13

DREAMS OF AMELIA

After John left for the airport on Monday afternoon, Laura went to the post office on Sadler Road and mailed Christmas packages to Steven in Paris and Jenny in Sydney. Then she drove down Fletcher Avenue to Peter's Point and took her laptop to the picnic tables to start writing her work of fiction. She typed, *Dreams of Amelia, A Novel, Laura Beck*. She had written biographies and backstories for her three main characters and a preliminary timeline for the action, but she still stared at the screen for the next twenty minutes not knowing how to start. "Why is this so hard?" she asked the pelicans perched on the roof of the change room.

"Are you talking to anyone in particular?" asked a female voice behind her. Laura jumped and turned around.

"Oh, Detective Davis. This is my first attempt at writing a novel, and I'm not doing very well," she said with a laugh. "Lately I've been talking to birds and chameleons—I guess I'm losing it! Are you here looking for me?"

"No, I like coming here to clear my head when I get a few minutes. The sound of the ocean washes away the chatter in my mind. And there are a few things about the Conti case that don't add up."

"I'm not sure what you mean. Is there anything you can tell me?"

"There was something strange found on Mr. Conti's body, but I'm not at liberty to talk about it at this time. What I can say is that the more we check into the man, the more complicated the situation gets. He had his fingers in a lot of pies and made a number of enemies along the way. And that doesn't include his son. We've identified the make of the gun that shot him, and we're looking into recent purchases and gun thefts in the area."

"I guess it would be better if you found the murder weapon, but that probably doesn't always happen. John and I spoke to Paolo yesterday, and he's very upset, but I'm not sure he'd harm his father. He seemed more concerned about his mother's health. Was Mr. Conti involved in illegal activities?"

"Yeah, and we're working with the FBI and IRS to put the pieces of the puzzle together. We're questioning his ex-business partner in New York, his neighbors, and his household help. We've looked at his phone records and his connection with quite a few local women. Your neighbor, Cassandra Harcourt's, number came up several times. I'll be contacting her tomorrow."

Laura didn't know what to say. She suddenly realized that the idea that Cassie had some kind of ongoing relationship with Conti had been in lurking in the back of her mind.

"Good luck with your writing, Mrs. Beck. I'd better get back to the station. By the way, there's a memorial service for Mr. Conti next Monday at St. Michael's Catholic Church. His son had him cremated but decided he should have a service for his father in the Church."

Laura thanked the Detective, then turned off her computer. It was difficult to focus on creating a work of fiction when she had a real-life mystery in front of her. She decided she should talk to Cassie and let her know the police would be questioning her on Tuesday. She took out her phone and was searching through her contacts for Cassie's number when her phone rang. It was Melissa, a good friend from St. Louis.

"Melissa, how are the wedding plans going? Did you find a mother-of-the-groom dress?"

"Yes, I found a fabulous designer dress, and I know I shouldn't have spent the money, but I bought the most amazing Jimmy Choo shoes."

"I can't wait to see you at the wedding."

"Actually, that's why I'm calling. We had to cut the number of guests to 400, and I'm afraid I'm going to have to uninvite you and John."

Laura sat in stunned silence. Melissa, her partner Bill, and Mel's son, Peter, had been like family to them for over a decade, and she couldn't believe they were being 'chopped' from the wedding. Laura and John had been the only St. Louis friends who had gone to the trouble and expense of attending Bill's daughter's wedding in Denver the year before. Mel droned on about her son's wedding plans.

"If you're still in Florida in March," said Melissa, "maybe I'll come down for a week to recover from the wedding."

"Yeah, maybe. I have to go, Mel." Laura hit the end button on her phone. It was another betrayal by someone who was supposed to be her friend. Recently, Melissa and Bill's new friends were affluent and socially well-connected—unlike Laura and John. *And she wants to come here and spend a week talking about a wedding I wasn't invited to?*

Laura had an image flash through her mind of picking up Melissa at the airport and before they walked into the Becks' new house, Laura laid down on the front step and let Mel walk on her back in the amazing Jimmy Choo stilettos. *I refuse to be anyone's doormat!* Holding back tears, Laura picked up her laptop and headed to the car.

CHAPTER 14

THE TAIL

A my walked along Centre Street in Fernandina Beach on Monday after-noon, deciding which antique store would hold a Christmas gift for her niece. She often used her intuition to find whatever she was shopping for in the least amount of time. Amy's brother, James, his wife Evelyn, and their daughter, Hannah, lived in Bloomfield Hills, Michigan only a mile from where she'd grown up. Her father, Ward, had been an accountant for a major auto manufacturer. He was analytical and authoritarian and had little use for Amy's and her mother, Pamela's, psychic abilities. Her mom had worked part-time at the local high school while Amy was growing up and occasionally gave psychic readings to friends and family.

Ward would give Pam and Amy 'the look' whenever they spoke about spirituality or contact with the other side, and they knew enough to keep quiet in his presence. It wasn't until Amy's dad had passed away that she began her career as a psychic medium. Her brother worked as a biochemist and admitted that he often used his intuition to aid in his work. As Amy thought about her dad, it dawned on her that with Doug, she'd married someone just like Ward! Maybe subconsciously she was trying to please her father when she married Doug.

As Amy entered the Eight Flags Antique Market, a chill ran up her spine, and she had the feeling someone was watching her. She quickly turned around, looked across the street, and saw a young man stop and turn away from her as he pretended to answer his phone. *It could just be my imagination, but something about that guy is familiar.* Swiftly, she walked to the far end of the store and peered out a window that was covered in vintage clothing. She watched as the man crossed Centre Street and walked past the store. *Doug! That guy works with him.*

Amy wandered around the shop for several minutes, unable to concentrate on finding a gift for her niece. *He must be following me. Why else would he be on the Island? Should I confront him or avoid him?* Amy decided confrontation was the best way to handle the situation, and she walked out of the store in the direction the young man had gone. She turned the corner and saw him leaning against a 1930s, mud-colored pickup truck. She was disturbed by the smug look on his face.

"Ms. Temple. Good to see you again. My name's Albertson, and we met last year in the Atlanta office."

"Yes, I remember you. What do you want?"

"Mr. Masterson wants to talk to you. In person. You can't trust the phones—too many little critters out there."

Amy wasn't surprised that Doug thought their phones were bugged. "Why didn't he come himself?"

"He had to leave the country for a meeting, but he'll be back tomorrow. Can I let him know you'll be returning to Atlanta—real soon?"

Dozens of questions went through her mind, but Amy knew she wouldn't get any answers today. "Tell Doug I'll drive back on Wednesday, and I'll see him at the apartment on Thursday morning."

"That should work. Have a good day," Albertson said as he walked down the street to a black sedan parked in front of the historic redbrick courthouse.

Damn! I wish my intuition worked better with my own life.

***

Faith was pulling weeds around the scarlet Knockout roses in the front garden when Amy drove up to the house on Hopeful Court. "Amy, did you find what you were looking for in town?"

"I found something that I wasn't looking for." Amy told her of the encounter with the young man from Doug's company.

"Mercy! What is going on? Are you sure you have to go back to the city? Would you like me to come with you? I don't mind, because our lawyer asked me to drop into his office as soon as possible. You can stay with me so you don't have to spend time at the apartment."

"That would be great, Faith. I don't understand what this is all about, and I get a feeling that there's something serious happening, and I haven't got a clue how it involves me. Some psychic I am, huh?"

Laura drove around the corner and waved to the two women standing by the front garden. *I hope these women become true friends, unlike my old pal Melissa,* she thought as she pulled into the driveway. Walking over to Faith's house she was greeted by strained smiles.

"Is everything okay?"

"We have another mystery on our hands," commented Amy as she described what had happened and the feeling that it might have something to do with Conti. "So we'll be heading to Atlanta for a few days. We're going to miss Wining Wednesday at Cassie's."

"Laura, why don't you come with us? There's more than enough room at my home. Have you ever been to Atlanta?" asked Faith.

"We've driven through on our way to Florida, but I've never seen the city. Are you sure you want someone tagging along?"

"It would be a pleasure to have you. And I'll call Cassandra and let her know we'll be away on Wednesday."

"I can call her," said Laura. "I need to talk to her anyway. Detective Davis told me that the police will be contacting her about her relationship with Mr. Conti. It seems they had some sort of connection."

Amy gave Laura a knowing look, and it didn't take Faith long to figure out what the relationship between the murder victim and Cassie might have been.

"Oh my! Well, if you want to call Cassandra that's fine. We'll leave around 9:00 on Wednesday morning and arrive for a late lunch. I'd love to show you my city," said Faith, knowing how difficult it was going to be returning to Atlanta without Charles being there. Having company in the house would make the experience easier.

"A road trip will be great, Faith. Thanks for the invitation."

Laura called John as she entered the house and told him of her forthcoming trip. "I could never have imagined everything that's happened since we bought this house. I wanted something new in my life, and I've gotten so much more than I expected."

"Does Amy know what her ex wants? She'd better be careful, and so should you. Those military-type guys can be scary."

"We'll be careful. I've got to let Cassie know that the police are going to call her. I have a good idea what she and Conti were up to."

"Let me know what happens, Laura. Be safe," answered John.

CHAPTER 15

MORE LIES

On Tuesday morning, Cassandra bolted upright in bed, frightened by an elusive dream. A wave of anxiety washed over her that verged on a panic attack. She'd frequently experienced this sensation ever since she was a teenager. She'd been to so many shrinks over the years she felt like she could write a book about the modern psychiatric experience. Yet the anxiety was always a breath away.

She pushed down the feelings and went to wake up Allison for school. She stopped at the bedside, looked down at her sleeping child, and said a silent prayer of thanks for the beautiful girl who made her a mother. Cassie was devastated when she'd learned she couldn't have children of her own, especially when her first husband looked at her as a failure and decided to move on. She gently kissed her daughter's cheek. "Time to get up, angel eyes!"

The ringing phone startled Cassie, and she had a knot in her stomach as she went to answer it. Good news never came this early in the morning.

"Hi, Cassie, it's Laura. I hope I didn't wake you."

"No, Laura, I've been up for a while. Is there something I can help you with?"

"Actually, I wanted to warn you that I spoke to Detective Davis with the Fernandina Police Department yesterday, and she'll be calling you today about Mr. Conti. She said your cell number came up several times when they checked his phone records." Laura waited for Cassie to confirm what she already suspected.

Cassie was silent for a long moment. She feared this day would come, but all her years of experience as a lawyer failed her as she struggled for something to say.

"Laura, I have to get Allison ready for school. Can we meet after she leaves for the bus?"

"Sure, come over when you can."

It was over an hour later when Laura led Cassie out to the lanai for coffee and cranberry muffins. Laura had bought the cranberries with plans to string them for the Christmas tree, but she put them to better use.

Cassie started the conversation. "I don't know why the police want to talk to me, I barely knew Mr. Conti."

"How did you meet him?"

"Well, I first spoke to him about the Gordons. I was checking their references before I hired them to clean the house and take care of the yard. Mr. Conti seemed very nice on the phone, and I enjoyed talking to him. Then in August, I was staying overnight at the Jacksonville Hyatt on business and stopped in the bar for a drink before I went to my room. I heard someone talking to a server that sounded like Eduardo. I introduced myself, and we had a wonderful conversation."

"Did you have more than a conversation?"

"No! We just talked that night. He was so charming and listened to me. We—talked several times over the past few months."

Laura looked at Cassie's body language as she picked at the muffin on her plate. *Lies*, Laura thought, *more lies*. Something snapped in Laura's carefully controlled persona. Maybe it was her newfound courage in being on her own, or the pain from her conversation with Melissa, or her long-suppressed anger at Cassandra.

"Bullshit."

"What?" Cassie answered, stunned at the remark.

"Bullshit, Cassie. I don't believe you weren't involved with Conti. The first time his name was mentioned, your reaction was so over the top that I knew something was wrong. It was obvious you had a personal connection to the man, and Amy picked up on it too. Does Robert know?"

Cassie began to cry softly. "I don't know. I think he might suspect something, but I'm not sure. Robert has anger issues, and I don't want to tell him. Please don't say anything. I have to protect Allison!"

"It's not my place to say anything. Why did you do it?"

"Marrying Robert was a mistake. I wanted some stability for Allison, and I thought an older, secure father figure was the answer. But he has a dark, abusive side that only surfaced after we were married. I guess I should have talked to his first two wives before I accepted his proposal, instead of afterward. I think he paid off his other wives to keep quiet about his volatile temper. He's never physically harmed us, but his anger can be explosive. That's one of the reasons I wanted to move to Florida before he was ready to retire, and I used the high-school thing as an excuse."

"So you thought cheating on him was a smart thing to do?"

Once again Cassie was shocked by Laura's directness, and so was Laura. This was so unlike the mild-mannered housewife from St. Louis.

"No! I didn't mean for it to happen. Eduardo was just so charming, and he made me feel like a desirable woman again." Cassie stood up and began to pace around the lanai.

"It had been so long since I felt someone wanted me. I knew he was seeing other women, but I didn't care. I wasn't looking for a commitment. He gave me thoughtful gifts, and he was so romantic and attentive when we were together. And now he's gone, and my life is a mess." Cassie sat down on the loveseat and put her hands over her face.

"Well, the first thing you should do is call Detective Davis and tell her the truth. It's all going to come out sooner or later. And you'll have to talk to Robert. He was here on Thanksgiving weekend, wasn't he?"

It took a moment for Cassie to understand what Laura was implying. "You don't think Robert found out and would confront Eduardo, do you?"

"You'd know better than me. What do you think? Does Robert own a gun?"

"Yes, he has an extensive gun collection, but he'd never shoot anyone! Even if he did find out about the affair, Robert would never kill another man."

"I hope you're right." Laura looked at her ex-friend Cassie and saw the anguish in her eyes. "Are you going to stay with Robert?"

"Three strikes, and you're out. How can I face another divorce? Robert is fine as long as he's the center of attention and gets what he wants, when he wants it."

"But is that the type of relationship you want to model for Allison?"

"No, no. This is all going to get out, isn't it? Small towns thrive on salacious gossip. I'll have to face the music, but first I need some time to decide what I want to say before I speak with Robert and the police." Tears began to roll down her face as she silently sobbed.

Laura walked over and placed her hand on Cassie's shoulder. All her anger at Cassandra melted away. There would be time later to revisit their past and heal the old wounds from their youth. Laura walked into the kitchen and brought out a box of tissues.

"I almost forgot to tell you that Faith, Amy, and I are going to Atlanta tomorrow for a couple of days, so we won't be here for your wine night."

Cassie wiped her eyes. "I wish I could go with you and escape this craziness. Most of all I dread telling Allison about everything. Thanks, Laura, for warning me about the police. I think I'll head home and decide what I want to say to Robert."

"Good luck, my friend," Laura said as she walked Cassie to the front door.

CHAPTER 16

CONFESSION

B etsy Biddle was watering the potted red and pink poinsettias on her back patio when Detective Davis arrived at Cassie's house on Tuesday afternoon. The bionic busybody, as Amy had called her, scurried across her lawn toward her neighbor's yard after the policewoman was let in the front door. She was straining to hear the conversation when the screen door to the lanai opened, and the two women walked outside. Betsy crouched down and scampered along the fence toward the back of Cassie's house. *How delightful. I'll be able to hear what they're saying.*

"I'll speak to my husband soon and tell him everything. I think my marriage is over."

"When did your relationship with Mr. Conti begin?" asked Detective Davis.

Betsy gasped as she realized what was happening. *Heavens! I can't wait to tell the bridge club about this.*

"It was a few months ago," Cassie replied in a soft voice. She briefly told the story of her affair with Eduardo. "But I haven't seen him for a while. Robert has been here a lot lately, and I didn't want to take any chances."

"Did your husband know about Mr. Conti?" the detective asked. "Was he in town on Thanksgiving?"

"Robert was here that day and left on Friday morning. I'm not sure if he's aware of the affair or not. Even if he sounds shocked when I tell him, he's famous for his great performances in court, so I won't really know. Detective, my husband wouldn't harm anyone."

"But is capable of hiring someone to handle a situation like this?"

Betsy was wondering the same thing as she stood quietly, pressed against the weathered, wooden fence. She'd always thought Robert was too big for his britches—an arrogant Yankee who looked down his nose at her. She could imagine the cuckolded husband seeking revenge.

"I'm certain he wasn't involved," Cassie said. *He did go out for a while after Thanksgiving dinner, but I'd better not mention that.* "I'm more concerned with how to tell my daughter."

"I don't have children of my own, but I've witnessed many families in turmoil over the years. Children sense when there's something wrong, and I'm sure your daughter's main concern is with your well-being. Honesty is always the best policy with teenagers, though there may be some over-the-top drama for a while."

Cassie nodded. "You're right about the drama that will ensue. And I'm sure Allison won't miss Robert's nasty temper." She regretted the words the instant they left her lips. The last thing Cassie wanted was for her husband to be a suspect in the death of her lover.

"Well, if you think of anything else, please call me. Here's my card."

Betsy Biddle hurried across the lawn and went into her lanai. She still wanted to eavesdrop as the detective left so she stayed outside. Millie was at the sliding door barking and trying to get to her owner. "Hush, Millie. You'll give me away."

Cassie looked over at the Biddle house as she walked the detective to her car. Betsy quickly opened the sliding door and went inside, admonishing her dog for making so much noise.

"Thanks, Detective for coming here instead of asking me to meet you at the station. I appreciate your discretion."

"Let's hope we can solve this crime and soon."

Cassie sat at her ornate mahogany desk in the small office and wrote out what she wanted to say to her daughter when Allison got home from school. Cassandra knew she couldn't put it off any longer, and she wanted her thoughts to be clear and appropriate.

"Mom, I'm home. You wouldn't believe what this jerk said to me at school today!"

"Sweetheart, we need to talk," Cassie said as she held her daughter's hand and led her to the sofa. She talked about the affair and that she would be asking Robert for a divorce. Allison's reaction to Cassie's actions and the decision to end the marriage was typical of a 14-year-old, with lots of tears and histrionics.

"What about me? How can you do this to me? Now I won't have a dad again."

Cassie let her daughter vent for half an hour and was surprised by what Allison said at the end of her tirade.

"I need some space. I'm going to call Madison and see if I can stay with her for a couple of days. I love you, Mom, but I need to get away from you right now."

With a heavy heart Cassie answered, "I'll call Madison's mom and see if it's okay. I don't blame you for being angry, and I respect your need for time apart."

Allison packed a bag for a three-night stay at her friend's house, deciding that would be long enough to punish her mother, and she'd still be home for the weekend. There was a slight grin on her face as she realized that she wouldn't have to put up with her stepfather any more. Robert's bad temper always made her fearful, but she wouldn't let her mom know that she was truly relieved about the separation.

After dropping off her daughter, Cassie drove to the beach near their home. Walking along the shore, she decided to face the music and called Robert. She explained about her affair with Conti and being questioned by the police. Then she suggested they get a divorce. Robert hung up without saying a word, which was almost worse than the verbal barrage she was expecting.

Cassie sat down on the cold sand and watched several pelicans glide over the surface of the waves in unison, with their wings almost touching the water. *Free as a bird. Wait, I'm free! I thought another divorce would devastate me, but I feel like a huge weight has been lifted off my shoulders,* she thought as she stood up and walked toward the water. She took a deep breath of the cool ocean air and closed her eyes as she listened to the waves gliding to the shore. *We're going to be okay. I can increase my hours at work and pick up a few new clients. Allison and I are going to be just fine on our own.*

The wind was picking up as she drove home, and she realized she would be alone for the next few days. Pulling into her driveway, Cassie saw Laura opening her mailbox and walked over to give her an update on her once-again messed-up life.

"So, Allison is away for a while?"

"Yes, I'll pick her up after school on Friday. That should give her enough time to stop being furious with me. Sometimes parenting is harder than I thought it would be."

Laura saw the soul-weary look on Cassie's face and decided she shouldn't be alone right now. "Faith, Amy, and I are leaving for Atlanta in the morning. Why don't you come with us? I'm sure it will be fine. A road trip could take your mind off everything here."

"I can't, I shouldn't, I don't want to be a burden, I—"

"Cassie, come with us. I'll call Faith and make sure it's okay."

Cassandra stood looking at Laura for a long moment. "You're a good friend. Yes, if it's all right with Faith, I'll come with you. Laura, you are just the person I need in my life right now to help me see things clearly. Thank you, and I'll call Faith to make certain it's fine."

CHAPTER 17

ROAD TRIP

The ladies of Hopeful Court gathered at Faith's house on Wednesday morning and loaded their suitcases in the trunk of the champagne-colored, four-door Lexus. Not surprisingly, Betsy came out to see what was going on and marched over with her hands perched on her hips.

"What's this all about? Are y'all going somewhere special? Is the 'fearsome foursome' out to save the world?"

"Hi, Betsy," said Amy. "We're going to Atlanta for a couple of days. Faith needs to take care of a few things and so do I. Cassie and Laura are coming along for the ride."

"Humph, I guess my invitation got lost in the mail," answered Mrs. Biddle.

"Next time, we'll be sure to include you, Betsy. And I think we're more like the 'fearful foursome,'" said Faith.

"Actually, I like it!" Laura added. "The fearsome foursome—newfound friends fighting crime and solving mysteries."

"Humph," Betsy said again and toddled home.

Amy offered to drive, and they headed up Amelia Island Parkway under the enchanting canopy of oak trees that lined both sides of the road. Amy stopped short, as the traffic light at Fletcher Avenue turned yellow, surprising the young man in the old Volvo driving behind them. A dull thud let them know that they'd been rear-ended, and Amy put the car in park and got out to see the damage. Laura got out as well and told Faith they'd check the rear fender.

"Oh no, oh no!" said a teenager as he backed up quickly. "I'm so sorry! I thought you'd go through the yellow light."

Amy looked at both bumpers and decided there was no real damage. "Don't worry, it looks like there are just a few scratches. Just be more careful."

"Thanks, lady. I'll watch it!"

As Amy and Laura got back in the car, they noticed a black sedan with dark-tinted windows, three cars behind the Volvo. *It looks like Albertson's car. Is Doug having me followed?* Amy wondered.

While driving north on Highway 95 toward Savannah, the women shared stories of their lives. Cassie filled them in on her conversations with Detective Davis, Allison, and Robert. She turned her head and gazed out the window at the passing golden-brown marshes of the Low Country, before she began the story of her relationship with Conti. The other women listened intently but kept their comments to themselves. They knew how difficult it is to share something that was painful and humiliating.

"It feels good just getting this all out," said Cassandra. "Keeping secrets is hard work. Thanks for listening."

Laura decided it wasn't the right time to force Cassie to revisit her actions from high school, but it still bothered Laura that she didn't have any clarity about their relationship. She turned the conversation in a new direction. "Faith, tell me about Charles. I'm sorry I never had the chance to meet him."

As a wistful look crossed her face, Faith told the story of her marriage. "The boys couldn't have asked for a better father, and he was the most attentive man. Except for a youthful indiscretion and a recent midlife fling, he was a devoted husband."

Do many Southern women talk about infidelity so nonchalantly? Laura wondered. *I would never refer to it that way if John cheated on me.*

"Charles was a wonderful man," said Amy. "He was kind and generous and was coming around to accepting that Austin is gay. Your turn, Laura— tell us more about your family."

Laura talked more about John and the children and her life in Missouri. She told them of many things about the Midwest that she enjoyed, like the friendliness of the people, the courteous drivers, and their competence in completing public projects on time. She also discussed the things that drove her crazy, such as many people's assumption that everyone was religious and Republican and that there was something wrong with you—or sinful—if you weren't. Finally, she told them the story of her friend, Melissa, and how she and John were chopped from the upcoming wedding.

"How extraordinary!" commented Faith. "Did you tell your friend how disappointed you were that you were uninvited?"

"I emailed her later and said how hurt we were and how I felt she didn't respect our friendship. Her answer was that reducing the guest list wasn't an easy task and sometimes being a friend means understanding, caring, and support. She was saying that *I* was being a bad friend because I didn't support her decision to insult us. And she had wanted to come to Amelia Island for a week to recover from the wedding!"

"Unbelievable," said Faith. "With a narcissistic friend like that . . ."

Amy had a story to tell, as well. "I got a call last night from a client I worked with several years ago. At that time Jackie wanted to know about her missing cousin. It turned out that her cousin was fine and just needed to get away for a while. This time Jackie was concerned that a ghost was haunting her house."

"Were objects moving or were there sounds in the night?" asked Faith.

"No. Her son, Ned, and his college friend stopped by her house before they flew to Las Vegas for a long weekend. The next day, Jackie was dusting her son's room and noticed a black cardboard box on his dresser but she didn't have her glasses on to read what it said. She opened the box and saw some powder inside but didn't think anything of it.

"After her son got home, his friend disappeared, and when Jackie asked where he was, Ned told her that his friend was upstairs getting his dad."

"Oh my gosh, Amy. Was his father in the box?"

"You got it, Faith. The friend had picked up his father's ashes and didn't want to take them to Las Vegas, so he left them at the house. Now he was taking them back to college with him. Later Jackie told her son that the next time one of his friends leaves a family member in their home to please let her know."

"Did she think the dad's spirit was there?" said Cassie.

"Yes, she was paranoid that his ghost was in the house, and every sound she heard made her jump. I told her she didn't have anything to worry about, and I didn't feel there was anyone haunting the house."

As they neared Macon, Laura noticed that Amy looked in the rearview mirror more than once and wondered if she was concerned about the dark sedan they'd seen when they got back in the car after they were rear-ended. A short time later, they turned north on Highway 75, and Amy swerved into the right lane and, at the last second, got off at the first exit. Everyone in the car was flung to the side as Amy stopped the car on the shoulder. "Sorry, ladies. I wanted to lose our tail."

"What are you talking about?" asked Cassie.

"There's been a black sedan following us since we left, and it looks like the car that Doug's coworker was driving when he confronted me in town. There's also a white panel van that I noticed as we crossed the bridge over the Amelia River when we left the Island. That vehicle seems to be following the sedan or us or both."

"Could it be the police? Or the FBI? Or someone else involved with Conti?" asked Faith, sounding alarmed. "What should we do?"

"Why don't we get lunch around here. Then we can drive to Atlanta and see if I'm just being paranoid or if we see either car when we get back on the road."

The women agreed, and each of them silently wrestled with their thoughts and fears. Except for Amy, none of them had ever been involved with a murder case, and it was a troubling sensation.

"I know where we can go for lunch. A sorority sister lives in Macon, and she's taken me to a wonderful local place." Faith directed them to Mimi's Comfort Food Cafe, which was less than ten minutes from the highway. "Comfort food is just what the doctor ordered!"

The women looked around as they walked into the restaurant, making sure no one was watching them. "I feel foolish even thinking we're being followed," said Cassie as they were being seated at a side booth. "I hope we're just overreacting."

"This menu is great! There's every kind of comfort food imaginable. I'm going with the meatloaf and mashed potatoes," said Amy.

"Biscuits and gravy or cheese grits and fried green tomatoes? Maybe I'll order them all," added Faith. "And sweet tea of course."

Laura said, as the waitress came to take their order, "I'll have the grilled cheese sandwich and tomato soup, with a cup of hot tea."

"And I'm having the all-American standby—a cheeseburger, fries, and a regular Coke," said Cassie. Calories and diets were the last thing on their minds as they ordered the food that fed their souls and calmed their nerves.

Ninety minutes later, they were on the road again, and the apprehension returned. After twenty miles, they began to relax, when there were no signs of the black sedan or white van.

CHAPTER 18

BUCKHEAD

The heavy traffic on Highway 75 continued on Highways 85 and 400, and Amy was relieved when she exited at Peachtree Road. She gave the ladies a quick tour of Buckhead, then turned down Faith's street, past large houses with manicured lawns set behind stone walls and privet hedges.

"This area is lovely," said Laura. "I had no idea Atlanta was so beautiful. You don't see any of this from the highway."

"Thank you, Laura. We're very proud of our city, and we're fortunate to live here," answered Faith. "We—I mean I . . ." Faith's voice began to waver as she once again realized Charles was no longer a physical part of her life. She closed her eyes and began to breathe deeply so she wouldn't break down.

"And there is the Country Club where Faith and I first met at a fundraiser," said Amy.

"It was friends-at-first-sight. Jeremy, one of Charles' coworkers, had previously worked for Doug's company and introduced us. We were seated at adjacent tables, and Amy and I were able to talk during the dinner. We hit it off immediately, and Charles and Doug became golfing buddies. They even played on Amelia Island a couple of times."

"That's right," said Amy. "I'd forgotten about their trips to the Island."

Faith let out a deep sigh as they pulled up to the Proctor house. Everyone was silent as they unpacked the car and went inside. Faith steeled her heart and became the consummate Southern hostess.

"Please make yourselves at home. Amy, you can take Austin's bedroom; Laura, I'll put you in Miles' room; and Cassie can have the guest room. I called our cleaning lady, and she freshened the rooms this morning."

Suddenly, a wave of sorrow washed over Faith. "I think I'll rest for a while if you don't mind. It's being home again after . . ."

Amy hugged her friend. "Don't worry, I'll entertain Cassie and Laura until dinner. Get some rest."

The three women unpacked, then met in the kitchen for afternoon tea. Amy showed Laura and Cassie around the antique-filled house before she found Faith's exquisite porcelain tea set in the dining room buffet and returned to the kitchen to put on the kettle.

"We're all originally Northerners, aren't we?" said Cassie. "I'm still not used to being in the South, but there's so much to admire about the beauty and charm of Southern living. Although I'm not sure I'll ever like collard greens and some of the other favorite foods down here."

"Doug introduced me to shrimp and grits, and now I can't get enough," Amy said with a laugh. "I wish the dish wasn't so high in calories and cholesterol. I always have it when I'm in Fernandina since they have the best local shrimp in the state."

"When I think about the Island, I automatically think about Conti," said Laura. "Cassie, is it okay if we talk about it? I have this feeling that there's something I should do to help solve the mystery—that there's a reason I found him on the beach."

Cassie slowly stirred a spoon of sugar in her tea. "I want to find out what happened too. Since I was involved with Eduardo, it worries me that a killer is still out there and may know about my connection to him. Especially now that I can't rely on Robert to be there with us."

Faith walked into the kitchen. "Mind if I join you? I couldn't sleep, and the company of friends is just what I need."

"We were talking about Conti and how we're all drawn to his sad end. Why don't we pool what we know and try and figure out how we can help the police," said Amy.

"Perfect," added Faith. "The fearsome foursome—freelance detectives! Amy, I always wished I could help you with your cases. Wait, I know—I have a hand-tooled, leather journal we can use for the clues." Faith found the journal and a pen and handed them to Laura. "Since you want to be writer, you can write down our thoughts."

"Thanks," Laura said. "I need some motivation to get me started on my writing. This is like a cozy!"

"A what?" asked Cassie.

"A cozy mystery novel, where an amateur sleuth—often a smart, intuitive, middle-aged woman—works with the police to solve a murder. Except we have four intelligent women, including one psychic medium. Maybe this is why we were meant to move to Hopeful Court and find one another."

"You're right," said Amy. "I do feel a strong connection to each of you, and the fact that we're all together right now may be synchronicity. Now, why don't we tell what we know about Mr. Conti and his murder, so Laura can start taking notes."

A while later, the women had detailed everything they knew about Eduardo Conti and his untimely death. There were so many unanswered questions. Had the police found the murder weapon? Did they know who owned the gun? Who was on their list of suspects other than the obvious people? Cassie was the final person to speak, and she talked about the man's charm and generosity.

"It wasn't my intention to become involved with him, but the first time he kissed me, it was like I'd never truly been kissed before. It was tender and erotic at the same time and just incredible. The whole thing was totally unplanned, unexpected, and amazing. His touch was so gentle, and I felt desirable for the first time in a very long while."

Cassie's eyes had a faraway look as she continued her story. "The last time I saw him was when he dropped off a gift late one night. It's an antique, musical jewelry box. I told Robert I'd picked it up at a second-hand store in Fernandina. The music doesn't play anymore, but the detail in the wood inlay is lovely."

"That was probably the night that Betsy saw Conti's car leaving the neighborhood," added Laura.

"You're right. I hadn't connected her comment to that night."

"Well, ladies, I think we deserve a fabulous dinner to celebrate our sleuthing. It's great having friends to share this with; I'm often struggling with a case on my own. I'll call my favorite restaurant, Pricci's, and reserve a table. A Wining Wednesday in Atlanta," said Amy.

CHAPTER 19

HIS AND HERS

When the ladies returned to the Proctor house after dinner, Laura remembered to call Ronnie Gordon and postpone Shirley's cleaning day until the following Tuesday. Then plans were made for Laura to accompany Amy to her apartment the next morning while Cassie went with Faith to the lawyer's office.

Amy slipped under the covers in Austin's bed and was just about to turn off the bedside lamp when she saw Charles sitting in a chair in the corner of the room. Once again, Amy heard his lament in her mind—he was sorry for the mistakes he'd made, and he loved his wife and boys.

"What mistakes, Charles?" she asked out loud. "What are you talking about?"

"Tell Faith—tell her to find love again," Charles said before he disappeared.

Faith gently tapped on the bedroom door. "Amy, are you awake? I thought I heard voices," she said as she opened the door. Amy wasn't sure how her friend would respond to the message she'd received.

"I had a brief visit from Charles and again he apologized for his mistakes and said he loved you and the boys. Then he said—"

"Please tell me. I can face whatever it is."

Amy smiled as her friend sat on the end of the bed and placed her hands together as if she was in prayer. "It wasn't anything bad. Charles wants you to find love again. He wants you to have a full, happy life and find someone who will love you."

"Mercy! That wasn't what I was expecting. Does he feel guilty about leaving us or about his indiscretions? Even from beyond the grave, he's a mystery to me. How can he even imagine I want another man in my life? He's been gone such a short time."

"Maybe he's moving on to a level in the spirit world where he won't be able to communicate with us for a while. I believe that can happen. It was a final message of his regret, his concern for you, and his desire that you'll be open to love again."

"This is all too much. I think I'll take one of the sleeping pills the doctor gave me," Faith said as she hugged Amy then went to her room. She walked into the closet and ran her hand across Charles' suit jackets. She inhaled the scent of his shirts, and tears began to flow. Climbing into bed after taking a sleeping pill, she reached over and touched the pillow where her husband's head should be.

She wept as quietly as possible so she wouldn't disrupt her guests. *I miss you beyond words. What happened, Charles? Why did you leave me—and the boys? We need you, and I don't ever want to love anyone else. How could you even suggest that?* It was several hours before Faith slipped into a fitful sleep.

The following morning, Amy and Laura took a cab to the apartment building where Doug was waiting. They agreed that Laura would wait at a coffee shop down the street and would help Amy load some of her things in her car that was parked in the underground garage, after she talked to her husband. Walking into her apartment, Amy saw Doug standing on the balcony talking on his phone.

Memories flooded back to the first time they'd met through mutual friends, three years earlier. Doug was a strong, handsome, fascinating man who charmed her with his humor and wit. She'd loved how grounded he was and connected to the physical world in a way she would never be. There was an immediate allure and an undeniable attraction between two very opposite people. A quick courtship led to a simple, sunset wedding ceremony on a Maui beach and a move to Doug's hometown of Atlanta.

They had spent countless nights talking about their past adventures, and he'd seemed captivated by her abilities, the people she'd assisted, and the cases she helped solve. Doug had traveled all over the world and had tales of working with foreign dignitaries and celebrities. They complemented one another, and for the first couple of years, the marriage was wonderful. But when things began to unravel at Doug's company, he started to pressure Amy about using her psychic abilities to help him, and when she refused, he became verbally abusive. The end of the marriage was as quick as the courtship.

Amy looked around the apartment and realized how little they'd acquired as a couple, and it was mostly 'his' and 'hers' instead of 'ours.' She would leave behind most of the things they bought together. They were painful reminders of another failed marriage.

"Doug," Amy called to him when he was off the phone. "Why did you want to see me?"

The look on Doug's face showed that he still had feelings for Amy. It was a mixture of sadness and regret that it had all gone so wrong. "Amy, how's Faith doing? It must be tough for her losing Charles like that."

"We're trying to help her through it. Two neighbors from Amelia came here with us. What was so urgent that you sent Albertson to the Island?"

"You've been asking about the dead guy, Conti, and I don't think you know what you're getting yourself into."

"Did you have me followed from Florida? I'm sure there was black sedan tailing us."

"No, it wasn't me. Damn, that's what I was afraid of. Conti pissed off a lot of people in the PSC and PMC biz. And that doesn't include the assholes up in Jersey. Man, you got to let this thing go. I don't want to see you hurt."

The genuine concern in Doug's eyes made Amy's heart pound. Her intuition was telling her what he was saying was true, and investigating the murder could put her in danger. She walked over and put her arms around her soon-to-be ex, and he hugged her back.

"Thank you for worrying about me. I promise I'll be careful." Amy released him and smiled until she spotted divorce papers sitting on the coffee table. "I guess this is the next step. I'll have my lawyer look them over, and I'll mail them back to you. I think I left some moving boxes under the guest bed. There are a few things I want to take with me now, and I'll arrange a time to pick up the rest. Albertson said you were out of the country. Is it a new job?"

"Yeah, there's a pharmaceutical exec that has to spend a few months in Mexico City, and we're protecting his family. The wife and young daughter will be under my watch."

"Wait. There's a place—an area of the city that you should avoid," Amy said as her eyes focused high on the ceiling when an image came into her mind. "It's Saint Angel or something like that. Please be careful when you're in Mexico for your sake and the family you're guarding."

"Thanks, Amy. I'll be vigilant. I trust your vibes. I guess we still have each other's backs."

Doug helped Amy pack clothing, photos, and books. He reached into his desk drawer and pulled out a small handgun and ammunition. He loaded the weapon. "Amy, I want you to take this."

"Oh, no. I really don't want a gun in my new house."

"I'm not taking no for an answer," he said as he placed the gun in the final box.

Making two trips, they carried the boxes and suitcases down to her car in the parking garage. As Amy got into the driver's side, she looked into Doug's eyes and smiled. They knew there were reasons why they'd been drawn to each other but equally impelling reasons why they couldn't stay together. He had shown her how to be strong and grounded, and she'd softened his hard edges. It was time to go their separate ways.

When Amy parked the car, walked up to the coffee shop, and pulled up a chair beside the table, Laura noticed a subtle change in her appearance. There was a peaceful look on her face, not what Laura was expecting from someone picking up divorce papers.

"Everything's okay," said Amy. "Closure is a wonderful thing. Doug helped me carry the boxes to my car. It's interesting that I'd saved some moving boxes. Maybe a part of me knew the marriage wasn't going to work out."

"Did he have us followed?"

"No, but he thought it might be someone connected to Conti, maybe from a private military company. Or it might be an enemy from Conti's checkered life up North. Doug wanted to warn me to be careful and stay away from the case. He isn't sure who's involved and who might be listening to our phone conversations. "

"Wow. I've never been tailed before or even imagined I ever would be," Laura answered. "Incredible but also extremely scary."

While she was ordering a latte from the cashier, Amy's cell phone rang, and she found herself talking to Detective Davis from the Fernandina Beach police. When the conversation ended, she filled Laura in on the latest news as she sipped her coffee.

"Detective Davis is a friend of the Fergusons, and she learned that, as she said, a 'minor celebrity' was renting their house for a year. The detective Googled me and found my cell number on my website. She wants to know if I can help with the Thanksgiving murder."

"How ironic that on the same morning you're warned to stay away from the Conti case, the police ask for your assistance. What did you tell the detective?"

"I told her I'd let her know when I'm back on the Island. One thing for sure, if I do work with them, I'll possibly have access to police information, and that could help us in our investigation. I know Doug's right that there are some dangerous guys out there but I've been drawn into this case, and I don't think it's going to be easy letting it go."

"I feel the same way, that this was all meant to be—synchronicity as you called it before. Wait. If your calls are being monitored like Doug thought, someone could know you're talking to the police. "

"You're right, I'll be careful. Thanks for the heads up. Maybe you should be a mystery writer instead of writing a past-life romance."

"Writing about past lives is safer than real-life murders."

"You're right again. Now, are you ready to meet the ladies at the Dekalb Farmers Market?" asked Amy. "It's huge and has everything you could ask for—fresh produce, a great bakery, and foods and spices from around the world. It's fun that we're each cooking a dish tonight. We'll be nourishing our bodies and our spirits."

CHAPTER 20

THE BIG CHILL

Faith overslept on Thursday morning and had to rush to the lawyer's office with Cassie in tow. She was grateful for the company and tried to maintain a brave face for her guest. Everything seemed surreal to Faith, and she didn't know when she'd feel normal again. Each day was a struggle to maintain some equilibrium and manage the fallout from Charles' death. It was easier when she was in Florida, where she could push the memories to the back of her mind.

The lawyer gave Faith a package of documents to read and several she needed to sign. She left his office feeling heartsick but smiled when she saw Cassie in the waiting room. She knew her neighbor had major problems of her own. *Misery loves company,* she thought.

"Let's have an early lunch before we meet the ladies," Faith said as they walked to the car, and she placed the documents in the trunk. "There's a tea room and gift shop around the corner." Entering the store they both stopped in their tracks. They were overawed by an elaborate display of Christmas decorations.

"Oh heavens! What am I going to do about Christmas this year? We traditionally have a party on Christmas Eve, but I can't face it without Charles. My parents won't be here, so it will only be me and the boys."

"I'd planned on spending Christmas in Boston, but it's probably not a good idea. Confronting the friends who'll pity me over my third divorce isn't something I want to deal with. In many ways, Boston is a small city, and word will travel with lightning speed once I hire a divorce lawyer." Cassie walked around the shop looking for an ornament for her daughter as a distraction from her painful thoughts.

"I'll talk to Allison first, but I think we'll stay in Florida over the holidays. Since my parents passed away, there's less of a reason for us to return north. Maybe I can fly Allison's best friend, Clara, down on the 26th, and she can stay until the New Year."

At the same moment, both women realized they wouldn't have a man to kiss at midnight on New Year's Eve. Their eyes locked, and each of them knew what the other was thinking.

"It's the little things that can affect you the most," said Cassie. "Like being alone on New Year's Eve or Valentine's Day. For me, this is nothing new, but it will be hard for you, Faith, especially in the first year when you have to face each holiday without Charles."

"Thank goodness I have my beautiful boys to help me through. Life would be unbearable without them."

"You're right. Allison is a lifesaver for me. And we have each other—new friends that will help us cope and survive. Now, time for lunch and then grocery shopping with the FF."

"The FF?" asked Faith.

"The Fearsome Foursome!"

***

The kitchen was buzzing with activity as the ladies made dinner on Thursday night. "Christmas music or oldies?" Faith asked as she plugged her iPod into the speaker. "Oldies," came the agreement. "Red velvet cake or sweet potato pie?" was her next question. "Red velvet cake!" was the unanimous decision.

"I've never felt such camaraderie with a group of women like this," said Laura. "It's great, and I'm so glad I met you all."

Faith laughed, "It's y'all, Laura, now that you live in the South. You have so much to learn, missy."

"I do, don't I?" she said with a laugh. "Can you turn me into a proper Southern belle, Faith? I could surprise my children when they come to our place in Florida."

"I'm not sure if I can accurately describe what it means to be from the South. It's more of an attitude rather than the things you say or do. What do you think, Amy? You've been here for a few years. Have you changed because you live in Atlanta?"

Amy laughed, "I move a little slower, I speak more softly, and I feel a greater connection to the land than I did growing up in Detroit. It's wonderful to live in different places and internalize the best from each area."

"I'm looking forward to part-time living in Florida, and I'll be curious to see if it changes me in any way," said Laura. "Now, I'd better get started on my veggie lasagna."

Faith was happy that her kitchen was filled with laughter. She was looking for her Dutch oven and realized that Charles had used it last but hadn't put it back in the correct place. He'd become interested in cooking the past few years and delighted in creating dishes he saw on the cooking shows.

The ladies worked beside side each other, preparing dinner as they listened to the music. They joined in on the next song on the iPod—*I know you want to leave me, but I refuse to let you go.* They danced around the kitchen singing along to the music, with whisks, spoons, and spatulas swirling in the air. Cassie said, "That's the song from the movie *The Big Chill,* you know, when they were dancing in the kitchen after dinner. What's it called?"

"*Ain't Too Proud To Beg,*" Laura and Amy said in unison.

"That's it," said Cassie. "And we're just like the characters in the movie—except there are no men around!"

Laura's cell phone rang at that moment, and she was still singing as she answered. "Hey, Mumma! What's that noise? Are you at a party?" asked Jenny.

"If you want to call four middle-aged women making dinner a party, then yes, I guess it is," answered Laura. "Just a minute, sweetie, I'll go in the other room so I can hear you better."

Jenny filled Laura in on her life in Sydney and how it was giving her a new perspective on the world. "We were just talking about how living in new places changes you," Laura said. "I'm sure Steven will find the same thing working in Paris. I can't wait until you're both back home, and we're all together again."

"Me too, Mum. But until then it's amazing to experience something different. Say hi to Dad when you talk to him. Love you."

"Love you, Jenny. And I want you to meet the ladies of Hopeful Court when you're back. Be safe, my beautiful daughter."

Laura returned to the kitchen, and a wave of gratitude washed over her as she contemplated this unexpected new life. She missed her family, but she knew they needed to follow their own paths. As she observed the activity in the kitchen, she realized that she was the only one who still had a husband this holiday season, and her gratitude expanded tenfold.

Watching Cassie laugh and talk while making a salad, Laura saw the fun-loving, free spirit that attracted her to Cassandra as a young teen. *The eternal child within,* Laura thought. *Too often our youthful joy gets mired down in decades of sadness, loss, and disappointment. But what caused Cassie to change in the first place?* Laura left those thoughts behind as they continued to make dinner, relishing the energy created by a group of women enjoying the sharing of song, conversation, and good food.

Faith took photos of her friends with her smart phone as they worked in the kitchen and sent them to her sister, Amanda, in San Francisco. Amanda had called Faith earlier, concerned about how she was doing without Charles. Faith wanted her little sister to know that she was more than surviving and starting to recover from the worst loss of her life.

CHAPTER 21

GHOSTLY VISION

Faith and Laura drove together, with Amy and Cassie following behind in Amy's car, as they made their way back to Amelia Island on Friday morning.

"Tell me more about the book you're writing, Laura," Faith said as they drove. "I know it's about a teen that finds her love again on Amelia Island, but why did you decide on this kind of story?"

"Well, I've always thought that if people believed in the past lives of their soul, they would be more tolerant and compassionate toward their fellow human beings. If you knew a part of your soul would return as another sex, race, ethnic group, religion, or sexual orientation, then there would be less hateful, destructive prejudice in the world."

"I understand what you're saying, but I've been raised to believe that reincarnation doesn't exist and that people who have that belief are heretics. But I do think there should be more tolerance in the world. It pains my heart when someone verbally attacks my son Austin because he's gay."

"I want to reach young adults—actually adults of all ages—with this message, and originally I thought I'd write a self-help book, but a romance novel seems like it would get my ideas across more powerfully. I want my words to inform, inspire, and entertain. I also want to give the reader a sense of Island life."

"A story of star-crossed lovers on Amelia Island. How romantic!" said Faith. "And young people aren't as jaded as people our age, so there's a chance their hearts and minds are more open. I think appealing to them by including teenage characters is a good idea."

"We're all connected at a spiritual level, and we hurt ourselves when we hurt another," said Laura. "More understanding and love in the world is a much better future than the prejudice and fundamentalist fanaticism that's being espoused these days."

"That is a fine message, Laura. I'm beginning to see the world in a new way lately, questioning what I was taught. Do you remember a past life with your husband?"

"Yes, I've discovered three lifetimes when we were together. One when we were engaged but he died before we were married; another when John was my father; and another when I was a man and he was my wife."

"Heavens! I hadn't considered that possibility. I don't know what to think."

"It gives me a sense of confidence that our love transcends time and survives death," said Laura. *Should I have said that? I wonder how Faith feels about Charles' passing.*

"I believe our souls go to heaven, but I'm not sure about reincarnation. Anyway, I hope your novel is a best-seller," added Faith.

An hour after they began the journey, Laura called Amy on her cell and said they were stopping for gas at the next exit. Amy replied that they would drive slowly so Faith could catch up with them.

"Look at that car up ahead," Laura said once they were back on the highway. "It looks like the sedan that was following us to Atlanta. I wonder if it's tailing Amy again."

"Oh my, you could be right. Write down the license number, and we can have the Fernandina police check into it. You should call Amy and let her know. Tell her we'll stay behind the sedan and see what happens."

The car that was tailing Amy finally veered off after they crossed the bridge to Amelia Island, almost four hours later. There was no doubt in their minds that the car was purposely following them. When they were back in the cul de sac, Amy thanked the ladies for going on the trip to Atlanta, and they agreed to meet on Sunday evening for a cocktail.

Laura walked along the beach later that afternoon as a storm brewed over the ocean. Massive dark clouds covered the sun, and the ocean turned a sickly green. *The water's the same yellow-green color the sky turns in the Midwest when there's a tornado warning. That's so strange!* A fog rolled in quickly, and the shoreline was draped in mist. As Laura started to make her way back home, something drew her attention to the water. She saw a lone figure—a woman with short brown hair and wearing a long, white trench coat was standing near the waves.

If I didn't know any better, I'd think that woman is a ghost. She looks so eerie. Then it dawned on Laura that a ghostly vision on the beach was how she could begin her novel. She rushed home to put down her thoughts. Laura started writing her book that afternoon, channeling the energy she'd felt in the past few days and the inspiration of the woman by the ocean.

Laura called John that evening as she sat on the sofa, admiring the Christmas tree. She filled him in on the trip to Atlanta and her success at beginning the novel. "I love you, John, and thank you for loving me."

"I'll always love you, Laura. Where's this coming from?"

"I guess I just feel fortunate to be married to you, and it would break my heart if we weren't together. Last Christmas, Faith, Cassie, and Amy were with their husbands, and this year none of them are because of death, infidelity, and a breakdown in trust. "

"Don't worry, honey. It's you and me forever."

"I'm so glad! You never know what the future holds. I couldn't have imagined that this Christmas, Steven would be in France, Jenny would be in Australia, and you, Jack, and I would be spending the holidays in Florida."

"Me neither! Goodnight, Laura. Sleep well, and I'll call you tomorrow."

A short while later, Laura was reading in bed when Jack called from Mizzou.

"I can't wait until these stupid exams are over and I can come down."

"I thought you'd be out with Kate on a Friday night."

"She's at the library with a study group. We're going to meet up later. Tell me about Atlanta, Mom. What did you think of the city?"

Laura started to describe the city, Faith's house, and how much she enjoyed being with the ladies. Then she talked about the woman on the beach and how it had inspired her to start writing. Suddenly, she noticed a strange odor in the room. "Jack, there's a weird smell in the room. It reminds me of my old bedroom in Andover when I was a teen. Wow! Now there's a—a glowing white orb up by the ceiling with a gold ring around it and a purple ring around that one."

"Mom, what is it? Are you okay?"

"Fine, fine, but I can feel a strange energy around me—I don't know how to describe it. Wait, the lights are flickering. Oh my God, they just went out, and I'm in total darkness. Ahh!"

"MOM!"

"Jack, it's okay. The lights came back on. I felt a cold blast of air go right through me, and then it was over."

"Holy crap. What do you think it was?"

Laura's heart was racing as her mind was trying to make sense of the experience. "Well, the odor reminded me of the smell of leather. Do you remember me telling you about the summer before my senior year of high school, when I was a camp counselor and we had Indian names?"

"Yeah, Mom, I remember."

"My name was Shanika of the Shawnee tribe, and I made a dream-catcher out of feathers, a wooden hoop, and leather cord. It hung over my bed for years. That's what came to mind."

"What the heck do you think it means?"

"I have no idea. Nothing like this has ever happened before. The orb felt like a spirit energy, but it wasn't negative. It was more like it was trying to get my attention and communicate something. I wish I knew what it was."

"Do you think the house is haunted? Maybe it's sitting on an old Indian burial ground or something. Do you know what was there before the houses were built?"

"I haven't got a clue," answered Laura. "I'll have to do some research into the history of this part of the Island. Don't worry, Jack, I'm fine. Go meet up with Kate and have a good night. I'll text you if anything else happens."

"Night, Mom. I wish you weren't alone. Love you and be careful."

It was several hours before Laura could sleep. She was tossing and turning all night while images of Indians dominated her dreams.

***

Cassie picked up her daughter after school on Friday at the same time that Laura was encountering the lady on the shore. Allison was calm and happy to be home until she started to unpack her suitcase and put away her schoolbooks.

"Mom! Did you go through my things when I was gone?"

"No, Allie. I haven't been in your room. Is there something missing?"

"No, but my journal is on the left side of my desk drawer, and I always leave it on the right."

"Maybe you were distracted before you left. I wouldn't be surprised. I'm sorry about this mess," Cassie said as she walked into Allison's bedroom and hugged her daughter. "Let's order some pizza for dinner."

Cassie looked through the kitchen drawer for the pizza menu and noticed that papers had been moved. She had a sickening feeling that someone had been in the house. She went to her bedroom and looked through her closet and dresser. If she weren't such a meticulous neat freak, she wouldn't have noticed that her belongings were slightly out of place. She looked in her jewelry box and verified that nothing was missing, but things had definitely been moved.

Cassie checked all the locks on the outside doors, but there was no damage that she could see. Whoever it was, they knew what they were doing. *I don't want Allison to be afraid in her own home so I won't say anything to her right now.* She decided to wait until Saturday morning to call the police, when Allison would be at her art class. There was no point in upsetting her daughter any more than she had to. She'd also get the security system activated, something she'd neglected to do after they moved in last summer.

Cassie's conversation with the police the next morning didn't make her feel any better, especially when she learned there'd been other break-ins during the past few days. Cassie asked them to wait until Monday morning, when her daughter was at school, to come to the house to investigate. She was told about the other break-ins—one was at a home in the Amelia Island Plantation, and the other had been at an historical home in downtown Fernandina Beach. In both cases, possessions were moved but nothing was missing.

Someone is searching for something, and he's definitely a professional, Cassie thought. *I'll have to find out if there's any connection between me and the other homeowners. Maybe the police will be able to help when they come on Monday.*

CHAPTER 22

HOME TOUR

"Mom! My art teacher gave me four tickets to the Holiday Home Tour today. She has some family flying in this afternoon and can't use the tickets. Can we go, please, please?"

Cassie smiled as her daughter got into the car. "Sure, honey. Is there anyone else you want to invite?"

"Nah, all my friends are already going or they've gone, like, a hundred times, and don't want to go again."

"Well, would you mind if I invite a couple of my friends? Then we can go out for dinner."

"Do you have to invite Mrs. Biddle? She gives me the creeps."

Cassie laughed, "No, Allison. I was thinking about Mrs. Beck, Ms. Temple, or Mrs. Proctor. Is that okay? I'll call and see if at least two of the ladies are able to join us."

"Sure, Mom."

Cassie phoned her neighbors, and Amy and Laura agreed to meet them at the Amelia Island History Museum at 2:00. From there, they would take the trolley to the houses on the tour and have an early dinner at a waterfront restaurant. Dressed for the festive season, they hopped on the trolley to visit the first house on North 6th Street. Each house had been lovingly restored, and local florists and designers decorated them for the tour. Carolers wore costumes from the age of Dickens, and pirates and other characters representing Fernandina's past wandered the streets.

"This house is perfect," Laura said as they toured the parlor at the first home.

"Perfect for what?" asked Cassie as she admired the antique decorations on the Douglas fir tree in the corner.

"A character in my novel is from the 1920s. My heroine remembers a past life on the island, and her counterpart would have lived in a house like this."

"Mom, Mom, come and look at this dollhouse," called Allison from the dining room. Cassie joined her daughter, grateful that some normalcy had returned to their relationship. Allie had agreed they should spend the holidays in Florida, and Clara would join them after Christmas.

At the second tour house on North 4th Street, Amy enjoyed the extravagant decorations but felt someone was watching her. Out of the corner of her eye, she saw an old woman on crutches with a single leg. She knew immediately that she was looking at a ghost and smiled when she saw the old lady's mischievous grin. Amy wondered how many other visitors today would sense the one-legged ghost and have the feeling that someone was watching them but wouldn't see anyone in the room.

Amy walked outside to the enchanting formal garden in the backyard. Laura, Cassie, and Allison joined her, and they all marveled at the beauty of the grounds. Amy described her encounter with the apparition in the house.

Faith laughed, "There is a long tradition of ghosts haunting old Southern homes. I wouldn't be surprised if you meet others today, Amy."

They walked next door to the third house on the tour, and carolers greeted them as they ascended the front steps. "I know it may seem strange that I don't belong to an organized religion and I still love Christmas," Laura said as they strolled through the house. "I guess it's the pleasure of the traditions, the beauty of the decorations, and the joy I feel this time of year."

"Mom, look in the backyard. There's a club house!" said Allison as she ran out the back door to the elaborate children's playhouse.

"Sometimes Allie seems so mature, and other times she's still a little girl to me," Cassie said to her friends. "I'm glad she's overcome most of the trauma of the past week, but I didn't want to tell her that I'm sure someone broke into our house when we were away."

"Cassie! Oh my word," Faith said, concerned that other houses could have been violated too—including hers. She hadn't notice anything was missing when they returned from Atlanta. "Was anything taken?"

"No, things were just moved around, and it happened at two other homes on the Island as well. It's like someone was looking for something specific. I've contacted the home security company to get my alarm activated. It's overwhelming, but I don't want to worry Allison, so I told her that with Christmas coming I wanted to make sure our presents didn't disappear."

"I'll drop by later and see if I can pick up any information about the break-in," added Amy. "Sometimes I can get psychic impressions about a crime scene even if there hasn't been a violent act."

"That would be great, Amy. Thanks—all of you—for your support. Everything would be much more difficult without your friendship."

They got on the trolley for their final stop on the tour, a lovely Victorian house on South 7th Street. They drove past some smaller historic homes that Laura thought were perfect for other characters in her novel. Her life had become an adventure, between scouting locations for her novel and dealing with real-life mysteries. She was certain that Cassie was correct in her belief that it was a targeted, professional break-in and that others in the neighborhood shouldn't be concerned.

"When we get together tomorrow night, we should go over all the clues again about the crime. If Amy comes up with any psychic impressions at Cassie's, maybe we can help the police," Laura commented as they toured the last home.

After returning to the History Museum, they walked to a waterfront restaurant. "It's so strange seeing palm trees standing next to traditionally decorated Christmas trees. Our first Florida holiday season is going to be so different from what we're used to," said Laura. "No heavy coats or mittens, just sunshine and sand."

CHAPTER 23

SECRET PANEL

Cocktail hour at Cassie's on Sunday night brought more surprises to the ladies of Hopeful Court. Amy had arrived earlier and went through the house trying to get impressions of who could have broken in while they were in Atlanta. She told Cassie that she had spoken to the police and would see Detective Davis after the memorial service for Conti on Monday.

"It was a man who moved with military precision," Amy began as Faith and Laura joined them in Cassandra's living room. "I got the feeling he was looking for information, because I could see a series of numbers in my mind but I'm not sure what they meant. When I entered Cassie's bedroom, I was drawn to a jewelry box on her dresser, but we didn't find anything unusual inside it."

Cassie walked into her bedroom then returned with the antique box that Eduardo Conti had given her shortly before his death.

"My great-grandmother used to have a jewelry box similar to this," said Faith. "May I see it? If it's the same kind as the one she had, there's a secret compartment." She opened the box and ran her fingers around the burgundy velvet fabric inside, feeling for a small indentation. Faith located the spot she'd been looking for and pressed hard. There was a distinct click and the bottom panel was released. Faith turned the box over and gently opened the wood panel.

"Is there anything inside?" asked Cassie.

Faith removed a small piece of folded paper. Opening it, they saw a series of numbers and letters. '271214TC8667xjiu7439821.'

"What on earth do the numbers mean?" questioned Cassandra. "And why did Eduardo hide them in the music box and give it to me? Do you have any idea, Amy?"

Amy held the paper and closed her eyes, feeling the energy left by the man who wrote the numbers and letters down. After several moments she opened her eyes and looked at her friends.

"This is beyond strange. I get the impression of a ship, a large one but also medicine or something medical. I have no idea how the two relate to each other."

"A medical ship?" asked Cassie. "I don't remember him ever talking about anything like that. What could it mean?" Cassie walked into the kitchen and the three other women silently followed her. They took a cup of mulled cider that Cassie had prepared. The wheels were turning in each of their heads trying to decipher what the numbers could mean and how they would relate to a ship and medicine.

Amy was still looking at the slip of paper when she noticed words in tiny print on the back. "Look at this. It says, 'Resolve to Dissolve.' What was Conti up to?"

Allison walked into the kitchen holding the box they had left in the family room. "Wow, this is wicked cool! A secret panel! Mom, did you find anything inside?"

Amy showed the paper to the young teen. "Geez, what does it mean?"

"That's what we're trying to figure out," answered her mother.

"Mom, these first six numbers could be a date," said Allie. "It's the way they write it in Europe with the day first, then the month and year. We learned about that in school."

"Allison is right," said Laura. "They do the same thing in Canada. Let me get the journal and we can write down everything that comes to mind." Laura retrieved the leather journal and a pen from her purse. "Okay, I've written the numbers and letters and the message on the back. It looks like the date is December 27, 2014. Whatever is going on, will happen two days after Christmas."

"And we have Amy's impressions of a large ship and medicine. I'm at a loss how to put it all together but we have some time before it will 'go down' as they say on TV," added Cassie. "Amy, put the paper in a plastic bag and you can give it to Detective Davis. Maybe the police will be able to figure out the rest of the numbers and the message on the back."

Amy laughed, "I'm not a very good detective because I shouldn't have put my fingerprints on the paper. You'd think I'd know better."

"Don't worry, Amy. I'm sure the police will be able to determine if yours are the only prints or not," said Faith. "Dear Lord, this mystery gets more strange and interesting every day!"

"It's kinda exciting," added Allison. She looked at her mother and remembered that someone Cassie cared about had died. "Sorry, Mom."

"It's alright, Allie," Cassandra said as she hugged her daughter. "I understand how you feel. It's time for bed sweetie, you have school in the morning."

"Do you ladies want to drive with me to the service for Mr. Conti tomorrow?" asked Faith when Cassie returned to the kitchen after tucking Allison into bed. "At first I wasn't sure if I could face another funeral, but I feel that we're a team," Faith added. "The Lord has brought us together for a reason, but only He knows what it is!"

"I would appreciate the company," said Cassandra. "An officer is coming early in the morning to investigate the break-in but we can go together," she whispered so her daughter wouldn't hear.

"That will be good for me," answered Amy. "I'm meeting Mrs. Ferguson at 10:00 to pick up the key to the house next door and sign the rental agreement. It will be strange moving into a furnished home and living with other people's belongings but it's the best option for now."

"It will be wonderful to have you close, Amy. Your friendship and support mean the world to me," said Faith.

"We're all glad you're moving here, Amy. We need each other right now."

"Thanks—all of you. It means a lot to me to have your friendship, too," Amy said with a smile. "Oh, Laura, will you bring the journal tomorrow and we can go over what we've discovered so far? I'll bring the note with me to give to the police."

The women agreed to meet at Faith's at 10:30 the following morning.

CHAPTER 24

BOOM!

Monday, December 8, turned out to be a cold, blustery day on Amelia Island. The forecast had been for cooler weather, but the drop in temperature was dramatic and unexpected. There was a freeze warning for the coming night, and Laura thought about covering some of the palms in her garden. She was glad she'd brought her crimson wool coat with her from St. Louis. She'd definitely need it today when they went to the memorial service for Eduardo Conti.

Looking out the front window, she saw the police at Cassie's house, who were there to investigate the break-in. At 10:30, she joined the ladies in Faith's driveway as Cassie told them the police didn't find any fingerprints or signs of forced entry. The home security company had arrived a short time after the police left, and Cassie felt better.

"Last night I was going over my notes about the case, and it dawned on me that the killer may have left footprints in the sand because it had rained earlier in the day," said Laura. "I wonder if the police were able to recover any prints right after the crime. They didn't ask John or me to show them the shoes we were wearing, although I didn't get too close to body."

"I can add that to our list of questions for the detective," answered Amy.

Cassie was silent during the ride into downtown Fernandina Beach. Amy began humming a tune that surprised Laura. "Amy, why are you humming *Row, row, row, your boat gently down the stream?*"

Amy laughed, "I have no idea! It's been going through my head all morning. I wonder if it has something to do with the case, but I can't for the life of me figure out what it is."

"You should mention it to the detective. You never know what might actually be a clue," said Faith.

They were surprised at the number of vehicles lining the streets and had to walk several blocks to the church. Small groups of well-dressed men sauntered up to the front door, amid the local police and others who were obviously members of law enforcement agencies. *It looks like half the population of Amelia Island is here,* Laura thought. *There's nothing like an unsolved murder to captivate the locals and draw them to the spectacle of a funeral.*

Laura spotted Paolo Conti, a woman who she assumed was his mother, and an elderly man who reminded her of a character out of *The Godfather.* She decided it was probably Paolo's grandfather. The women walked inside the church, and Amy led them up the stairs to the balcony. They found seats along the railing that provided an excellent view of the people sitting below.

Laura took out the journal and wrote down the names of everyone she recognized or who appeared interesting: Betsy Biddle; Laura's real estate agent, Janice; Sheila, the woman who worked at the police station; Andrea, her hair dresser; the lady in the white trench coat from the beach; Ronnie Gordon; and another woman she could only describe as a 'cougar,' with platinum blond hair and a full-length sable coat.

"That's Doug's boss," Amy whispered and pointed to a man who was walking down the aisle. "And those men following him look like his competitors from the military security business. Wow, this is a bizarre group of people to have on the Island."

The organist began playing, making it difficult for further conversation. Eduardo's son led his mother and grandfather down the center aisle, and they sat in the front row as the priest walked to the lectern. In front of the altar, there was a table that held an ornate urn surrounded by massive floral arrangements. A poster-sized photo of Conti was set on an easel to the right of his remains.

Cassie's eyes filled with tears as the priest began to pray. The feeling of loss was overwhelming; her Italian lover and her marriage were now both gone. She was alone once again, and she began to sob. Everyone in the balcony stared at the attractive, dark-haired woman. There was little doubt in many minds that this was one of Conti's 'woman friends.' If she had been a friend of the family, she would be sitting in the front pews instead of the balcony.

Faith put her arm around Cassie's shoulder and began to cry as well. Attending a memorial service so soon after Charles' funeral cracked the fragile shell Faith had placed around her heart. The priest finished his sermon, then Paolo walked up to the lectern to speak. He did a masterful job of talking about the highlights of his father's life while omitting the less-savory aspects of the man's personality and questionable business dealings. To Laura, it didn't sound like the speech of a murderer, and she was more convinced than ever of Paolo's innocence.

Conti's ex-business partner was next to speak, and his words were not as kind. Laura got the impression that Albert Maxwell was quite delighted that Conti had been 'taken out.' "What do you think of him?" she quietly asked Amy.

"Definitely a suspect," Amy answered. *The murderer is here,* Amy thought as she used her psychic sense while focusing on the people in the pews below. All of a sudden she saw the spirit of Eduardo standing beside the large photo on the easel and glaring at his ex-partner. "He's here," Amy whispered. At that moment, the photo went flying down the steps in front of the altar. "Conti knocked it over!" Amy exclaimed.

Before Laura could respond, there was a huge explosion outside the church, shaking the building and rattling the stained glass windows. It was pandemonium as people rushed outside to find the cause of the noise, and officers from several law enforcement agencies ran across the street to a black Mercedes SUV that was now a ball of fire. Acrid smoke rose high into the morning sky as the church emptied.

Doug's boss, Ivan Whitman, ran over to his burning vehicle and let out a stream of profanity that made even the most hardened police officers cringe. Betsy sidled up to Amy, Faith, Cassie and Laura, and—for once—she was speechless. Amy whispered to Laura, "Look to your left and observe what you can about how the people react. I'll take the right side."

Amy watched the two military-looking men who had followed Whitman into the church hurriedly walk down the street and disappear around the corner. Laura noticed the look of fear on the faces of two women to her left—the lady in the white trench coat and the lady in the black fur coat. *They must be two of Conti's other woman friends. I wonder if their houses were the ones broken into. They certainly look frightened,* Laura thought. *Like Cassie, they must be worried about their connection to Conti. This is turning into a dangerous situation for everyone who knew the man.*

Detective Davis was swiftly moving away from the scene when she saw Amy. "Ms. Temple, are you still able to come to the station at 3:00?"

"Yes," Amy answered. "I'll be there."

"Amy, why do the police want to talk to you? Do you know something about the murder? You're a psychic, aren't you? Did Conti's ghost tell you who shot him? Is it someone we know? Should I be worried about a killer on the loose?" Betsy Biddle had found her voice again.

CHAPTER 25

CLUES

The four women drove to the Florida House Inn on South 3rd Street after they had convinced Betsy that they would talk to her later about the case. The Inn is the oldest, continuous hotel in Florida, built in 1857 to house railway workers. Fernandina was the beginning location of the first railway built across the state, which ended in Cedar Key on the Gulf coast. The Florida House Inn had recently been renovated and offered a lunchtime menu of Southern specialties. The ladies had a few hours before Amy was expected at the police station.

After ordering lunch, Laura took out the journal and asked for impressions about the memorial service. She wanted to get as much information as possible before Amy talked to the police.

"I'll start," Amy said. "An infuriated Conti was in the church and knocked over his photo. I think people mistakenly thought the blast caused the photo to topple over."

"Oh my, Amy. You're right that the photo fell before the bomb went off. The whole thing was so upsetting that I didn't remember they were two separate events. Did Conti say anything to you?" asked Faith.

"No, he was only there for a few moments before the big bang. I also had the impression that the killer was in the building, but I couldn't zero in on who it was. Okay, the information I've received includes: a ship; a medical connection; *Row, row, row your boat*; and the murderer was at the church today. This is definitely the strangest case I've ever worked on."

The server brought their lunches and seemed overly interested in the conversation. Amy looked around the room and realized their conversation about the Thanksgiving murder was the focus of attention. *We'll have to be more careful when we're discussing this in public*, she decided. "We should probably lower our voices. There are too many curious people in this room."

Laura nodded as she added the notes to the journal. Quietly, she contributed her own thoughts. "I don't think Paolo Conti was involved, but what about his grandfather? He looked like he was an extra in *The Sopranos*. Then there's Conti's ex-partner, who still seems angry and could have wanted revenge. His eulogy was filled with vitriol."

"What about all those military-looking guys?" added Cassie. "I wonder if the warring factions that you talked about, Amy, are responsible for the car bomb. Whatever they're fighting over is serious, and somehow everyone involved with Eduardo is a target."

"I agree," said Laura. "Did you notice the two women standing near us outside the church? One was wearing a white trench coat and the other a black fur. They both seemed very upset. Actually, I saw the woman in the trench coat on the beach the other day, not far from Conti's house. I'm guessing they were 'seeing' Eduardo, too."

Cassie looked down at her lunch, knowing that Laura was right. "I never imagined I'd run into Eduardo's other lady friends. Do you think it could it have been one of them who shot him? Or maybe one of their husbands? My head is spinning."

"Don't worry, Cassie. I'm sure the police are working hard to solve the case. I hope they can give us more information today," said Amy.

As they were leaving after lunch, Faith's phone rang. "Excuse me, ladies, it's my sister calling." Not wanting to venture outside into the chilly air, they remained beside the fireplace in the Inn's quaint, mermaid-themed bar.

"Happy news, ladies. My sister, Amanda, was able to get us tickets to see Pastor Jeffrey Stanton! He's going to give a sermon at one of those megachurches in Orlando and has agreed to speak in the Amelia Island Plantation Chapel on Thursday night. He'll be making a presentation after the Island Chamber Singers performance. Amanda was on his website today and noticed the change to his schedule. He must owe a favor to someone who lives on the Island. I've seen him on TV, and he's so handsome and such a charismatic speaker."

Laura looked at Cassie. "Is that the same Jeffrey Stanton we knew in high school? I'd heard that he was a famous religious speaker."

The color drained from Cassie's face. "Yes, it's him. I'm not sure I want to hear Jeffrey speak. I don't agree with his message."

"Please come with us, Cassie," said Faith. "We're such a great team."

Cassandra was silent for a few moments and then sighed. "You're right, Faith. We need to stick together. I'll go with you on Thursday."

After returning home, Amy picked up her car and drove to the police station. Detective Davis was interested in Amy's psychic impressions about the murderer being at the memorial service; the ship; the medical idea; and the nursery rhyme about rowing a boat. The detective was especially intrigued by the slip of paper that was hidden in the jewelry box that Conti had given Cassie the week before Thanksgiving.

"Cassie's daughter suggested that the first numbers are a date with the day first. It makes sense, but I don't understand what the rest of the numbers and letters mean."

"The date is followed by TC2667, then *ycdxjui* followed by seven numbers," said Detective Davis. "I'm going to have to give this some thought and talk to my team. We'll dust the paper for any fingerprints other than yours and Mr. Conti's."

"Do you know who set the car bomb? It shook everyone—figuratively and literally," Amy added.

"We're trying to determine who planted the bomb and why. Thank goodness no one was hurt. These events are highly unusual for the Island. And since there are suspects from several states involved, we're working with the FBI."

"I also wanted to ask you about Paolo Conti's mother and grandfather. Do you think they were involved?"

"We don't think so, but we're continuing to investigate the family and Conti's ex-partner from New Jersey."

Amy asked, "There were two women at the service, one in a white trench coat and one in a black fur. Were these ladies personally involved with Conti, like Cassie was?"

"Good investigative work. Yes, they were dating Conti, too, and it was their homes that were burglarized around the same time that Ms. Harcourt's house was broken into."

"Could the killer be one of these ladies or their cuckolded husbands?"

"We're checking them out. This case is more complex all the time," answered the detective.

"Laura Beck was wondering if any footprints were found in the sand beside Conti's body since it had rained earlier that evening. She said that she and her husband weren't asked to show the police their shoes."

"No, the only prints were Mr. Beck's. An officer on scene noted the make and size of his shoes and determined that the murderer wiped away any prints before he left. It made us believe that it was a professional or someone local who would think about prints in the wet sand."

"Do you know the make of the gun and who might own it?"

"It was a Ruger LC9. It's a small pocket pistol, and we're still checking the state database for sales and thefts. I'll keep you updated on what we find, and please let me know if you have any additional information or psychic impressions. Thanks for your help, Ms. Temple, and please thank the other women too."

Laura was at her mailbox when Amy returned home. Amy gave the journal back to Laura and filled her in on what the police had discovered.

"There are still so many unanswered questions," commented Laura. "Do you have any other feelings about the murderer and if he's still on Amelia Island? I worry that we're in danger."

"Yes, I do feel that he's close by, and I don't understand why," said Amy. "If it's a professional hit man, I guess he hasn't found what he was looking for. If it's the information that was hidden in the jewelry box, it's now in the hands of the police."

Laura added, "But that person probably doesn't know they have it. I wonder if he'll keep on looking."

"That's crossed my mind too. I need to put the case out of my mind for a while," said Amy. "I'm moving into my temporary new home tonight. It'll be good to let Faith have some private time. Yet we'll all be close so she won't be alone if she wants some company."

CHAPTER 26

BROKEN ANGEL

On Tuesday morning, Shirley arrived to clean Laura's house. She showed the young woman around and gave instructions on what she wanted cleaned. "I saw your brother at the memorial service for Mr. Conti yesterday but I didn't see you," Laura exclaimed.

"Oh, Mrs. Beck, Ronnie thought I would be too upset. But he told me there was a bomb, and I woulda liked to see that! Just like in the movies."

"Yes, Shirley, it was just like in the movies. Why did your brother think you'd be upset?" Before Shirley could respond, Laura's cell phone rang. "Excuse me, Shirley, it's my son. Steven, it's so good to hear your voice. I miss you!"

"I miss you too, especially at this time of year."

"Tell me more about what it's like to live in Paris," Laura said as she walked out to the lanai and wrapped a purple throw around her shoulders. She settled into the love seat, anxious for her son to share his experience.

"I like working and living in a major city, and I'm experiencing that newness along with the unknown of a foreign land," Steven began. "Commuting to work on the subway, going without a car, and living in a small apartment is hard to get used to. I usually stop in a bakery on my way to the subway for a *pain au chocolat*—it's like a croissant. Then I muscle my way through the crowded underground tunnels and head to my office in a massive glass building."

"Wow, it must be strange living in an enormous city like Paris. It's huge compared with St. Louis. What are your co-workers like?"

"The people have a different vibe, they move and speak and work in an unfamiliar way. When I first got here, I was scheduled to meet with people to simply get to know them before we'd work together, something I'd never encountered in the US. When people are out of the office, their work goes undone until they return, and decisions are held off until they can weigh in. The sense of 'everything has to get done right now' that I grew up with in the US is simply not true here. The work–life balance is important, and no one's expected to pull long hours simply to complete regular work. This is totally new, and it's refreshing."

"I can see that, honey. I know Europeans take their vacations, unlike the people in the States."

"There are other differences too, like the computer keyboard. There are 3 sets of switched keys—the A and the Q, the W and the Z, and the M and the semi-colon. It was hard to get used to!"

Laura added, "I had no idea their keyboards weren't the same as ours."

"There's also, as one might expect from the French culture, a greater emphasis on the quality of the food provided at work. Coming from an office that offered sandwiches and light salads, I'm amazed by the lunches. There's a full kitchen that makes pastas, meats, vegetables, and rotating specials every day. Starters, entrees, and desserts are the norm, and no one ever eats at their desk!"

"You are a foodie like your father," Laura laughed. "I can't wait to visit. Be safe, my darling son, and we'll give you a call on Christmas Day."

"Love you, Mom," Steven said.

Laura choked back tears as she went back into the house. It was hard being apart from her children, but once again she felt a deep pride in their accomplishments. She decided to focus on the murder case as a distraction. Sitting at the kitchen table, she opened the journal Amy had given back to her and began to brainstorm. She knew in her heart that Paolo wasn't involved, but she started her list with his scary-looking grandfather. On the same page where Amy had noted the type of gun that was used in Conti's murder, she listed the other suspects:

New Jersey partner, Albert Maxwell;
a private military company;
Doug's private security company, run by Ivan Whitman who
had his car bombed;
a vengeful lover including the lady in white and the lady in black;
an enraged husband;
or someone else with a personal grudge.

Then she remembered that Amy had said something about ammunition that Doug's company was supposed to buy from Conti. Maybe that was the connection between the private military company and private security company feud—and the car bomb. She figured the police had already put that together. Laura heard a crashing sound and went running into the Jenny's bathroom. Shirley was standing beside an angel statue that was in pieces on the tile floor.

"Oh, Mrs. Beck! I'm so sorry."

"It's okay, Shirley, lets pick up the pieces." The women were cleaning up the mess when Laura heard a voice coming from the kitchen.

"Hey, Mrs. Beck, the back door was open. Do you need help with anythin' else while Shirley's cleanin'?" Ronnie called out.

Laura walked into the kitchen and saw Ronnie leaning over the kitchen table reading the open journal. She was angry that he had just walked into the house and was snooping.

"Ronnie, no, I don't need help right now, and next time please knock before you come in."

Ronnie's face turned bright red as he looked at Laura. "Yeah, sorry. I'll be back in an hour to pick up my sister," he said as he slipped out the sliding door to the lanai.

Shirley quietly walked into the kitchen. "Please don't tell my brother I broke the statue."

Laura decided that her brother intimidated the young woman. "Don't worry, I won't say anything. I can get my daughter another angel statue when she visits the Island."

Laura went back to the journal and reread all the entries looking for some clue she might have missed. After five minutes she gave up and went into the garage to retrieve the Christmas decorations she hadn't put out yet. She had brought down three boxes and had left another ten at home in St. Louis. *This will be a minimalist holiday. It makes me realize what decorations and traditions are really important and the ones that I can let go. Change is good, but it's also difficult in many ways.*

CHAPTER 27

P I

A my woke with a start on Wednesday morning and bolted upright in bed. She looked around and didn't recognize her surroundings. It took her a moment to realize she was in her newly rented home on Amelia Island. She tried to recall her last dream, and the memory slowly returned. She'd been standing by the wharf in Fernandina Beach where the tour boats leave for Cumberland Island, Georgia across the St. Mary's River. A heavy fog was rolling in, and she heard sirens in the distance. Suddenly a hand gripped her shoulder, and she spun around to face Eduardo Conti with an angry look on his face.

"Protect my girls!" he screamed at her.

Amy wasn't surprised that she'd awoken at that moment. She immediately wrote down every detail of the dream so she could review it later—after she had her first cup of coffee. She was standing in the kitchen, still in her robe, when there was a knock at the door.

"Laura. You're up early, please come in. Here, let me get you some coffee. Is there something on your mind?"

"I had the strangest dream last night. I could hear a baby crying and looked all through our house in St. Louis, but I couldn't find it. Then I was back in our old house in Andover, and a baby was crying there too. I woke up feeling so sad. I don't know anyone who's pregnant, and I have no idea what it all means."

Amy described her unusual dream, and both women sat in silence for a while trying to get some clarity. "I wonder who Conti meant in my dream when he said 'my girls.' Cassie and the other two women? Are they in danger from whomever broke into the houses?"

"I wish I knew and if they really are in peril," answered Laura as they walked into the living room. Something caught Laura's eye as she walked past the front window. "Amy, look up the street. Is that the same type of car that followed us to Faith's house?"

Amy cautiously looked out the window as she entered the room. "Yes, it could be the same car or one just like it. Do you think it's time to confront the driver? Let me get dressed, and we'll go and see who it is." Amy quickly changed into jeans and a heavy knit sweater, and the women walked out the lanai and through the backyards so they could approach the vehicle from the rear. Laura banged on the passenger side window and waited while the tinted window descended. She was surprised to see a balding, heavy-set man with thick glasses and a goatee. Laura had expected a clean-cut military-type.

"Who are you and why have you been following us?" demanded Amy.

"I'm a private investigator," he said showing them his credentials. "And I'm not following you, lady. I've been hired to check up on Ms. Harcourt. Her husband wants the lowdown on her extramarital activities."

"You know that the man she was involved with is dead, don't you?" asked Laura. "Why would her husband want her followed now?"

The PI chuckled. "You know, once a whore always a whore. He wanted to see if she was datin' anyone else before takin' her to divorce court."

Amy and Laura were shocked. They didn't know Robert personally but were surprised he'd go to such lengths to hurt Cassie.

"You followed us to Atlanta to see if she was with another man?" said Amy.

"Yeah, lady. I tailed you until Macon, but I knew where y'all were headed. I ain't seen Ms. Harcourt with anyone else except you broads, but as long as I'm being paid I'll keep followin' her."

"Rest assured, Cassie is not involved with any man, and you can give that message to Robert," said Laura. "Did you break into Cassie's house?"

"Course not, lady. I follow and photograph, not break and enter. I'm no criminal." The man laughed as he put up the window and slowly drove out of the subdivision.

The women walked back to Amy's and sat quietly in the kitchen for a long time, working through the events of the past few weeks. "At least one mystery is solved," said Laura. "It wasn't anyone directly connected to Conti who was following us. Oh man, I forgot we had the license plate from the car that was tracking us, and we didn't give it to the police after we came back from Atlanta. Sometimes getting older and forgetting things stinks." Laura was lost in thought for a few minutes then said, "But if the investigator didn't break into Cassie's house, who did?"

"I don't know," answered Amy. "It still makes more sense that it was someone looking for information about the deal Doug talked about. That makes it more frightening, because it could be the people who planted the car bomb."

"At least the bomb seemed to be a warning and wasn't meant to hurt anyone."

"But mistakes happen all the time, and I don't want any of us to be on the receiving end of a violent threat," said Amy.

Laura poured more coffee in both mugs. "Do you think Robert could have anything to do with Conti's death? He could have hired someone and that person may have been at the memorial service."

"I'm not sure, but it's possible. Wow, we certainly got sidetracked from our conversation about our dreams. I have a feeling that everything will make sense—eventually."

"Should we talk to Cassie and let her know what's going on?"

"Her car is there, and we may as well get it over with."

Reluctantly, Laura and Amy walked to Cassie's to fill her in on the latest developments affecting her divorce proceedings.

CHAPTER 28

THE REVELATION

Cassie worked with clients in Jacksonville on Wednesday afternoon and all day on Thursday, knowing she needed to supplement her income with her divorce looming. She'd been angry when Amy and Laura informed her that Robert had hired a private investigator. Not only was she furious, she was frightened by the extreme measures her husband had taken and wondered if he was losing his grip on reality.

After dinner, Cassie picked up Allison's friend, Mandy, and drove the girls to a strip mall a short distance off the Island. Mandy's mother was picking them up later. Cassie pulled into a parking spot at the mall and said to the girls as they got out of the car, "Be careful. Watch your hand-bags, and make sure you stay together."

"Mom, we'll be fine. We're not children, geez!" said Allison as they walked away.

Cassie put the car in reverse but heard her phone chime with a text message. Picking up her cell from the passenger seat, she read a nasty and hurtful text from Robert. She tossed the phone back on the seat and put her foot on the gas, backing the car into a light standard behind her. The sound of crashing metal made her stomach churn, and she pulled forward and turned off the engine. Examining the damage, she saw that her rear fender was smashed in, but the taillight still worked.

I'm such an idiot! That's my second accident in three months. My insurance rates will be sky high, Cassie thought as she got back into the car and drove across the bridge over the Amelia River. *What is the matter with me? I can't do anything right. My life is in chaos, and I'm bringing Allison down with me. Why do I keep messing up?* Tears rolled down her cheeks as she drove to the Planation. Parking near the chapel, Cassie saw her friends walking toward the Zen garden on the right side of the building. She dried her eyes and put on her 'face-the-jury' face, not wanting to spoil the evening.

Laura, Amy, and Faith had arrived together in Amy's car. "I've heard of a nondenominational church but not an interdenominational one," Faith was saying. "Oh my, Cassie what's wrong?"

"I'm fine, really. I just smashed into a light pole, and it's just one more example of how I'm screwing up my life! I feel like Charlie Brown when he said, 'Everything I do turns into a disaster.'"

"Don't be so hard on yourself," said Amy as she put her arm around Cassie's shoulder. "To be human is to make mistakes. We so quickly forgive others but beat ourselves up about our own failures."

"She's right, Cassie," added Laura. "Let's go inside. The concert should start soon."

The women entered the chapel and found seats in the third pew from the back on the right side of the aisle. Floor to ceiling windows at the front of the room framed the twinkling lights on the decorated trees outside. The raised platform under the picture windows slowly filled with the Island Chamber Singers, and their excellent performance delighted the audience. As the final applause rang through the chapel, a lectern was brought to the center of the stage. A well-preserved, tiny woman with platinum-blond hair stepped behind the lectern and moved the microphone as low as possible.

"That was magnificent! Let's thank the Island Chamber Singers for their inspiring performance tonight." The clapping erupted then slowly died down. "Please give a warm welcome to our esteemed guest," said the diminutive woman, "a gifted international speaker and the illustrious leader of the New Life Evangelical Church in Boston—Pastor Jeffrey Stanton."

A distinguished-looking man stood up from the front pew and walked behind the lectern. His silver-gray hair, piercing blue eyes, and disarming smile drew a new round of applause. He was tall, slim, and impeccably dressed.

Jeffrey's certainly enjoying the adulation, thought Laura. *I had no idea he would be so successful and—according to his website—such a social fanatic. But he has aged well!* Laura glanced to her right and noticed that Cassie was not looking at their former high-school classmate. There were half a dozen young women in the pew in front of them whispering about the handsome preacher. Stanton raised his hands to quiet the audience. His smile was radiant, and Faith let out a sigh, along with many other women in attendance. The charismatic pastor began his speech.

"Thank you for that warm welcome. I'm so pleased to be spending this evening with the fortunate residents of this beautiful island. My old friend, Gilbert Findley, convinced me to experience the magic of Amelia Island first hand. We spent many nights debating theology at divinity school, although he eventually took a different and very lucrative path."

The audience laughed along with the pastor and listened with rapt attention, as he spoke for the next twenty minutes. He thanked his lovely wife who was in attendance this evening and his parents who were back in Boston caring for their six children.

"It's the children, God's most precious gift, that are the motivation behind my ministry. Regardless of the results of the last federal election, we must take a stand against the evils of the Godless left-wing fanatics. Planned Parenthood needs to be destroyed, and all doctors who perform abortions should be burned at the stake! We must bring God back into the hearts and minds of all our countrymen. Rise up my fellow citizens and follow me!"

The crowd cheered, and the applause was deafening.

"Even if he's old enough to be my father, I'd follow Pastor Stanton anywhere and do anything he asked, and I mean *anything!*" said a young strawberry-blond woman sitting in front of Amy.

Cassie moaned as if she was in pain. Her friends looked at her and wondered if she was ill. Then it happened. Slowly, Cassie stood up.

"Enough!" Cassie said quietly and then shouted, "Enough!" Jeffrey Stanton and everyone in the chapel turned and stared at the woman who spoke. Finally, a look of recognition crossed the pastor's face but was quickly replaced by a look of fear.

"You hypocrite! Tell them, Jeffrey. Tell everyone here about us. You preach violence against people involved with abortions, but you don't mention the fact that you forced me to get an abortion when I was 15 years old. Did you know that the so-called doctor you found botched my abortion? You went on to have your six children, but did you know that I could never have a child of my own because of it? Did you know that the embryo split, and I was pregnant with twins?"

Gasps could be heard throughout the building. Conversations erupted followed by a woman wailing at the front of the chapel. Cassie picked up her purse and ran out the door to her car. She quickly got in and drove away.

"How could you do that? Force a girl to get an abortion? You of all people! And how could you not tell me?" Mrs. Stanton screamed at her husband, then ran out of the room. Stanton stood with his hands glued to the sides of the lectern until he was able to recover his composure. With as much dignity as he could muster, he walked down the center aisle and out of the building after his wife. The chapel emptied quickly as discussions continued about the evening's unexpected turn of events.

Laura, Faith, and Amy followed the crowd out to the parking lot. "Should we phone Cassie?" Faith asked as they got into the car.

"I think we should give her some time. She'll call us when she's ready to talk," Laura answered. *Now I know what came between us, but why didn't she tell me? Didn't she trust me enough to let me in on something so traumatic? We were both so young, but I could have helped her deal with her pain.*

121

CHAPTER 29

YOU'VE CHANGED

"**M**om, have you seen it?" Jack asked when he called his mother on Friday morning.

"What are you talking about, honey?" said Laura.

"The YouTube video from the Plantation chapel last night. Someone used their phone to video that pastor and his wife. They didn't get Ms. Harcourt but got a great reaction from the Stantons and the crazy response from the crowd."

"I'll take a look at it later, Jack. Thanks for letting me know. Your flight gets in at 6:00 on Sunday night, doesn't it?"

"Yeah, and I can't wait to hit the beach. I'm so glad my finals are over," answered Jack. "I'll text you when I'm boarding the plane to let you know if the flight's on time."

"Have fun with your friends in St. Louis this weekend. It's wonderful that you'll see most of them before you come for Christmas. Love you."

"Love you too, Mom."

Laura had been baking cookies and using royal icing to glue together the gingerbread house she had made earlier. Jack would have to decorate it by himself this year, without his siblings to help. She took the final batch of cookies out of the oven before she turned on the computer to check

YouTube. Watching the video, she was thankful the person had missed Cassie's part of the event. *I wonder what the fallout will be for Jeffrey. I need to talk to Cassie, but I think I'll wait until tomorrow.*

She went on Pastor Stanton's website and saw that it was 'under construction,' and no information was available about when it would be back up. Instead of feeling glad that Jeffrey was reaping what he sowed all those years ago, she only felt sadness for everyone involved. Laura opened the kitchen drawer and took out her high-school diary that she had found among Jenny's books and tried to uncover some clues to what happened to Cassie. She read several entries in which her ex-friend had made comments that now made sense. *Hindsight is a wonderful thing. But why didn't Cassie tell me what happened to her?*

***

Just as she was leaving for the airport to pick up her son on Sunday, Laura received a text from Cassie. They agreed to meet at 9:00 the following morning. Laura knew that Jack would probably sleep in late Monday. Once again, she was grateful that Jacksonville airport was so close. Driving to the airport, she passed several large trucks carrying yellow pine trees to the two pulp and paper mills on the Island and was amazed when she'd heard that there were hundreds of trucks every day. She'd also been surprised when she'd read that the small port in Fernandina Beach supplied 90% of all the goods that were shipped to Bermuda, from toothpicks to cars. Trucks carrying large shipping containers to the small port on Amelia Island were also common on the highway.

"Hey, Momma," Jack said as Laura hugged her son as he greeted her in the bright, open concourse outside of security at the airport.

"It's great to see you, sweetie. Your new bed is set up, but I thought I'd let you unpack your boxes. Now you have a third bedroom to keep clean."

"And this one will be full of beach sand!"

After Jack finished unpacking, mother and son spent a joyful evening catching up on everything that had happened in the past month. "You've changed, Mom. You seem more—I don't know how to put it—maybe comfortable in your own skin. More sure of yourself and what you want to do with your life."

Laura smiled. "I do feel more confident. Having to face so many extraordinary things on my own, in such a short time, has shown me how strong and resilient I am. It makes me confident I can accomplish more than I ever thought I could. Maybe I will be a successful author!"

"I have no doubt, Mom. You have so much to offer the world and in your own, unique way."

Tears welled in Laura's eyes. Her son's words were so kind and supportive, and she didn't know what to say.

"And it's not just me who thinks that. Steven and Jenny and lots of our friends appreciate your advice. You've touched more lives than you know, and you'll influence even more people with your book."

"Jack, do you remember when I applied for that sales job and was worried that I wouldn't be successful? You told me that sales was 'just talking to people.'"

"Yeah, I remember."

"I recalled that conversation when I was wondering if I could write the dialogue in my novel and decided that dialogue was 'just people talking to each other.' Your words gave me the confidence to start the novel. I guess there are many times when we have a positive impact on people without being aware of it."

Laura and Jack talked late into the night. She filled him in on Cassie's pregnancy in high school and Jeffrey's actions and her hope that Cassandra would reveal the whole story soon. Laura described Amy's and Faith's recent life changes and how impressed she was by her new friends' strength and resilience. Finally, she talked about the characters in her novel.

"What is it about Kate that makes her special to you, Jack? I'm writing about teens falling in love, and I need some advice," Laura said. "It's been quite a while since I fell in love with your dad."

"Wow, Mom, let me think. I guess it's the way we connect with each other. We enjoy the same music, the same movies, and the same art. It's just easy with her. We don't have to compromise in every situation. And we have similar beliefs on why we're here, why we met, and why we're together. We understand each other, and we make each other happy every day, so that's good enough for me right now."

"Thanks for sharing that with me. They say opposites attract, and many times they do, but I agree that if you're with someone whose basic beliefs and interests are the same, it's easier to share your life. Your origins and life experiences may be different, but if your goals are the same, it can be a good match."

"Yeah, even though we grew up in different parts of the country, how Kate and I see ourselves and our place in the world is similar. And we make a conscious effort not to hurt each other."

"You are wise beyond your years, Jack. You must be exhausted—time for bed. I love you so much."

Jack gave his mother a bear hug. "I love you too, Mom."

CHAPTER 30

THE EXPLANATION

Laura kept yawning the following morning as she walked to Cassie's house after Allison had left for school. *Jack is right, I am different and in a good way.* Cassie answered the door, and the ladies sat in the family room, sipping coffee and making small talk. At last, Cassandra was ready to come clean about what happened in high school.

"It was at a party at the Stantons' for all the kids who were working in Maine that summer after sophomore year. I'd had a crush on Jeffrey since middle school, and I was amazed that he was paying attention to me. After the other kids left, we kissed for a long time, and he asked me out the following weekend."

Cassie poured more coffee in both of their mugs. "It was on that first date that we had sex, and it was the only time. My periods were erratic, and I didn't know I was pregnant for many weeks. I wasn't sick at all, and the first part of the summer went well until I realized I was pregnant."

"It must have been hard to tell Jeffrey."

"It was horrible because he accused me of sleeping around and said it probably wasn't his baby. We met several times in a park in the small Maine town where we were working. He'd had an inheritance from his grandfather and said he knew how to fix 'the problem,' as he referred to my

126

pregnancy. He made the arrangements for the abortion in a city an hour away. I was terrified, but I trusted Jeff to find a good doctor. Instead he found a sleazy old man who ruined my life."

"But why didn't you tell me? You were my best friend, and you completely avoided me," Laura said. "I could have helped you or at least been a shoulder to cry on."

"Laura, I couldn't tell anyone. My cousin got pregnant a few years earlier, and her parents sent her to a boarding school in a different state until she had the baby. She gave it up for adoption, but she never came home again. I knew my dad would send me away too."

"But why did you shut me out of your life?"

"Because I couldn't take the chance of slipping up and telling you. It was easier just to put a wall around my heart and force you to stay away. I surrounded myself with people I didn't really like so I wouldn't reveal my secret."

"Cassie, you were a traumatized girl, and Jeff was a frightened boy. It could have happened to anyone. It must have been a terrible burden," Laura said as she poured more coffee into her cup. "How did you know it was twins?"

"I heard that wretched doctor say something to the nurse about 'them,' and I knew it was twins. In my heart I believed they were identical twin girls."

"Have you forgiven yourself?"

"Yes. It took many years, especially after I found out the abortion was botched, and I was infertile. It was devastating and cost me my first marriage. When Faith said she had tickets to see Jeffrey, I thought I might be able to finally forgive him too."

"Yeah, they say we need to forgive others because we are only hurting ourselves when we don't."

"I know," added Cassie. "But it was what he did with the rest of his life that made me unable to forgive him. His fanaticism about abortion and advocating violence against Planned Parenthood and doctors added insult to injury. How many people have his words harmed over the years? How many traumatized young women are there who are told they'll burn in hell if they choose to end an unplanned pregnancy?"

Laura took Cassie's hand in hers. "I understand completely. I could feel my blood pressure rising just listening to Jeffrey speak. I don't care how you feel about abortion, no one should incite violence, especially someone who's supposed to be representing God. No wonder so many young people today say they're not affiliated with an organized religion."

Several minutes passed in silence. Laura stood up began to walk around the room. "I know how you feel about adding insult to injury. On a much smaller scale, that's what I felt after the conversation my friend Melissa. She devalued my feelings, suggesting I was wrong to take her snub as an insult.

"Where is the tipping point, Cassie? What is the one event or emotion that changes a relationship with little chance of going back? Even if we forgive someone, should we resume the friendship knowing that we're likely to get hurt again because we can't change others, we can only change ourselves?"

"I think friends and family are different because you normally don't sever the ties with family," added Cassie. "It's part of the human experience where we balance forgiveness with protecting our emotional boundaries."

"LCMC. It's my New Year's resolution. Less criticism, more compassion, but you're right about needing to set boundaries."

"I guess it's also about facing our demons and shedding light on the darker aspects of our personalities. And realizing that more of our lives are behind us than ahead."

"Oh, I wasn't sure if you knew," Laura said, "but there's a YouTube video of Mrs. Stanton's reaction at the chapel and Jeffrey walking out. Whoever took it was sitting close to the front and didn't get their phone out fast enough to record your comments. At least that's one good thing."

Cassie smiled—not the reaction Laura expected. Then she began to laugh and Laura laughed too. "What's so funny, Cassie?"

"It's a strange new world we live in. Our sins are out there for everyone to see. The Internet could make Catholic confessionals obsolete because everyone will know about your misdeeds right after they happen."

"You're probably right. But do you think it will change people's bad behavior?"

"Regrettably no. And you're right that Jeff and I were just kids when I became pregnant, and I'll work on forgiving him. I hope Allison can forgive me—once again. She's almost the same age as I was when I got pregnant. Maybe this will be a lesson that will save her from the misery that I went through."

"She'll forgive you in time, Cassie. You're a great mother, and she's a wonderful girl. I feel bad for Jeffrey's wife and children. But people love to forgive a sinner, and I'm sure he'll publically repent and regain his followers. How many televangelists, athletes, actors, and politicians have done awful things, and it ended up helping their careers?"

"It seems to happen all too often," Cassandra said.

"It's funny that some are forgiven but others aren't. Maybe this is the thing that will make the good pastor stop inciting violence against healthcare workers," Laura added. "His life was built on a lie, on shifting sand, and you were the earthquake that sent his world tumbling to the ground."

The women sat in silence. "This has been an open wound in my psyche for such a long time," said Cassie.

"And to a lesser extent in mine too," Laura said. "I feel like a dark cloud has finally disappeared, and the sun is shining. I'm glad we're friends once again."

CHAPTER 31

RICKY

Jack was eating breakfast when Laura returned home from Cassie's. She briefly described her conversation with Cassandra and her feelings about what had been a shadow on her soul all these years.

"And it will make it easier visiting you when you move to Boston. I won't have a knot in my stomach going back, and it is a wonderful place to live. It was incredible how the city rallied after the terrible marathon bombing. I pray nothing like that happens again in Boston—or anywhere else."

"I'm excited about moving there, and I really liked the city when I went for my interview," said Jack. "I hope Kate can get a job in Boston too. Her parents aren't wild about the idea of her living as far away from Seattle as possible, but for me it would be great."

"I hope she does too. It can be lonely when you move to a new place. I've been lucky with this move to Amelia and found an old friend and two new ones. After you get dressed, I can drop you off at the beach if you like. I need to pick up a few groceries."

"Thanks, Mom. It's cool out, but that sun on my face will feel so good. Oh, is it okay if I take the murder journal with me? I like a good whodunit."

E. Louise Jaques

"Wow," said Laura, "I never thought of it as a 'murder journal,' but I guess that's what it is. Maybe you can see the situation with fresh eyes and help us solve this mystery. I added some notes from Amy's dream about Conti and the strange experience I had with the glowing orb in my bedroom. I'm not sure if it's all connected."

After leaving Jack at the beach, Laura drove down Amelia Island Parkway under the lovely canopy of oak trees to Fletcher Avenue. Heading north, she was mentally reviewing her grocery list when a dog ran out in front of the car. She slammed on the brakes then pulled to the shoulder with her heart pounding and her knuckles white from gripping the steering wheel. A boy ran out, grabbed the dog's leash and started disciplining the puppy. Laura got out of the car and walked over to the young man who was struggling to settle the animal down.

"Thanks for stopping, lady. I know he looks big, but he's still a puppy, and a dumb one. They're coming tomorrow to put in the electric fence."

"I'm glad I was able to stop in time," Laura said as her heart rate returned to normal. She looked to the right and realized the boy's house was next to Conti's massive home. Then something else caught her eye. The boy was wearing expensive binoculars around his neck. Her intuition kicked in, and a small voice in her head said *he saw something Thanksgiving night.*

She didn't want to frighten him, so she asked him his first name and a few questions about his dog. When she saw him relax, Laura said, "Ricky, those are great binoculars."

"Yeah, they're my dad's, but he lets me use them. I like looking for dolphins from our balcony."

"It's too bad what happened to your neighbor, Mr. Conti. Where you home on Thanksgiving night?"

Ricky lowered his eyes and started fiddling with the binoculars. "Yeah, my mom and dad finally stopped yelling at each other when they heard the sirens. The cops came and talked to my parents, but they didn't see anything."

"You seem like an observant guy, Ricky. Did you see anything at Mr. Conti's house the night he was shot?"

The dog started barking and jumping around the boy's legs. "Stop it, Buddy! Why do you want to know, lady?"

"My husband and I were the ones who found Mr. Conti's body. We want to help the police find whoever did this so he won't hurt anyone else. Sometimes don't you just feel you need to do something, even if it doesn't make sense?"

"I feel that way lots of times. My mom says she doesn't understand anything I do." Ricky was quiet for several moments, and Laura could feel the boy's internal battle. Finally he admitted, "Yeah, I saw something that night. I was out on the back deck and Mr. Conti was talking to a man by the pool. I couldn't see the guy's face—even with the binoculars—just his back. Then they walked down the boardwalk to the sand. But that's all I saw 'cause my mom called me in for dessert. I didn't tell anyone. I was scared that the man would come after me if he knew I saw him."

"Ricky, get in here," called a teenage girl from the front door. "And bring that stupid dog with you."

"That's my dumb sister."

"Ricky, before you go, would you be willing to talk to the police about what you saw on Thanksgiving night? Of course, your parents would be there too."

"Ricky—now!" called the teenager.

"Yeah, maybe. My name's Ricky Thompson." The boy and dog ran into the house.

Laura had a good feeling that this could be a break in the case, and she called Detective Davis with the information. Resuming her trip to the grocery store, Laura marveled at how much her life had changed since she'd left St. Louis.

CHAPTER 32

THE LAMP

A single book protruded from a shelf jammed with a hodgepodge of used books. *It looks as though someone started to take out this book then stopped,* Amy thought as her hand reached to the top shelf in the antique shop on South 8th Street in Fernandina Beach on Monday afternoon. *Wow, it's a second printing of 'Edgar Cayce on Reincarnation' by Noel Langley, published in March 1968. What a great find and perfect for Laura to read for background information for her novel. Thanks to whoever you are on the other side who brought this volume to my attention—I'll make sure she gets it right away.*

After paying for the book, Amy returned to the antique store on Centre Street where she had previously encounter Albertson. She still needed a Christmas present for her niece. She was careful not to pick up too many objects because she'd often get overwhelmed with images about the previous owners, and it usually wasn't a pleasant experience. *It's hard getting into the Christmas spirit knowing I'm going to be alone this year.*

Walking up a side isle, she smiled as a young woman and her tiny daughter modeled vintage hats and fur wraps. Turning the corner, she saw a brass lamp like the one Aladdin found in the ancient fable. Her niece loved the Disney movie, and this would be a perfect gift. As she was about to pick it up, another hand appeared and reached for the lamp. Amy looked up into the face of a handsome man with a dimpled smile and wavy, dark hair that was greying at the temples.

They both laughed. "Please," said Amy, "go ahead. I can find something else for my niece."

"That's funny, I was going to buy it for my nephew. He loves that Aladdin movie. He's watched it a hundred times."

"My niece too." Amy looked at the beautiful dark eyes in the attractive face and realized something about him seemed familiar. "I'm Amy Temple, have we met before?"

"I don't think so. I just moved here a few weeks ago from Detroit. My name's Nate, Nate Jones," he said. "And I insist that you take the lamp."

"Oh my gosh. I grew up in Bloomfield Hills. Maybe our paths have crossed before," Amy said as she placed her hand in his outstretched hand. An electric shock ran through her body unlike anything she'd experienced before.

"I lived in Grosse Point, so I don't see how we could have met," Nate said. "But you look familiar too. Wait, haven't you been on TV? Something about a missing child?"

It took a few moments for Amy to catch her breath. Never had she felt such a strong, instant attraction to a stranger before. It was exhilarating and unsettling at the same time. She didn't want to let go of his hand. "Yes, I'm a medium, and I sometimes work with the police on missing-persons cases. The last one was in Atlanta when I helped them find a toddler."

"That's it. I knew I'd seen your face before, and a beautiful face it is."

Amy blushed at the compliment and finally removed her hand from Nate's. She continued to stare into his deep brown eyes. *I've loved him before.* Still gazing at one another, Amy said, "Did you move here with your family?"

"No, my son lives in Brooklyn, and my wife passed away two years ago. I took an early retirement and decided to leave the cold, snowy, Michigan winters behind."

Amy's body relaxed slightly before it began to vibrate with anticipation. "I just moved here too,' she said. "I don't have children, and my soon-to-be ex-husband is living in Atlanta. I needed some space between us."

"That's understandable. Amy, please take the lamp. I can find something else for my nephew. But here's my card in case you happen to find another one in town." Nate retrieved a card from his wallet and handed it to her, as Amy did the same with her business card. Sporting a final smile, Nate turned and walked away.

When he was out of sight, Amy picked up the lamp and started to rub the side. *Please Genie of the Lamp–please have Nate call me!* This was the first time she had met a man and known instantly that they had loved one another in a past life. She carried the lamp to the checkout and decided she would keep it for herself and find another gift for Hannah.

With a newfound joy in her heart, she walked down the street to a store called Twisted Sisters and bought the perfect present for her niece. She found lovely gifts for Faith, Laura, Cassie, and Allison too. She'd already picked up gifts for Miles and Austin, so her shopping was complete. Leaving the store with her packages, she thought, *it's incredible how a chance meeting with a stranger has helped me find my Christmas spirit. This truly is a magical time of year.*

CHAPTER 33

CHRISTMAS COOKIES

Tuesday, December 16, was warm and sunny. Miles, Austin, and their friend Beau Weatherly arrived at Faith's just in time for lunch. The plan was for Beau to stay the night, then Miles would drive him to Jekyll Island, Georgia, the following morning. The Weatherlys had a home on St. Simon's Island, not far from Jekyll, and they would meet at the historic Jekyll Island Club for lunch.

Faith was delighted to have the company and was grateful that her boys were with her for the holidays. A couple months earlier, Miles had talked about staying in Atlanta with his girlfriend, Stephanie, over Christmas, but he knew his mother needed him. As she prepared lunch, Faith had the sensation that someone was watching her, and she quickly turned but no one was there. *Charles? Is that you? Have you come to see your boys?* There was no answer, but Faith had the feeling that her husband was near.

"Mom seems to be doing okay," Miles whispered to his brother as they watched TV in the family room. "Is she being brave for our sake?"

"She's a strong lady, but I think she's holding it together for us. I'm surprised she hasn't cracked under the pressure, but maybe being away from Atlanta is a good thing."

"Should I ask her to come to Jekyll with us tomorrow?" Miles asked. "You know, include her in what we're doing?"

"Great idea, bro. I know Mom wanted to see that turtle place on the Island. And she said something about a new museum there. If we keep her busy, maybe she'll get through the holidays without a meltdown."

Miles walked into the kitchen and told his mother of their plan to all visit Jekyll Island the following day and meet with Beau's parents. Faith was delighted by the proposal and agreed it would be a good day trip.

The doorbell rang, and Miles walked to the front hall to answer it. Laura and Jack were standing on the porch with a large plate of decorated Christmas cookies. Faith walked out of the kitchen and introduced her son to her neighbors.

"Faith, we usually have a Christmas party, and my recipes made way too many cookies for just the three of us. I saw your sons drive up earlier, and I wanted to introduce them to Jack—and bring treats."

"Please come in, Laura. Would you like to stay for lunch?"

"Oh, no, thank you—we just ate."

Jack had already followed Miles into the family room, and the four boys were getting acquainted. Walking into the kitchen, Laura told Faith about her serendipitous meeting with Ricky Thompson and her conversation with Detective Davis.

"The police are going to contact the Thompsons and interview Ricky again. I hope they get a lead. The detective said they haven't located the gun or identified where it may have been purchased. There's no record of a gun of that make and model reported as stolen in Florida."

"Heavens, I wish they could find out what happened to poor Mr. Conti. In the back of my mind, there's always a fear that the killer is still out there and he might strike again."

"We should ask Amy if she's had any more psychic impressions. She's the only one of us who's ever been involved in a murder case before," added Laura.

Sandwiches were piled high on a large platter, and Faith carried it into the family room as Laura followed with sodas and a bowl of chips. The boys dug into the food—even Jack who had just finished lunch.

"Young men and their hollow legs," laughed Laura. "I have a feeling there won't be many cookies left by Christmas."

Faith flashed forward to their first Christmas morning without Charles and felt a searing pain in her heart. Pushing down the anguish, she took a deep breath and tried to focus on the present moment. "The boys seem to be getting along well. Laura, have you ever been to Jekyll Island?"

"No—isn't it in Georgia?"

"Yes, it's an hour north of here, and the boys and I are driving Miles' friend Beau there tomorrow to meet up with his parents. Would you and Jack like to join us? We can have lunch at the Jekyll Island Club and then visit the sea-turtle information center."

"I'll ask Jack, but it sounds good to me." Arrangements were made to meet at 10:00 the following morning, and Faith said she would invite Amy as well.

Laura left Jack at Faith's house and went home to work on her novel. Jack had given her a new confidence that she would be a published author and bring her vision of the world to readers. The idea that she could leave behind something tangible for her children, grandchildren, and great-grandchildren spurred her desire to keep writing. Opening her laptop, she thought how she might even have a future incarnation when a part of her soul would discover the book she had written in this lifetime.

Her challenge was to create a dramatic scene where the heroine and hero meet for the first time. Near the ocean was an obvious choice since they were on an island, and she decided to head to the beach to look for inspiration. She sent Jack a text saying she was going for a drive and would leave the door to the lanai unlocked.

First she drove south on Highway A1A and over the bridge to Big Talbot Island. A short walk along the beach led her to the incredible driftwood that dotted the sand. The driftwood were trees that had washed ashore and looked like intricate works of art. *There's so much natural beauty here. I want John and the kids to see this.* She took photos with her phone.

Her next stop was American Beach, which was slightly south of Summer Beach where her home was located. Laura drove into the public parking lot at Burney Park next to the town. She was fascinated by the history of American Beach, as it was one of the few beaches in the South that African-Americans were allowed to use in the early part of the 20th century. From the 1930s through the 1950s, it was a haven for blacks of all income levels, as well as prominent musicians and entertainers. There had been a hotel, nightclub, restaurants, and cottages that attracted Cab Calloway, Dinah Washington, and many others. Today the small town was largely deserted, experiencing a decline with the end of segregation.

Laura walked down the boardwalk, noticing the rustic beach houses and restored homes to her left and the multi-million-dollar houses and condos to her right that were part of the Amelia Island Plantation. *It's incredible that it wasn't that long ago that there were Whites Only beaches. Thank goodness things have changed.* Gazing over the ocean, she watched five pelicans glide over the waves in unison, reminding her of the Blue Angel airplanes in formation. She marveled at the fact this was now her home—at least part of the time. She liked being a splitter.

Strolling past the sea oats and dunes, she observed several children playing on the shore, chasing seagulls and terns as the birds took flight then settled on the sand a short distance from the kids. She noticed they were a mix of black and white children, and an idea popped into her head. *What if the young woman in my novel, from the heroine's past life in the 1920s, fell in love with a black man? That would have been a forbidden relationship in the South in that timeframe.*

Laura headed back to the parking lot and observed a sign on the wall of the change room. It was a notice about riptides and how to best escape them by swimming parallel to the shore until you were out of the current. *That's it! My heroine is caught in a riptide, and the hero saves her. That's a good dramatic way to have them meet for the first time. Wow, two great inspirations in one trip to the beach. Now I just have to get back to writing.* She was excited about having workable ideas for the novel.

Arriving home she noticed a package by her front door. Inside a gift bag was a book and note from Amy wishing Laura well as she wrote her novel. Laura smiled as she unlocked the door and entered her Island house. *Lots of pleasant surprises today!*

CHAPTER 34

JEKYLL ISLAND

The road trip on Wednesday morning had Faith, Miles, and Beau in one car and Laura, Jack, Austin and Amy in the other. Faith was looking forward to hearing the conversation between her son and his fraternity brother—she learned so much more about their experiences at college when she was in the front seat and the boys were in the back. It was like she was a fly on the wall.

Jack and Austin were comparing life stories while sitting in the back seat of Laura's car, and the woman talked in the front.

"Thanks so much for the book on Edgar Cayce. I'm sure it will help with my writing. I'm looking forward to reading it and using his insights in my work."

"How's your novel coming?" asked Amy, as they drove north on Highway 95, leaving Florida behind.

"Actually, it's coming together, and I have a clearer idea about how the story will unfold. I've avoided reading novels lately because I don't want to unconsciously be influenced by other authors. But related nonfiction books are great."

"That makes sense."

"When I moved here," Laura began, "my intention was to make a new start and leave the past behind, but important things from the past keep resurfacing."

"You mean Cassie and your friendship as teenagers?"

"Yes, that's part of it but other things too. That glowing orb that reminded me of my childhood bedroom in Andover, finding my old journal among Jenny's things, and lately I've have been reading spirituality books and a strange thing is happening. Just as I had a strong conviction that what I was taught in church as a child didn't ring true for me, the same thing is happening with some of the 'New Age' thought."

"What specifically are you questioning?" asked Amy.

"I can't fully accept a few concepts that I've been reading about. I realize that we're all on individual journeys and we're at different stages in our spiritual growth. I understand that many people feel the need for the support of an organized religion, either a traditional or an alternative one."

"Yes, I've seen many of my friends move from one spiritual master, guru, or leader to the next, always looking for someone to provide them with the answers. For them it is the best approach," said Amy, "but I don't feel the need to belong to a specific church."

"I don't either, and there are a lot of insightful people out there teaching about the soul. But the widespread idea that we need to suppress or even destroy the 'ego' is a problem for me. If we think of our egos as the human part of us—our minds and personalities, then why should we get rid of them? Didn't we choose to come here to learn and grow and experience all aspects of earthly life, the dark and light, joy and sadness, and the good and bad, in ourselves and others?"

"The attack on the ego has bothered me too," Amy said. "In each moment, we can feel the influence our soul—which springs from God—in our daily existence, but we have also chosen a human life. Why not accept that too? I try and deal with my negative emotions, not push them down or deny they exist. I think it is part of our experience in physical bodies."

"I agree, Amy. As a mother, I could see my children's personalities emerging right from the start, and I'm not taking about their natural temperaments. It was more than if they were calm or fussy babies—or 'fuzzy babies' as Jenny used to say about her little brother when he would cry. There were distinct personality traits that have continued through their lives, and I think it's important to acknowledge a child's ego. Maybe there needs to be a change in terminology to describe the difference between the negative aspects of our personalities and the positive ones."

"I haven't had the experience of motherhood, but I understand what you're saying," said Amy. "I've known identical twins who were very different—their interests and personalities. I guess the words we use do matter, and it's confusing. Is it a matter of semantics? I'm not sure."

"The other thing that's been on my mind is the concept of surrendering our will to God's will. That reinforces the idea that God is separate from us and He or She has created us for a reason and has a plan for us. I believe that we are sparks of God and co-creators of our lives, and our souls have decided why we're here, with divine guidance of course. I think that as spiritual and physical beings, 'we' are responsible for our lives."

"You're right, Laura. I believe our will is inseparable from God's, and maybe we need a shift in our attitude from surrender—and the suppression of the ego—to an embracing of all aspects of who we are—mind, body, and soul. Like you, I think we should continue to explore our dual natures by hearing what others have to say but ultimately deciding for ourselves."

"Amy, I'm so glad that I can talk to you about all the my spiritual ideas and questions. Because I want to include these concepts in my novel, they've been on my mind."

Laura followed Faith's car as they exited from the highway and drove east on Highway 17 toward Jekyll Island. The South Brunswick River was on the north side of the road and the marshlands on the south side.

"The marshes are beautiful at this time of the year, even though the grasses are a pale brown rather than the bright green of summer or the gold shade of fall, which is why the Georgia barrier islands are called the 'Golden Isles,'" said Amy.

"Wow, look at that ship in the river. I've never seen anything like that before," exclaimed Jack.

The massive vessel was the size of a container ship, but the sides were high, solid metal with the pilothouse on top. "That type of ship carries all kinds of vehicles," Austin said. "Cars and trucks are transported to Europe and Africa from the ports in Georgia and Florida."

"Cool," answered Jack. "I noticed all those cars at the Georgia port a few miles back and wondered why they were there. I've seen container ships but never a ship like that."

"See, Jack," Laura said, "even when you're out of school you're still learning."

"And look at that great suspension bridge, Mom. Do we go across it?"

Amy answered the question, "No, the cutoff is right before the bridge. We're almost there."

After paying the entrance fee to the Island that is designated as a national park, the two cars followed the signs for the historic Jekyll Island Club. The impressive building was originally opened in 1888 as a private recreational and hunting club for the wealthiest Americans, including the Vanderbilt, Rockefeller, and Morgan families. It closed in 1942, was purchased by the state in 1947, and operated as a resort until 1971. The club was restored and reopened as a hotel in 1985.

"Look at those remarkable oak trees with the huge branches trailing on the ground," said Faith as they walked from the parking lot to the main entrance. "This island is a marvelous combination of natural splendor and manmade beauty. The cottages built by the various families who belonged to the club are Victorian wonders."

Beau greeted his parents and teenage sister who were already seated in the elegant restaurant. They had a delightful lunch, and Amy was grateful that no uninvited ghosts interrupted her meal. After saying goodbye to the Weatherlys, the ladies and young men walked to the Georgia Sea Turtle Center.

"Mom, I'm learning even more today," joked Jack. "The preservation and rehab of the turtles is really something."

"Yes, it's interesting to see the actual turtles they've rescued from Florida to Massachusetts. Look, that one is named Chatham after the town in Cape Cod where it was found."

"This poor turtle was run over by a boat motor. It's amazing he survived."

"I'm glad we came here today and saw a new part of the area, Jack. There's so much to see on the southeast coast. We'll have to visit Savannah soon too," said Laura, "when your dad and Kate are with us. I'd also like to tour Charleston, South Carolina. I hear it's one of the most fascinating cities in the country and only a four-hour drive north."

CHAPTER 35

THE RO-RO

Jack drove back to Amelia Island in the car with Faith, Miles, and Austin. Amy and Laura drove in the second car and continued their conversation from the drive to Jekyll Island.

"Since I moved to Amelia, I've been thinking about what I believe and how I can explain it so people will understand," said Laura. "I want to include some of the concepts in my novel in a direct, simple way."

"Good idea, Laura, especially since it will be about a teenage girl. What are you thinking about saying?"

"I've read a lot about the law of attraction and identifying important desires and then sending our requests to the Universe, without worrying about the details. But what if our dreams are like beams of light, fueled by our intentions and positive emotions? And even though we send them to our Source or God, through our higher selves, we remain connected them."

"I see what you mean," answered Amy. "And our beams of light could attract other beams of similar vibration to bring our dreams into earthly reality. But we don't severe our ties with our intentions and dreams."

"Right, we entwine our wills—and lights—with the universal will and attract the people and situations that help us manifest our desires."

Amy laughed as an idea popped into her mind. "Do you remember in the first Ghostbusters movie where the laser beams from their weapons 'crossed streams' and created an explosion? Maybe as our intention beams cross with others they create an impact in our physical world."

Before Laura could answer, her cell phone rang. "Mom, I think I figured out one of the clues to the murder," Jack said as he waved from the back seat of Faith's car.

"What are you talking about, sweetie?"

"We just passed the Georgia port again, and Austin and I were talking about the huge ship we saw on the way in that carries cars and trucks. Miles said it's called a 'ro-ro' because the vehicles roll on and roll off the ship. I remember from the journal that Ms. Temple had the song Row, Row, Row Your Boat going through her head and the mention of a ship."

"Jack, you're brilliant! Of course, that's the kind of ship that could be a clue! Thanks, love, I'll see you at home."

Laura told Amy of Jack's insight, and Amy called Detective Davis with the information. "So we have a ship that carries vehicles and that ties in with the nursery rhyme," said Amy. "I'll talk to the police again soon and see what they come up with."

"On a lighter note," Laura began, "have you finished your Christmas shopping?"

A slow smile crossed Amy's face. Laura looked at her friend and laughed. "Amy, what's up? You have a 'cat that swallowed the canary' look."

"Well, I was in an antique store the other day and as I reached for a brass lamp for my niece, so did someone else. It was incredible, Laura—there was this gorgeous man who wanted the lamp too. We started talking, and for the first time in my life, I met someone who I knew I loved before."

"That's so exciting! Are you going to see him again? And who got the lamp?"

"I bought it, and I'm keeping it. I found another gift for my niece. And Nate and I exchanged numbers. He's a widower and recently moved to the Island. But I think I'll wait until the New Year to call—but if he calls me first, who knows!"

"You never know what's around the corner. I'm glad it was a pleasant surprise this time. Did you rub the lamp and ask the Genie to make Nate call you?"

Amy laughed. "Yes, I did!"

The women were silent the rest of the drive home. As they crossed the bridge over the Amelia River, Amy's mood began to change. An uncomfortable feeling washed over her, and the closer they got to Hopeful Court, the more anxious she became. Walking toward her house after Laura dropped her off, Amy wished she'd had the security system activated. She unlocked the front door and stood quietly in the front hall, listening for any noise inside the house. Then she heard a familiar sound.

Walking into the kitchen, she saw Doug with a Bud Light in his hand. The noise had been the distinct sound of a beer can opening.

"What are you doing here? You can't just break into my house!"

"Sorry 'bout that, but I waited outside for hours and I was getting thirsty. Thanks for buying my brand of beer."

"A force of habit, I guess. Now, what do you want?"

"You found something Conti left behind, didn't you? You and your friends. My contact with the local cops couldn't get his hands on it."

"Talk to the police, Doug. I'm not telling you anything," Amy said as she walked to the front door and opened it wide. "Now please leave."

Doug walked toward her with the beer in one hand and grabbed her arm with the other. "Listen, Amy, I'm trying to protect you. There are some dangerous guys out there, and I don't want you to be caught in the middle. And get your security system hooked up."

"I can take care of myself. Now please go!"

"I left my burner cell number on the counter. Call me when you come to your senses."

Amy locked the door behind her ex and watched out the front window as a dark SUV drove around the corner. Doug climbed into the passenger side.

Deciding she needed to clear the negative energy in the house, from Doug and any other unknown source, Amy made herself comfortable on the sofa to begin meditating. She progressively relaxed each part of her body then focused on her breathing. With each breath in through her nose, Amy felt an emotional pain or discomfort. Each breath out through her mouth was forceful, as she imagined blowing up a balloon.

Instead of suppressing or denying her negative emotions, Amy felt she should experience them completely before releasing them into an imaginary balloon that would float away into the ionosphere. She'd developed this meditation technique over several years as she learned to effectively cope with the pain of rejection, ridicule, and loss.

After 45 minutes, she felt clear and calm with heavenly energy flowing through her body. *Thank you all, every loved one and angel guiding me from the other side today.*

CHAPTER 36

A CHRISTMAS STORY

On Thursday morning, Faith remained in bed for a while after awakening. She remembered watching the Weatherly family at lunch the day before and realized she'd never have her family intact again. Finally, as she got out of bed and walked down the hall to look in on her sleeping sons, she felt a cool breeze behind her. *Charles is that you? Why did you leave me? I want you here with us. What will Christmas be like without you?*

Faith stepped into a hot shower and sobbed as the water poured down on her tear-swollen face. She dried her hair and wrapped her robe tightly around her. Entering the bedroom, she was surprised that her sons were sitting on her bed. Miles handed his mother a cup of coffee, and Austin held out a box of tissues as he pulled back the covers and guided her into the waiting bed.

"Thank you, my beautiful boys. I don't know how I would survive without you," Faith said as she dried her eyes.

Miles went into the kitchen and brought two additional cups of coffee and a tray of warm biscuits and raspberry jam. Austin turned on the TV and put a disc in the DVD player, then both boys sat in the bed on either side of their mother. Together they watched their favorite seasonal movie, *A Christmas Story*, and laughed at the end when Ralphy and his family watched as the waiter chopped of the head of the duck or the 'Chinese turkey,' as they called it.

"It was an accident, Mom. It's nobody's fault. I know Dad didn't leave us on purpose," said Miles as they watched the movie credits role.

"Yes, my darling, I know. Your father would never hurt you boys on purpose."

"He wouldn't hurt you either, Mom," said Austin.

Faith smiled and prayed that her sons never found out about Charles' affair—that is, his affairs. *They should only have good memories of their father. It wouldn't serve any purpose to sully his memory.*

The three Proctors spent the rest of the day putting up a Christmas tree and decorating the house. Lighted garlands were placed around the front door and on the fireplace mantel. Elaborately decorated wreaths were hung on the front door, in the family room, the dining room, and the kitchen. Sprays of holly and southern magnolia leaves were tucked into every nook and cranny.

"I'll call Miss Amy and see if she's free for dinner," said Faith. "She must be feeling disoriented spending the holidays in a strange house."

Amy was delighted when Faith called and invited her to dinner. Austin was setting the table when Amy arrived, and she had a flashback to the day after Thanksgiving when all their lives had changed forever. *If Charles hadn't died, we would still be in Atlanta, and I wouldn't be involved in another mystery. And I wouldn't have met Nate Jones.*

"We never finished our dinner together last month, did we?" said Austin as they filled their plates and walked into the dining room.

"It seems like yesterday and yet like a lifetime ago," added Faith.

"How quickly our lives can change," said Amy. "I want to thank you, Faith, Miles, and Austin for being my family this Christmas. I love you all."

"A toast," Faith began, "to Charles, to family, and to all our wonderful memories. Cheers!"

***

At the same time, Laura and Jack were finishing dinner while they watched the movie *A Christmas Story*. It was a Beck family tradition, too.

"I'm going to my room to call Kate," said Jack when the movie was over. "We're trying to decide what to do for New Year's Eve."

"Say hello to her for me. I'm going to read for a while before bed." Laura picked up a novel but couldn't concentrate. She noticed that Jack had left the crime journal, as she preferred to call it, on the coffee table. When no new bright ideas came to her, she turned on her computer and looked up ammunition on the Internet. *What could possibly be so important about the type that Conti was involved with? I don't see anything that explains it. It's sad and frightening how easy it is for anyone to buy guns and ammunition online.*

Going over the clues to Conti's murder again, she was startled when the house phone rang. "Hello."

A husky voice on the other end said, "Leave it alone." Then the line went dead.

There was no doubt about the menacing tone of the message. She went around the house closing blinds and making sure the doors were locked. Laura didn't want to frighten her son and decided not to tell him about the call. She was glad that John was arriving the next day. Later, she would contact the other ladies and see if they'd received calls as well.

CHAPTER 37

BOSQUE BELLO

Cassie picked up her daughter from school on Friday afternoon. "Are you excited that it's Christmas break? We still have some shopping to do. How about going to St. John's Town Center in Jacksonville tomorrow?"

"Yeah, Mom, that'll be great. But today can we go to a cemetery?"

Cassie laughed, "Are you looking for the ghost of Christmas future, Ebenezer?"

Allison giggled, "No, Mom. I have a history assignment over the break. We have to go to one of the cemeteries on the Island and find the headstones of a family. Then we have to write down the births and deaths of all the members and research the year when one of the people passed away. And we have to check if the people might still have family on the Island."

"That's an unusual assignment, honey. Is it something the history class does every year?"

"No, our teacher's new, and she wants to learn about Amelia Island and the people who've lived here. Some of the kids are going to use their own families, since they've lived here, like, forever."

"Which cemetery do you want to go to?"

"Sally Wright told me that Bosque Bello cemetery is on North 14th Street, so it's not too far. Then I could find a family and work on the paper next week."

Ancient live oaks, covered with Spanish moss, greeted them as they drove into the older part of the cemetery. Cassie parked the car on an unpaved road, as gray clouds began to sweep across the sun. Warily, they began to tour the gravesites, walking past family plots surrounded by crumbling brick walls or rusty, wrought iron fences. A cold wind started to blow, and they wrapped their coats tightly around them.

"Some of these statues are wicked cool!" said Allison as she took out her phone and started taking photos. "Mom, do you see any families that I could use for my report?"

Cassie carefully walked past several plots and saw one that might be appropriate. "Here, Allie. This family has four members buried here; the father, mother, and two daughters. Oh my, the two girls died on the same day—August 10, 1928. And the mother passed away one week later. The father lived for another decade."

"Wow, the older girl was sixteen and the younger girl was ten. That's crazy that they died on the same day. I wonder if it was an accident."

"Probably, sweetie. If it were an illness, it's doubtful they would have died on the same day. The timeframe is interesting because it was during the Roaring 20s. We'll have to do some research on what was happening that year."

"Okay," Allison said as she began to write in her notebook, "Mr. James Marshall Ballantine died on March 25, 1938; his wife, Lucy Bohun Ballantine on August 17, 1928; and Evangeline and Abigail on August 10. I wonder if the mom just couldn't go on without her daughters."

"It's very likely. I don't know what I'd do if anything happened to you."

The temperature began to drop as clouds completely covered the sun. They rushed back to the car. "The mom, Lucy Bohun, may have been a French Huguenot like the Harcourt family," said Cassie. "I remember that name from the research I did on the French Protestants who fled persecution during the late 1600s. Many of them went to other European countries before coming to America."

"Yeah, we learned about Jean Ribeault and the Huguenots who first came to the Jacksonville area. The French settlers got wiped out by the Spanish."

"We should drive down to Huguenot Memorial Park near the Mayport ferry sometime soon. It's not too far south of the Island on A1A."

Allison was quiet on the drive home. "Our family is just you and me again, isn't it, Mom."

"Yes, my darling girl. I've been thinking about what it means to be a family, too. Mrs. Proctor and her sons are their family now; Ms. Temple is alone; and the Becks still have a traditional family, but two of their children are far away this Christmas. And Mrs. Biddle has her dog, Millie."

"Millie is the yappiest family member I know."

"It's interesting, but lately I've been feeling that the ladies on Hopeful Court are becoming like a family."

"When we go shopping tomorrow, should we buy everyone a Christmas present?"

Cassie smiled at her daughter, "You are an amazing child with a loving heart. That's a great idea, and we can invite everyone over for Sunday brunch."

CHAPTER 38

CIAO ITALIAN BISTRO

A rush of love and gratitude swept over Laura as she saw her husband exit security at Jacksonville airport on Friday evening. John smiled and gave his wife and son a bear hug. The three of them laughed as they watched a rotund man with a long white beard and dressed like Santa dance through the concourse.

"No snow! Just palm trees and the beach," said Jack as they walked to the parking lot. "This is my kind of Christmas."

"Why don't we have dinner before we head home? I'm starving," John added.

The owner of Ciao Italian Bistro on Centre Street in Fernandina Beach greeted them warmly. He led them to a table near the back and brought them complimentary glasses of sparkling wine. Then the owner walked over to the corner table and began to speak in Italian to three well-dressed men. *They are right out of Central Casting–The Sopranos, Florida-style,* Laura thought. *I wonder if these men are here because of Conti or the mystery that revolves around the message he'd hidden in the music box. Were they the ones who called last night and threatened me?* Laura had decided to wait until they got home to tell John about the phone call.

As they ordered their dinner, Laura overheard the three men speaking French. It had been a while since she'd heard the language but she knew they weren't French Canadian and were obviously from Europe. She heard them say something about 'sisters.' Laura glanced at the table and was unnerved when all three turned and stared directly at her. She quickly looked away and began talking to Jack.

Laura's nerves were on edge the rest of the night. After Jack went to bed, Laura told her husband about the threatening phone call. "Did you call the police?" asked John, as they got ready for bed.

"No, not yet. I wanted to talk to the other ladies to see if they got calls too."

"Did you recognize the voice? Did he have an accent?"

"No, he didn't sound familiar and no accent that I could tell. I'm glad the security company is coming on Monday to activate the system. John, did you notice the men in the restaurant tonight were speaking French as well as Italian?"

"Yeah, I did, and I figured they didn't want anyone to know what they were talking about, since not many people in Florida speak French. Did you understand anything they were saying?"

"No, but did you see the look on the restaurant owner's face when he heard their conversation in French? He obviously understood what they said. I'll add the Europeans' presence to the journal and ask Amy to mention it to the police."

Slipping into bed beside his wife, John was glad he was there to protect his family. "This isn't what we expected when we bought a house on this peaceful island, is it?"

"It is unsettling and unexpected, but I'm still happy we bought the house. This Island has opened up a whole new world for me. I've started writing a novel, I've made new friends, I've reconnected with an old friend, and solved a mystery that's been troubling me most of my life. So all in all, I'm glad I'm here."

"I guess the pros outweigh the cons, but I sure wish I was here full-time."

"Me too, John!"

CHAPTER 39

WHEELS TURNING

Laura called Amy on Saturday morning and asked if she'd had an update from the police.

"No, and I thought I'd hear something from the detective because it's getting close to December 27, the day we thought something might happen."

"Any more psychic impressions? Or any word from your new friend, Nate?"

"No, Laura, I haven't felt anything new about the case. But I got an email from Nate this morning asking what I was doing on New Year's Eve when he gets back from Brooklyn. I haven't answered him yet."

"Oh, Amy, go for it. You're not divorced yet, but you can't let the chance to get to know Nate slip you by. If you feel more comfortable, you can invite him here on New Year's Eve. John is flying to St. Louis on the 28th, but he'll be back on the 31st. We can have dinner and watch the Times Square crystal ball drop on TV."

"Thanks, Laura. I'll get in touch with him and see what he has in mind. But since he's new to the Island too, he might not have specific plans. I forgot to tell you that Doug was in my house when we got home from Jekyll Island. He'd heard from someone in the police department that we'd found something left by Conti, and he wanted to know what it was."

"Did you tell him about the slip of paper with the numbers and letters?"

"No, I told him to talk to the police. And I called the home-security company to activate my system next week. I don't like that type of surprise."

"No kidding. I had my own unpleasant surprise the other night, and that's what I wanted to talk to you about. I got a call on the house phone, and a disguised male voice said 'leave it alone.' I have no doubt that he was taking about the Conti case. Maybe Doug's 'mole' at the police station heard that I'd called the detective about Ricky Thompson seeing something that night and told someone. Have you gotten any calls?"

"No, I haven't. I wish my intuition were working better. I feel like it's being blocked for some reason."

"Amy, I have to go. The guys want to go to the beach. I'm quite sure they won't be jumping in the ocean, but it's still great to walk along the shore. And thanks again for the book about Edgar Cayce."

"Talk to you later, Laura. I'll let you know about New Year's Eve. And thank you for the offer to join you and John."

The Beck family packed a picnic lunch and headed to Peter's Point Beach Park. Walking past the dunes, they noticed several horses and riders coming toward them. Following the riders was a girl with a large bucket and shovel to clean the beach if the horses left something behind.

"We've got to try that some time," said Jack. "I'll have to bring Kate here for a ride on the beach—maybe for spring break."

"I was thinking the same thing a while ago," said Laura.

"Our son the romantic," laughed John. "We've raised him well, Laura."

After setting up their chairs, John and Jack were throwing around a football while Laura read the crime journal, trying once again to make sense of the clues. *Only a few days until whatever is supposed to happen will go down. And all of us are still involved to some extent.* Laura jumped when her cell phone rang in her pocket.

"Hello, Mrs. Beck, this is Paolo Conti. Are you free to talk?"

How did he get my number? Oh, yes, I gave him my card with the information about Washington University in St. Louis. "Hello, Paolo, how can I help you?"

"My hotel room, it was broken into last night. My mother and grandfather left two days ago to go back to Milan, but I have continued to stay here to solve the murder of my father. The police will not update me, and they did not seem to care that my room was violated."

"I'm not sure how I can help. What I do know is that your father was involved with a private military company and a private security company about the sale of ammunition. But you probably already knew this."

"Yes, I have heard these things about a what—double-cross—that led to the car bomb. But do you think something else is happening—a triple-cross, perhaps?"

Laura was silent for a moment; she hadn't considered the possibility of another player in the drama. "It's not out of the question, Paolo. Did the police tell you that three houses were broken into after your father's death? They belonged to women who had been involved with your dad, but nothing was missing, as far as they could tell."

"Yes, the detective told me so. And as with the other break-ins, nothing was taken from my room. What could the unknown persons be looking for?"

Laura decided not to confide in Paolo about the note his father left with Cassie. "Sorry, Paolo, I'm not certain what is happening. Um, I have to go now. Good luck."

"Thank you, Mrs. Beck."

Laura wrapped the beach towel around her legs and gazed at the sunlight dancing on the water. Slowly she closed her eyes as the waves rolled endlessly to the shore. She quickly slipped into a light trance and let her mind wander. *What am I missing? There has to be something I'm not seeing clearly.* She ran through the case in her mind—Eduardo Conti; Paolo and his family; the conflict over the ammunition; the Jersey connection; the lady friends and their husbands; the clues from the music box; Amy's impressions of a ro-ro ship and a medical connection; the Europeans in the restaurant; or some unknown factor yet to come to light.

"Mom, do you want to throw the football?"

"No thanks, Jack."

"Were you sleeping, or were the wheels turning in your head?" Jack asked.

"You know me well, honey. I was trying to see what I've been missing. There are so many possibilities regarding the crime, and I don't know where we should focus. Maybe Ricky Thompson will help the police figure it out. He seems to be the only one who saw anything."

Jack sat in the chair beside his mother. "It's weird to think we're involved with some scary guys. I noticed those men in the restaurant last night that were speaking Italian. You've got to think they're connected to Conti."

"And they were speaking French and said something about 'sisters.' I'm glad the police are working with the FBI on the case. I'm sure they'll figure it out soon," Laura said. "Do you two want to tour Fort Clinch? It's something I've been wanting to do as research for my novel."

CHAPTER 40

FORT CLINCH

The Beck family paid the entrance fee at the state park-ranger station leading to Fort Clinch. The arching, moss-covered oak trees greeted the family as they slowly drove through the 1400-acre park at the northern end of Amelia Island.

"It's beautiful in here with the live oaks, palmettoes, and sea pines lining the hiking trails," Laura said. "The pamphlet says that the forest area is called a maritime 'hammock,' which is a Seminole word meaning 'shady place.' There are saltwater marshes on the west, and there's a fishing pier at the northeast side of the park."

"Look, there are campgrounds," added Jack. "Maybe we should go camping, Dad, we haven't gone in years. Remember when you, Steve, and me camped in the state park in southern Missouri? We rented that boat and got so sunburned we couldn't move."

"Yes, Jack, I remember. And we didn't catch a single fish, just got covered in mosquito bites on top of the sunburns."

"And in addition to insects, there are also alligators in this park," Laura said. "Something you didn't have to worry about in Missouri. I think a day trip is better than staying overnight in a cramped tent. We have nice comfortable beds in our Island home."

There were few guests and plenty of parking spaces near the Visitor's Center. "The fort construction began in 1847 and was named after General Duncan Lamont Clinch who fought in the Second Seminole War," Laura began. "The brochure says it was never really finished and didn't see any major battles, although it was occupied by both the Confederate and Union armies in the Civil War. It was acquired by the state in 1936 and was last used as a security and communications post in World War II."

They walked through the brick tunnel and emerged in the parade grounds. They toured the two-story barracks, the laundry, infirmary, kitchen, and carpenter shop. In the prison area, John said, "I can almost see a Union soldier cleaning his rifle while watching over an inmate."

"John, why did the soldiers have to clean their guns so often in the past?"

"It was because the bullets were covered with a primer. When the gun fired, the bullet left behind a residue that was similar to salt. If the guns weren't cleaned they'd corrode."

"So, the ammunition was corrosive."

"You got it."

They climbed to the top of the fort walls and stood beside the cannon replicas. "What a great view of Cumberland Island. It's remarkable that the Carnegie family has owned it for so long," said John. "And I think that platform halfway across the river is the border between Florida and Georgia. I remember seeing a similar one before."

"Isn't Cumberland Island where John and Caroline Kennedy got married?" asked Jack.

"Good memory, Jack. There are only a few dozen people living on the island full-time according to a book I read. There's a hotel that I'd love to stay at some time. Do you two want to walk down to the beach?" added Laura.

A cool wind blowing in from the ocean greeted them as they went through the 'sallie port,' or fort exit, turned left, and made their way to the shore. There were a few men casting their fishing lines hoping for a grouper or speckled trout for dinner. Laura's eyes drifted over the abundant shells looking for shark's teeth as they walked over the stone jetties to the small, sandy alcoves. She spotted a triangular-shaped object and bent down to pick it up. It wasn't a tooth but an arrowhead with a broken tip. As she held it in her hand, a frigid breeze rushed through Laura, reminding her of what happened with the light orb in her bedroom.

"Guys, look at this! I wonder how old it is and what type of stone it's made from." *And I have the feeling that it holds an important message for me.*

"Cool, Mom. Can I see it?" Laura handed the artifact to her son as a young boy and his father walked by. The boy looked at the arrowhead in Jack's hand.

"Dad, look. That's awesome! Maybe it's from the Timi—Timu . . ."

"Timucuan Indians," the gentleman said. "People often find sharks teeth in this area. The navy dredges the mouth of the St. Mary's River so the nuclear submarines can get to the Kings Bay Naval Base in Georgia. But arrowheads are rare."

"Would you like to see it?" Jack asked the boy.

There was a big grin on the boy's face as he held the piece of carved stone. His father took out his cell phone and photographed the arrowhead in his son's hand.

"Sir, what do you know about the Indians who lived in this area?" asked Jack.

"Well, the first Europeans who encountered the Timucuan were surprised at how tall they were. The men had long hair that they wore in a knot on the top of their head making them appear even taller. They had well-established villages and cultivated crops, as well as hunted and fished. You can see the remains of where they dumped their oyster shells on the northwest side of the Island."

"Didn't they have lots of tattoos, Dad?"

"Yes, the men received tattoos for accomplishments."

"Are they still living in this area?" John asked.

"No, they were basically a peaceful tribe but did have wars with the Europeans and other tribes. The ones who survived the wars were wiped out by European diseases, especially smallpox."

"Thanks for letting me hold the arrowhead," said the boy as he returned the stone to Jack and walked away with his father.

"What do you think it means, Mom? Did you find it for a reason?"

"Yes, Jack, I think I did, but at the moment I don't know why. There seems to be a connection to Native Americans in the things that are happening to me, and I'll have to figure out what it is."

"Let's check out the fishing pier while we're here. And I'm hoping Santa will bring Jack and me saltwater fishing rods this year." John said as they exited the grounds and walked toward the car.

CHAPTER 41

SUNDAY BRUNCH

Allison walked into the kitchen and whispered in her mother's ear, "It's like having three big brothers." Cassie smiled and realized Allie was beginning to see her neighbors as family.

"Here, sweetie, would you take these appetizers into the boys?" Carefully, Allie carried the platter of mini hot dogs and pizza rolls into the family room.

"Faith and Cassie, did you get a threatening phone call?" Laura asked.

"No, what happened?" said Faith. Cassie shook her head.

"Well, it was a disguised male voice and he said 'leave it alone.' I have no doubt it was about the Thanksgiving murder. Amy, have you heard back from the police about the ro-ro?"

"What are you talking about?" said Cassie.

Amy filled her in on their trip to Jekyll Island and Jack's idea about the ship that carries vehicles and the nursery rhyme. "No, I haven't heard anything new. What a conversation to have at a Christmas brunch! Everything about this season is unusual."

Faith sighed. She confided in her friends about the difficult day she'd had and how much her sons' support had meant to her. "I can't express how much I appreciate my boys and my friends."

Laura, Cassie, and Amy all moved in to surround Faith in a group hug. Allison walked in and realized what was happening and wrapped her arms around the women too. The timer on the stove chimed, and Faith began to giggle. The laughter was infectious, and they all joined in as they separated.

"This is just what I needed," Cassie chuckled. "Now let's get this food on the table."

"Lunchtime, boys!" Allie called out then got out of the way as Miles, Austin, Jack, and John rushed into the dining room and filled their plates. Then they returned to their video game in the family room.

The ladies sat in the living room with their plates balanced on their laps. "*It's beginning to feel a lot like Christmas,*" Laura sang. "And I'm grateful for all of you. Merry Christmas!"

"Merry Christmas," they echoed.

"And a happy New Year," Allie added.

"Speaking of New Year's," Laura began, "did you tell the ladies about your possible date, Amy?"

With the color rising in her cheeks, Amy told Cassie and Faith about her meeting Nate at the antique store and her instant impression that she had known him before. "And this morning he invited me out for dinner on New Year's Eve, and then we're going to join Laura and John to ring in the year."

"Cassie and Faith, if you're free, you're welcome to join us for dinner and champagne. John will be getting into Jacksonville at 3:00 on the 31st, but Jack will be in Seattle. It would be great to have the company."

"It sounds like a wonderful idea, Laura. I'll check with my boys, but I'm quite certain they'll be with their friends in Atlanta."

"Allie and I would love to join you. Her friend Clara Simpson will be here too, if that's okay."

"The more the merrier," said Laura.

"Mom, can I hand out the presents?" Allison asked.

"Sure, honey. Good idea. Allie thought that since we're becoming like a family we should get each of you a small gift."

Allison put on her bright red Santa hat and turned on a Christmas CD. She retrieved the gifts from the front hall closet and placed them under the tree. Cassie loved seeing the joy on her daughter's face. *Every small step toward a new normal is good for Allison,* Cassie thought.

"I have gifts for each of you, but you'll have to wait," said Amy.

"Me too," Laura added, "and I was going to give them to you on the 24ᵗʰ. We always open one present on Christmas Eve, and since two of our kids are far away, I thought I'd buy gifts for my new friends."

"And I wanted to invite y'all over Christmas Eve. Our traditional party will be a little smaller this year, but it will still be a celebration," said Faith. "I'll see if Betsy is available, too."

"Perfect," Laura added. "We'll take our gifts to Faith's on Christmas Eve."

"And I'll do the same," added Amy.

John and the boys came into the living room when Allison called them. She handed each a small package. Just as the last gift was opened, a blood-curdling scream came from outside. Everyone quickly rushed out the front door to find the source of the horrible noise. Mrs. Biddle was on her knees on the lawn, holding a limp dog in her arms.

"Millie, Millie," Betsy wailed, "what happened to you? Please don't leave me."

John carefully lifted the older woman to her feet. "Do you want me to take you somewhere? Is there a vet nearby?"

"Yes, yes, on 14ᵗʰ Street. Please hurry. There's still time to save her!"

John ran across the street and jumped into his car as Betsy rushed to the passenger side and got in with the dog. They raced out of the subdivision and down Amelia Island Parkway.

"Mercy, what next? I hope the poor little dog will be all right," said Faith.

"Did anyone see anything?" asked Miles.

They all shook their heads. "I wonder if she was hit by a car and crawled onto the lawn," said Jack. "That poor little dog. I hope she makes it."

"Let's help Cassie with the dishes," added Amy. "There's nothing more we can do for Betsy."

Everyone walked back into the house in a subdued mood. "Something doesn't feel right about Millie," Amy said as they began to clear the dining room table. The boys had gone back to their game in the family room. "I'm getting a psychic impression that the dog was harmed intentionally."

"Who on earth would want to hurt a defenseless dog? Did Betsy stick her nose into something she shouldn't have? And what could she have possibly found out?" Cassie asked.

"I'll talk to her when they get back," said Faith. "So many highs and lows this holiday season. What else could possibly happen?"

A short time later, John called to say that the vet had determined she'd ingested poison and pumped Millie's stomach. To everyone's relief, the dog was expected to recover.

CHAPTER 42

LETTER FROM PARIS

On Monday morning, Laura was thrilled to receive a package that Steven sent from Paris. In addition to gifts for each of them, Steve had included a lovely letter describing the holiday season in his temporary home.

Christmas in Paris

Christmas in the City of Light is a wondrous sight. The trees of the Avenue des Champs-Elysees dangle with icicle light strands of blues and whites. The storefronts and shopping areas are decorated in familiar ways, yet they retain a higher aesthetic quality that is somehow inherent to Paris. But as a North American, Christmas in France can underwhelm, particularly in how it's celebrated by the people. In the US and Canada, Christmas is a spectacle, a shop-till-you-drop frenzy of consumerism that is among the biggest events of the year, holiday or not.

To the French, though, the holiday remains what is a more traditional, smaller scale event with a focus on family time, specialty foods, wines, and other delicacies. Gifts, decorations in the houses, even Christmas trees, seem to be on the periphery—certainly not unusual inclusions in the festivities, but not the focal point they are across the ocean. So, on the one hand, the city can appear to be among the best in the world to spend the holiday with its iconic beauty dressed up with beautiful lights and decorations.

Yet you don't get the sense that people are doing the same within their homes, spending the time and energy and money to go 'all-out' in the way that is expected of us in North America. This is the greatest difference I've encountered, feeling that the buzz—maybe childhood giddiness—was missing.

And also my family was missing. Paris could have done well to have had them there!

I love you all,
Steven

"I miss you too, my darling son," Laura said as she kissed the letter.

"Are you talking to yourself again?" asked John as he walked into the kitchen.

Laura chuckled, "Yes I am! We got a beautiful letter from Steven with the gifts he sent. He's missing us as much as we miss him. It sounds like the Parisians have a low-key celebration compared to the US. I must say I enjoy the hoopla of the holidays. Sometimes it feels good to celebrate."

"I know what you mean. It's at times like these that I appreciate our family traditions. There are no guarantees that we'll even be here next Christmas, so we might as well enjoy."

"What made you say that, John?"

"I got an email this morning that an old friend from high school has terminal cancer. He was always so healthy and fit. It doesn't make sense."

"Oh, I'm so sorry. You're right, there are no guarantees, and even a long life is too short. Who knows what tomorrow will bring?" Laura thought, *I can barely handle what's going on today worrying about the Conti case, without thinking about the future. And there's a killer on the loose who knows I'm connected to the crime. I still can't wrap my mind around this whole thing. The joy of the season is mingled with the lingering fear of a dangerous person out there. It's all so surreal.*

Jack sauntered into the family room looking like he was still half asleep. His eyes lit up when he saw the package. "Is that from Steve or Jenny?"

171

"Yes, honey, it's from your brother."

"Can I open my present?"

"No, you have to wait until Christmas morning. The card says, 'Open on December 25.' And you opened a gift at Cassie's yesterday, and I have one for you to open on Christmas Eve."

"Yeah, you're right, I can wait. I'm going to meet up with Miles and Austin after breakfast, and we're heading to the beach."

"Steven sent this letter if you want to read it. Gosh, I miss my far-away children."

"Me too," added John. "Any plans for today, Laura? I want to finish my shopping if you don't need the car."

"I'd like to work on my novel today, so it's all yours."

John put on his jacket and picked up the car keys. "Maybe you can send your characters to Paris. We can scout locations when we visit Steven in March. You could develop some interesting story lines since it's a romance novel."

"Good idea, John. I'll have to think about it. It's nice using my brain for something creative—not just proofreading junk mail."

When she was alone, Laura opened her laptop and stared at a blank page. Ten minutes later she hadn't typed a single word. She stood up and began wandering around the house and stopped when she spotted the arrowhead on the front hall table where she'd placed it when they came home from touring Fort Clinch.

"What are you trying to tell me?" she asked the small stone cradled in her palm. "What is the connection between Native Americans and Eduardo Conti? And is Millie's poisoning tied to the case?" *And I'm talking to myself again!*

The house phone rang, and Laura jumped. Hesitantly, she picked up the portable phone and pressed the answer button. The same gruff voice she'd heard before muttered, "Do you get it now?"

"Who are you and what are you talking about? Why are you harassing me?" The line went dead.

CHAPTER 43

MIRROR, MIRROR

Crows' feet, wrinkles, and worry lines. A middle-aged widow whose deceased husband told her to find love again. Who would even want such a sad-looking woman? Faith sat in front of the vanity mirror in her bedroom on Monday morning, realizing her internal pain was showing on her face. *Chances are I'll be alone for the next thirty years before losing my mind in some nursing home.*

Miles walked past his mother's room and saw her staring in the mirror. "With all that you've gone through, Mom, you're still beautiful."

"I was just noticing all the 'life lines' on my face. I don't feel beautiful."

"Mom, you're incredible," he said as he kissed the top of her head. "We're leaving in a few minutes to meet up with Jack."

"Have fun, my love."

Widow. What a depressing word. I'm too old to be enticing and too young to be alone. Beyond romance, what am I going to do for the rest of my life? I can still work for my charities, but my heart isn't in it anymore. It feels like they're part of my past. What will the future hold for this forlorn Southern lady?

Faith was startled when her cell phone rang. She rose to retrieve it from the nightstand.

"Hello, Faith. This is Jeremy Baxter."

She was surprised to hear from Charles' young coworker who had introduced them to Amy and Doug. "Jeremy, what a surprise. Are you in Atlanta?"

"No, I'm spending the holidays with my parents in Jacksonville. I was thinking about your annual Christmas Eve get-together and want to drop by if you're still having a party. I'd like to see you and catch up with the boys."

"Yes, Jeremy, we're having a few neighbors over, and you're welcome to join us. I'm afraid that without Charles here to make his famous appetizers, the food won't be as elaborate this year."

"It's the company I'm looking forward to. I've got your address, so I'll see you on Christmas Eve. Goodbye."

The phone rang again, and gratitude filled Faith's heart when she heard her sister's voice. "Oh, Amanda, I'm so glad you called. Have you heard from Mother and Father? It's been days since they've been in touch."

"Yes, I just spoke with Mom. They were up early to watch the sunrise and are having fabulous time. I'm so glad you encouraged them to take their trip—after . . ."

"The funeral."

Amanda paused for a few minutes. "How are you, Faith? How are the boys doing? I can't fathom the pain you've all been through."

"As you can imagine, some days are better than others. I had quite the meltdown a few days ago, but Miles and Austin got me through the worst of it. One day at a time. Amanda, Mom hasn't called me for a couple of days and didn't answer my text messages, so I was concerned."

"I don't think she knows what to say to you. She hates anything stressful and sad, and Charles' death is both."

"You're right. Mother has always avoided confrontation or acknowledging when she's angry or unhappy. She pushes down her feelings and denies there's a problem. I don't think she and I are cut from the same cloth. I need to cry and grieve."

"Me too," said Amanda. "I'm the emotional type, especially at this time of year. Are you having your party tomorrow night?"

"Yes, it will be a small gathering with our neighbors. And I'm going to miss Charles' cooking. He'd become a good cook in the past few years. It turned out that he was quite talented in the kitchen, much to my surprise. And he took such pleasure and pride in his culinary creations."

"I'm glad that cooking brought him joy." Amanda was silent for a few moments. "What brings you joy, Faith?"

"I've been sitting here this morning trying to find an answer to that very question. What am I going to do for the rest of my time on earth? I can't put the burden of my happiness on my boys. They have their own lives to live."

"You're my wise big sister, Faith. I know you'll figure it out in time. I think you should call Mom and tell her you're having a Christmas Eve party. I'm sure it will make her feel good that you're coping with your loss."

"Thanks for the support, Amanda. I'll give you a call on Christmas Day. Love you."

Faith wandered into the kitchen and made of cup of herbal tea. *Charles' insurance will provide a decent life for the rest of my days, and I'm glad the boys' inheritance from their Granddad Proctor will pay for college. But what can I do that will inspire me and contribute to the world? What will bring me joy?*

CHAPTER 44

The sound of sirens interrupted their conversation, as Jack, Miles, and Austin walked north on the beach toward Peter's Point Beach Park. The smell of smoke assaulted them before they saw the flames coming from a house north of the park. Running up the beach toward the blaze, they reached the house at the same time as two fire trucks and several police vehicles.

"Holy crap!" said Jack. "That's Conti's house. You know, the guy that was murdered on Thanksgiving." Billowing smoke and towering flames shot toward the sky. An explosion shook the ground, and the boys backed away but were mesmerized by the awful sight.

"Was anyone living in the house?" Austin asked.

"I don't think so. My mom said Conti's son was staying at a hotel in town."

Miles said, "Do you think his son torched the house?"

"I can't see him doing that. He's supposed to inherit everything, so I don't think he'd burn down the house he was going to get."

The firefighters worked quickly to douse the flames, but it was too late to save the house. The acrid smoke permeated the air, and the boys began to cough and move away from the area. This was the second time in a month that the house was a crime scene.

"Man, this is not the quiet place my mom described when she told me they were buying a second home on a peaceful Florida island."

"We've had a house here for three years, and nothing interesting ever happened. This is some crazy stuff," said Miles.

Jack sent a text to his mother about the fire. Laura felt sick to her stomach as she read the message. *Oh my God! What next? Are we in danger of someone burning down our house too? Or one of the other homes on the street?* She called her neighbors to let them know about the latest incident.

"I'll call the detective to see what I can find out," Amy said when she answered Laura's call. "This is out of control, and I'm worried about our safety."

"I'm trying to down play it for Jack's sake, but I'm worried too. Let me know what the police have to say. Oh Amy, I also got another threatening phone call. Please pass that on to the detective."

"Did you press *69 and find out who was calling?"

"Oh, my God. I didn't even think of it, and I've had other phone calls since then, so it's too late. Another senior moment!" Laura said.

"We all have them," Amy added. "You'll get it next time."

"I'm hoping there won't be a next time. Talk to you later, Amy."

Hanging up, Laura walked into the family room and stared at the Christmas tree. *What have I done? Was moving here the right thing to do? I've put my family in danger and every week there's a new threat. Was I so unhappy before that buying a second home was the only answer?*

She walked over to the tree and lifted the Jiminy Cricket ornament from the evergreen branch. *Was it wrong to buy this house?* A small voice in her mind replied, 'No, for your spiritual and emotional growth this is the correct path.' In her heart, Laura knew this was part of her life journey, and it was essential that she dig deep to find her inner strength.

Drama and trauma are part of life and I need to gather all my resources—intuition, intelligence, and observation skills. I never thought my Christmas wish would be to help solve a murder!

Laura's cell phone rang, and her heart jumped in her chest. *Get a grip, it's not the house phone.* Laura was glad to hear her real estate agent on the line. "Hi, Janice, Merry Christmas! How are you?"

"I'm all ready for the holidays and looking forward to celebrating. I just wanted to let you know that Betsy Biddle called me this morning and is putting her house up for sale next week. I was wondering if you have any friends from St. Louis that were thinking of moving to the Island."

Laura felt like she'd been punched in the stomach and it took her a moment to respond. "Uh, no, I don't know anyone who's thinking of moving here. Did Betsy say why she was selling the house?"

"She was vague about the reasons but said she's moving to Arizona to be near her daughter. She made no mention of the fact that she was planning on moving when I saw her last month."

"Yes, she didn't say anything to me either. I guess her dog being poisoned has shaken her. Well, Janice, if I hear about anyone interested in the house, I'll let you know."

"Merry Christmas, Laura."

John arrived home with several packages. "Close your eyes, Laura. You can't see your presents before the big day."

"My eyes are closed. You don't have your usual hiding places this year. There's wrapping paper in Jenny's room if you need it—I mean when you need it." *I like having bits of normalcy in this anything but normal holiday season.*

The front door opened and Jack came rushing in. "Man, you should have seen the fire! It was wild. What an explosion. Glad no one was in the house."

"Me too, Jack. Did the neighbors' homes get damaged? The Thompsons live next door, and there are people living there."

"No, the firefighters were on top of it and put out the flames quickly. Who do you think did it, Mom?"

"It could have been an electrical problem and just a coincidence that is was Conti's house. We'll have to wait until the police investigate."

"Are you nervous, Mom? I mean, since we're connected to Conti, that someone deliberately set the fire and could do the same to us?"

"Honestly, Jack, I was wondering that too. But deep down I don't think we're in danger."

"I sure hope you're right."

CHAPTER 45

RUINS

Two days until Christmas, Cassie said to herself as she sat in her home office working on files. *And another week until a new year.* The doorbell rang, and Allie ran to answer it as Cassie followed close behind.

"Cassandra Harcourt?" asked a heavyset young man standing in the doorway.

"Yes."

"You've been served," he said handing her a large brown envelope.

Cassie felt like she was holding a document pronouncing her death sentence. She knew that inside the brown paper was the end of her third marriage. She was dreading seeing a written version of Robert's rage at her betrayal.

"What is it, Mom?"

"Just some legal papers. Nothing to worry about. Have you finished wrapping your presents?"

"Almost. Could you drive me over to Madison's in a while? We want to exchange gifts today."

"Of course, honey. Let me know when you're ready."

Cassandra sat in her office chair with a heavy heart. Taking out the papers she was shocked at what she read. There was an Affidavit of Irretrievable Breakdown of the Marriage, a Joint Petition for Divorce, and a Separation Agreement that required notarization. *Oh my God! Robert is agreeing to a no-fault divorce. And he's decided to let me have the Florida house, and he'll provide child support for Allie. He's even setting up a college trust fund for her. What happened to the man who had a private investigator follow me?*

Still in shock, Cassie thought about the last time she'd spoken to her husband and the venom in his words. She was expecting the worst and received the best possible outcome. Tears of relief began to flow, and she was amazed at the turn of events. *Robert must have heard about my confrontation with Jeffrey Stanton and the events leading up to my meltdown. His compassion triumphed over his anger. What a great Christmas surprise!*

Allie walked up to Cassie and placed her arms around her mother's neck. "Is it bad news?"

"No, actually it's from your father, and he's been very kind in his agreement to the divorce. He's even putting money aside for your college fund. Everything is wonderful, and we're going to be fine, just fine."

Cassie stood up and hugged her daughter. "It's you and me, kiddo. At least until you leave for college."

"That's a long time from now, Mom."

"It's much closer that you think, my love."

Cassie reviewed the divorce papers once more. An hour later she asked, "Are you ready to leave, Allie?"

"All set, Mom."

After driving her daughter to Madison's house in the historic district of Fernandina Beach, Cassie headed south on Fletcher Avenue and pulled up in front of the ruins of Eduardo's house. She got out and leaned against the hood of her car. It was shocking to see the total devastation of one of the loveliest homes on the Island. A wave of sadness washed over Cassandra, and she took a few deep breaths to grapple with all the events of the past month.

"I've seen you before."

Cassie turned around to see a young boy standing on the lawn at the house next door.

"You were a friend of Mr. Conti's, weren't you?" he said.

"Yes, I knew your neighbor. I'm Ms. Harcourt. Are you Ricky? My friend, Mrs. Beck, said she spoke with you about Thanksgiving night."

"Yeah, I talked to her, and then the police came back. My dad was really mad because he doesn't like getting involved."

"Ricky, I know you've told the story many times, but could you tell me again what you saw that night?"

Ricky picked several leaves off the oleander bush in his front yard. He ripped them into small pieces as he decided what to do. Reluctantly, he repeated what he saw and heard the evening Eduardo was murdered. Cassie listened intently, and parts of the overheard conversation Conti had with his probable killer played over and over in her mind. She was staring at the burned-out remains of the house when Ricky's question brought her back to the present.

"Who do you think shot him?"

"I'm not sure, Ricky. But don't worry, I know the police will catch the man who did this."

Since Ricky had confided in Laura that Eduardo was with a man on Thanksgiving night, they all agreed a woman was probably not responsible for the shooting. But there were other things that Ricky had told her that raised questions in the back of her mind.

CHAPTER 46

VIOLET

A t the same time Cassie was speaking with Ricky, Amy was talking on the phone to a new client in Charleston, South Carolina. The young woman, Marilyn Evers, was experiencing unsettling activity in her historic home on Legare Street just south of Broad Street. Recent renovations seemed to stir up poltergeist activities, and the woman was worried about her safety. Marilyn sent Amy a photo of the house on her smart phone.

"Let me work on this. I'll call you back," Amy said.

"Please let me know as soon as you figure out what's happening," said Marilyn. "I'm not sure if I should have bought this place."

Maybe it's the ghost of Christmas past, Amy thought. She turned off her phone and settled into a rust-colored Lazy Boy recliner that was obviously used by old Mr. Ferguson on a regular basis. She closed her eyes, began to breathe deeply, and focused on relaxing her body and mind. Normally she'd get emotional impressions or flashes of images when she went into a deep trance to investigate a situation. Today was different.

Amy envisioned the Evers home in her mind. *Who are you and why are you in this house? Can you tell me your name? What is your connection to this place?* There was only silence. Amy sat for several more minutes without receiving a single message.

E. Louise Jaques

Suddenly she felt an intense vibration like an earthquake was rattling the room. Her body began to vibrate as her mind was searching for an explanation. All at once, Amy felt her consciousness lift out of her body and zoom skyward, through the roof, above the trees and over the island. In an instant 'she' was flying northward like a bird on the wind over the coastline of Georgia and South Carolina. She began to slow and floated down directly in front of the Evers house.

Looking upward to a second-story window, she could see the figure of a young woman with a scowl on her face. Amy's astral body glided into the house, easily passing through the front door. She could hear music and moved down a narrow hallway into a semi-renovated kitchen. Amy could 'see' Marilyn rolling out dough on a butcher-block island, listening to jazz on her iPod, with her curly, auburn hair tied back with a pink ribbon. She was wearing a red apron that said, 'got vino?' in large black letters. Marilyn was not aware that Amy was present.

Next, Amy returned to the front foyer and ascended the stairs. As she turned the corner at the second-story landing, a blast of cold air knocked her backward. She came face to face with a female ghost whose energy was so intense that it took Amy's breath away.

"Get out!" a voice screamed in Amy's mind. "This is my house, and you'll be sorry if you don't leave."

Amy was startled and didn't know how to respond until she felt a hand on her shoulder. Turning around she saw her grandmother's spirit standing behind her. With new confidence, Amy decided to confront the girl. "I know you're upset, but please tell me your story. What's your name?"

"Get out!" the spirit ordered and swept past Amy leaving a blast of cold air behind. "Violet, her name is Violet Ashford." It was her grandmother's voice that Amy heard. Without a moment's notice, Amy's consciousness whooshed back into her body on Hopeful Court. Her body jolted backward in the chair as her astral body reunited with her physical body.

Oh my gosh. That was incredible. Instead of remote viewing or receiving intuitive flashes, I had an actual out-of-body experience. I could see and even feel the chill left by the ghost. Amazing! Amy felt dizzy and drained like she'd been on a giant rollercoaster—twice. Her mouth was dry and she carefully rose from the Lazy Boy to make a cup of tea. Her hands were shaking as she put water in the kettle and took down a mug from the cupboard. *And thanks, Grandma, for your help.*

While waiting for the water to boil, Amy turned on her laptop to the Evers client file and wrote down her impressions of the journey to Charleston. She'd ask Marilyn to check local records for information about the departed Violet Ashford. Amy had rarely encountered such a powerful earthbound spirit haunting a location. And never before had her maternal grandmother been there to assist her. Amy's and her mother's paranormal gifts came from Grandma Annie.

The hair rose on Amy's neck as she stood up to turn off the gas burner under the kettle. She felt psychically open and vulnerable and looked around the room for signs of an unwanted guest. She could feel a dark energy but didn't see anything. Cradling the warm cup of tea in her hands, she walked out to the front porch and sat in the rocking chair. Amy needed to talk to someone about her experience so she decided to walk over to Laura's house.

"Amy, come in. What's up?" Laura said when she answered the door.

"Have I got a story to tell you," Amy said as she followed Laura into the family room and flopped down on the sofa.

Amy described her incredible journey to Charleston and what transpired while 'she' was inside Marilyn's house. "That is the first real out-of-body experience, or OBE as some call it, that I've ever had. It was quite a head-trip. I don't think it's something I'd like to experience on a regular basis, but it was great seeing my Grandma. I'll call Marilyn later to tell her what I saw."

"Is it the energy of this Island that's making us connect to the other side more readily? Or could it be the intense emotions we have because of the murder case we're working on?"

"I don't think it's about the murder, because I've had such limited interaction with Conti's spirit. Usually, it's only cases that involve me, or someone close to me, that I have trouble connecting with, so I don't understand what's going on."

"On a lighter note, where is Nate taking you for dinner on New Year's Eve?"

CHAPTER 47

'TWAS THE NIGHT BEFORE CHRISTMAS

Christmas Eve is my favorite day of the year, Laura thought as she opened her eyes. I look forward to the feelings of joy and anticipation all year long. Laura panicked for an instant when she rolled over and realized that John was not in bed beside her. Then the heavenly aroma of French Roast coffee slowly reached her. At least half of my family is with me today.

"Good morning, Mrs. Claus," John said entering the bedroom with a tray of coffee, mugs, and chocolate croissants. "Another new tradition for our new home."

Laura was overwhelmed with love and gratitude. *It's the little acts of kindness that make a marriage last.* "Thank you, Mr. Claus, this is such a sweet surprise. Breakfast in bed can definitely become a new tradition."

"Any left for me?" asked Jack as he ambled into the room.

"Of course, love. Your dad brought an extra coffee cup. Any plans for today?"

"Nope, just hanging out and eating cookies. What time is the party at the Proctor's tonight?"

"Around 7:00. Jack, I'm glad you're getting along with Austin and Miles. The first holiday without their father is really difficult. You're a great son with a loving heart."

Jack came around the bed and hugged his mother. "Yeah, we're lucky our family is still intact, and it will be even better when Steve and Jenny are home. Come to think of it, can I take the car? I want to pick up a few things."

"No problem. Dad filled the gas tank last night so you're all set."

When Jack left with a cup of coffee in one hand and a croissant in the other, Laura lay back against the pillows. She thought of her parents and brother celebrating on the other side and wondered if they would 'join' the festivities that night. *When someone dies there's always a hole in your heart that can never be completely filled. Thank goodness I'll see them again—but hopefully not too soon. I wonder what they think of our move to Florida and me attempting to write a novel. I'm having a hard enough time believing it. There are so many improbable things happening right now.*

John walked back into the bedroom after replenishing the coffee and said, "What's going on in that head of yours? You have a far-away look on your face."

"I was thinking about Amy's out-of-body experience, the one I told you about yesterday. I wonder if it will ever happen to me. I'm not very psychic, so it probably won't, but at least I can add a description of her journey in my novel."

"Moving here has given you a lot of ideas for your story—a murder, a car bomb, a house on fire—and all within a month. Incredible when you think about it," said John as he poured more coffee in his wife's cup. "I know homicides can take a long time to solve, but I sure hope the police figure this one out soon. I don't like leaving you here alone, but I have to go back to work after Christmas."

"I know, John. I have the ladies as support, but I wish you could work from Florida and travel back to St. Louis when you needed to. Maybe someday—but for now, we can enjoy our island time together whenever possible."

After breakfast, Laura showered, dressed, and admired her new holiday sweater as she looked in the full-length mirror. Jenny thought Laura's seasonal sweaters were corny, but her daughter wasn't here to comment. Later in the day, her cell phone rang, and Jenny was calling from Australia.

"Merry Christmas, Mumma! I miss you guys so much. I had a fun night and a wonderful morning with my friend Chris and his family. I was so glad they invited me. It would have been pretty sad if I had to spend Christmas alone."

"Merry Christmas, sweetie. I'm grateful too that you were included in their celebration. How is everything?"

"We just got back from a walk on Bondi Beach, and it's 90 degrees outside. It was hilarious! There were hundreds of people on the beach in Santa suits, hats, and even bikinis. It's amazing that you and I are both close to a beach this Christmas. I wonder if Steven will be walking along the Seine River today. We sure are far apart this year."

"But close at heart. I can't wait until we're all together on the Island. I pray that by then the police have solved the murder of the Mr. Conti and life is peaceful and uneventful on Amelia again. Did Steven send you a letter?"

"Yes, I think he photocopied the one he sent you. There are a lot of differences here too."

Jenny went on to describe her holiday 'down under.' "I even made Chris and his family carry candles and sing *Silent Night* on our way to bed, like we did when we were kids. And they say 'Merry Chrissy' here."

Laura laughed and was happy some of their family traditions were still a part of Jenny's life even though she was half a world away. "What are you having for Christmas dinner—kangaroo and Vegemite?"

"Gross! No we're having a BBQ with lamb, beef, pork, and something called crackle. I think it's the pig's skin! And Chris's parents gave me a gift basket with chocolates and 'lollies'—or candy, as we call it!"

"Wish everyone a Merry Chrissie for me, Jenny. I can't wait until you're back and you can fill us in on all the details of your trip. Your Dad and brother are here to talk to you. Love you so much."

"I love you too, Mum. Have a great day."

CHAPTER 48

PROCTOR'S PROMISE

Faith awoke on Christmas Eve with the feeling she was being hugged. "Charles, is that you?" she said aloud. "Oh, how I miss you, especially today. I need your expertise in the kitchen and your jovial laugh greeting our guests tonight." Tears pooled in her eyes, but in Faith's heart there was a new resolve to make everything all right for her boys. It was almost like Charles' inner strength was infusing her spirit.

A knock on the door made her quickly wipe away the signs of sadness from her face as Austin walked in her bedroom. "You okay, Mom?"

"I'm fine. Just wishing your father was here. Austin, would you mind going to the grocery store with me today? I have several things I need for tonight, and I'd love the company."

"Of course I'll go. I have to buy a few things for your stocking since Dad isn't here. I had the strangest dream about him last night, but when I woke up I just knew what he wanted me to get for you. Weird!"

"Maybe Amy's talent for contacting the other side is rubbing off on you. Let's leave in about an hour."

Maneuvering through the crowded isles at the grocery store, Faith and Austin were both in a trance, not paying attention to their shopping list.

Finally, Faith's eyes rested on a type of cracker that was Charles' favorite for his smoked salmon and caviar appetizers.

"I'm glad your father enjoyed cooking the past few years," she said placing the box in the cart. "And all those cooking shows he watched, my goodness, I had no idea there were so many of them."

"Yeah, it surprised me that he took an interest in food. I'll help you with his recipes today. Was it a mid-life thing?"

"Perhaps he just got tired of my cooking, which I admit is very repetitious. Culinary creativity has never been of much interest to me."

"You don't have to tell me."

"Is my cooking really so bad, Austin?"

"Just teasing you, Mom."

Faith stopped in the middle of the frozen food isle and looked at her son.

"Mom, what's wrong?"

"I just had the strangest thought—a cooking program for underprivileged teens through the YMCA. Now where did that come from?"

"Maybe Dad is sending you a message. I've read about programs that partner restaurants with groups that train kids to work in the food industry."

"Oh my heavens, Austin, that's it! I've been trying to figure out what to do with the rest of my life, and the charities I've worked for all these years don't seem to feel right any more. I can set up a program through the Y to help young people not only learn the skills they'll need to work in a restaurant, but life skills too. You know, like money management and how to succeed in a job interview."

"That's a great idea, Mom—and Dad. I know he's here putting ideas in your head."

"I can raise money for a scholarship fund, 'Proctor's Promise.' I'll get in touch with Mrs. Clarkson at the YMCA and see if we can work together. Oh, honey, this is so exciting. I have hope for the first time since your father passed. It will honor his memory and help others. Now let's finish this shopping."

Austin dropped his mother and the groceries at home before he left for the strip mall off the Island to buy the gifts he'd dreamed about. Faith put on her favorite Christmas music and hummed as she made hors d'oeuvres.

Her heart was happier than it had been since Thanksgiving weekend when her world had changed forever. *Thank you Charles for the inspiration! I promise to follow up in the New Year when I return to Atlanta.*

Miles walked in the kitchen while talking to his girlfriend, Stephanie, on his cell phone. He began sampling his mother's creations, and she shooed him away. "Wait until tonight. And don't forget to clear out the front hall closet so our guests can hang their coats."

The young man smiled at his mother and noticed a lighter air about her as she sang and chopped vegetables. "Steph, I think things are going to be okay around here," he said walking into the family room. "I wasn't sure how my mom was going to be on her own, but she seems to be doing pretty good. Sometimes parents surprise you. But I still miss my dad."

"Be strong for your mother, Miles. And I miss you, and I love you."

"Can't wait to see you after Christmas. Love you, too, Stephanie."

CHAPTER 49

REDNECK YACHT CLUB

"Thanks, Nate, I'm looking forward to it!" Amy said goodbye to her new friend who might become more than a friend someday. *I can't believe he invited me to go to Brooklyn with him next month to meet his son. He must feel as strongly as I do about our soul connection. And I'm so glad he Googled me, knows what I do for a living, and is okay with it.*

Amy was startled when her phone rang. "Oh hello, Marilyn, I was just about to call you."

"I know you said you'd contact me soon, but I couldn't wait. I have a house full of people coming tonight, and I don't want anyone to be freaked out."

"It was an unusual reading," Amy began, "I had an out-of-body experience, and my astral body actually traveled to your house. I saw you in the kitchen rolling out pie dough, and you had on an apron that said 'got vino.' Is that correct?"

"Incredible, Amy. I was wearing that apron yesterday and making pies. You have such a gift. Did you find out who or what was disturbing the house?"

Amy described the spirit she encountered and what had transpired. "After the holidays, you might want to investigate the name Violet Ashford and see if she lived in the house at some point. In the meantime, why don't you talk to Violet and invite her to be a part of your celebration tonight. Tell her, out loud, that you're sorry she's upset about the renovations, but you'd like her to join the party. That may be enough to quiet her activity when your guests are there."

"It's worth a try. Merry Christmas, Amy. I'll let you know what I find out about Violet."

It feels so good when I can help someone solve a problem. I hope Violet behaves tonight. She has such a forceful energy I'm sure she could disrupt the party, Amy thought as she wrapped the last few presents for her friends. She was placing the gifts in a large bag when her phone rang again.

"Hello, Detective Davis. I guess the police have to work on holidays too. Have you found out the cause of the fire at Conti's house?"

"The fire marshal has identified the origin of the blaze, and it was deliberately set. They're still working on the investigation. There is a new person of interest in the case. We've discovered that Mr. Conti had a second illegitimate son who's living in Miami. His mother contacted Conti's lawyer when she learned of his passing. She'd been out of the country for the past few weeks."

"I'm not surprised with Conti's history of womanizing. Is this son a suspect in the murder or the fire or both?"

"The son, 19-year-old Riley Stone, has an alibi for Thanksgiving night, but it isn't very credible. He said he was in Jacksonville Beach partying and crashed at a house in Yulee not far from Amelia Island. Mr. Stone said he only knew the nickname of the guy he was with—Bonesaw—and he couldn't remember exactly where the house was located because he was too intoxicated."

"Seriously, the guy's name was Bonesaw? And he expects you to believe it?"

"He told me he remembers seeing a sign for a Redneck Yacht Club and the house was near there on Highway 17."

"Seriously, again. Does that really exist?"

"Yes, it does. It's a boat launch on the west side of the highway. He said his 'friend' drove him back to Jacksonville Beach the next day, and we have a surveillance video of him checking into a motel. So it's inconclusive if he was where he said he was on Thanksgiving night. We know he and his mother had a troubled relationship with Eduardo. Ms. Stone was not happy with the money he had provided over the years."

"Is there proof he's Conti's son?"

"Yes, Ms. Stone had a paternity test done shortly after her son was born, and she's made a claim on the estate. We'll see how it shakes out, but in the meantime we're investigating all possibilities."

"Do you have an update on the paper we found in the music box or the information on the ship connection?"

"Nothing so far. But we have cleared Paolo Conti to leave the country and return to his family in Milan. Keep in touch, Amy, and have a Merry Christmas."

"Same to you, Detective."

There's something the detective isn't telling me. I'm not sure if she's trying to protect us or doesn't trust us not to say something that would jeopardize the case. They must be getting close to solving the murder if they let Paolo go back to Italy. Or maybe they're just being compassionate and letting him go home for the holidays to be with his ill mother.

Amy was dressing for the party when the doorbell rang. A smiling deliveryman was standing at the door holding a large box. "Merry Christmas, ma'am. Somebody is thinking of you today."

Opening the box in the kitchen, Amy was shocked to see two dozen long-stemmed red and white roses and a candy-cane striped vase. The card said, 'I wish we were together today. Looking forward to New Year's Eve! Love, Nate.' *My goodness. What a romantic guy. I can't wait to tell the ladies.* Amy arranged the flowers in the vase and placed them on the dining room table. She sent Nate a text saying she was thrilled with the roses and was excited about their date. *Honestly, I feel like a silly schoolgirl with her first crush!*

CHAPTER 50

YOU'D BETTER WATCH OUT

Luminaries lit the walkway to Faith's front door. The twinkling lights of the Christmas tree shone through the picture window, and Amy paused for a moment as she reveled in the beauty of the scene. She took a deep breath of the crisp evening air.

"I really love this time of year," a voice said behind her.

Laura walked up, placing her left arm around Amy's shoulder while holding a large bag in her right hand. "Even with everything that's happened, I'm still grateful to be here this Christmas Eve."

"Me too," said Amy. "There have been so many wonderful surprises that more than compensate for the unpleasant ones. Shall we join the others?"

Raucous laughter came from the family room where, Miles was telling John, Jack, and Austin risqué jokes. They were standing near the roaring fireplace, which was decorated with a glowing evergreen wreath and garland. The women followed the female voices to the kitchen, where preparations were underway for a feast of appetizers and desserts.

"There you are," said Faith. "We were wondering if you were all right, Amy."

"I was on phone with my brother, and my niece was unusually talkative tonight. When she opens up to me, I let her go."

"Jenny was the same way when she was a teenager. She'd have these moments when she'd share everything that was going on, and I always stopped what I was doing to listen. I never knew when it would happen again."

"I sometimes regret not trying to have another baby. It would have been wonderful to have a daughter," said Faith as she placed pralines and bourbon brownies on a three-tiered silver platter. She looked up and saw smiles on the faces of the women. "Okay, I know what y'all are thinking. Austin comes pretty close."

The sound of the doorbell interrupted their laughter, and Faith hurried to the front door. "Hello, Jeremy, please come in. It's been a while. I apologize for not speaking with you at the wake. I was overwhelmed, as you can imagine."

"Once again, Faith, I'm sorry for your loss. I was always grateful to Charles for taking me under his wing when I joined the company. It was a pleasure working with him—on everything."

"Thank you for the lovely fruit basket. The boys are in the living room, and they're looking forward to seeing you."

"No problem. I'm anxious to talk to Miles and Austin too. We have a lot to catch up on. And a glass of holiday cheer sounds good."

For the first time, Faith had an uncomfortable feeling around Jeremy. She had paid very little attention to the young man when they first met at the country club and the few times they had been together since. He was a little too slick, and his smile seemed insincere. Returning to the kitchen, she whispered to Amy, "How well do you know Jeremy Baxter? He used to work quite closely with Doug, didn't he?"

"Yes, and Doug never confided in me why he left the company. I always thought there was something a little off about him. But the one good thing he did was to introduce Doug and me to you and Charles. I'll be forever grateful for that."

"Me too, Amy. He unnerved me a little tonight, but I'm probably over-reacting. It was just something in his manner . . ."

"Mom," said Allison as she bounded into the kitchen, "can I please have some eggnog? I promise I'll just have one glass."

Cassie smiled at her daughter, "Okay, but just one. You know there's brandy in it."

"Thanks, Mom. Do you want me to take one of these plates into the living room?"

"Yes, and we're right behind you with the rest of the food."

Austin sang along with a Michael Bublé CD, '*You'd better watch out, you'd better not cry,*' as the ladies placed the food on several tables that were set up by the Christmas tree.

"A toast to family and friends, old and new," said John as he handed cups of eggnog to the women. "And let's raise our glasses to Charles, who is with us in spirit tonight."

"Cheers!"

Amy saw a smirk cross Jeremy's face as Charles' name was mentioned and was glad Faith was facing away from him. She placed several appetizers on a plate and walked over to Jeremy who was standing at the bar.

"Hello, it's been a while. What brings you to Amelia?"

"Oh, my parents live in Ponte Vedra, and I'm spending Christmas with them. I thought Faith could use a little support at her party this year, so I drove up for the evening."

"That was nice of you, Jeremy. Have you been in touch with Doug lately?"

"Um, ah, no, I haven't seen him for a while. Sorry the two of you broke up."

Amy instinctively knew he was lying and wondered why he denied seeing Doug. "Sometimes marriages just don't work out. How is the new job going?"

"Good, good. But we certainly miss Charles. He was an important link in the chain."

"Miss Amy," said Austin as he walked behind the bar, "can I refill your eggnog?"

"Yes, thank you. You're a great host. Your father would be proud." When Amy turned around, Jeremy had left and was sitting beside Miles on the sofa, deep in conversation. She walked across the room to where Laura was standing.

"Amy, did you talk to the police today? Is there any news on the case?" asked Laura.

Cassie and Faith joined them by the glowing lights of the tree, and Amy filled them in on everything the detective had told her. "I really think they're holding back information. I was surprised that they let Paolo leave the country. I'm sure his family was relieved. Speaking of family, Mr. Conti had another son, and this story is wild." Amy told them about Riley Stone and his alibi for the time of the murder.

"That is the most unbelievable tale I've ever heard," said Faith. "Good heavens, do the police believe him?"

"As far as I know. What I was most surprised about was the fact they had nothing new on the mysterious numbers and letters on the paper we found in the music box. I wish my intuition was working better on this case."

"Amy, it's not your responsibility. It's the police who have to solve the murder. You've done everything you can, and so have we," said Laura as she picked up a praline from the platter. "This is wonderful. Pecans, butter, brown sugar—what else is in the pralines?"

"Heavy cream and love," Faith answered. "It's my grandmother's recipe, and the brownies are from Grandma Proctor's recipe. That reminds me—I've decided what my next project will be and how I'll be able to make a difference in the world and honor Charles' memory." Faith went on to describe her plans for Proctor's Promise.

"That's amazing, Faith. I can help when I'm in Atlanta," said Amy. "I have quite a few clients that I can call when you decide to start a fundraising campaign."

"And I can help with any legal questions you have about setting up the scholarship fund," added Cassie.

"I don't have any special skills or contacts, but I can stuff envelopes and proofread promotional materials," said Laura. "Anything I can do to help."

"Thank you, everyone. Now, who's ready to open presents?" Faith asked her friends.

CHAPTER 51

CHRISTMAS MORNING

The weather was clear and chilly the following morning as the four households on Hopeful Court began to stir. Laura was the first to awaken in her home. She put on the coffee, took the cinnamon rolls out of the freezer, and turned on the oven. There would be time later for John's special omelets after the presents were opened. Her cell phone rang, and she quickly answered it so the noise wouldn't wake her sleeping men.

"Merry Christmas, Mom."

"Oh, Steven. It's great to hear your voice. Merry Christmas to you. Thank you for the gifts and the lovely letter. I guess you've been up for a while."

"Yeah, I was at my neighbor's this morning to open presents, and I'm going there later for dinner. I figured you'd be up already. I know Mrs. Claus is an early riser."

Laura laughed. "You know me very well, sweetie. Now tell me everything."

Steven filled in the details of his Christmas Eve and day so far. Laura could tell by the tone in his voice that he was homesick. "We miss you so much, Steve, and next year we have to make sure all five of us are together. These huge distances between us are too difficult."

"You can say that again. But I'm glad I'm having this incredible experience, even if it's hard sometimes."

"Is that one of the kids?" John asked as he walked into the kitchen.

"Steven, here's your dad." Laura poured coffee into two mugs and brought one to her husband, along with the phone, then popped the rolls in the oven. Walking into the living room to turn on the Christmas lights, she looked through the front window and caught sight of someone rounding the corner at Betsy Biddle's house. *Is someone looking to buy the house? What would they be doing there so early on Christmas morning? And the For Sale sign isn't even up yet. Maybe it's someone from the real-estate office.*

Laura walked outside to her front porch to get a better view, but there was no further activity at her neighbor's house.

"Looking for reindeer?"

"Good morning, Jack. Merry Christmas! I thought I saw someone at Mrs. Biddle's, but it's probably my imagination."

"Merry Christmas, Mom," Jack said and gave his mother a kiss on the cheek. "I smell coffee and cinnamon buns!"

"Your brother is on the phone with Dad. I think you can catch him before he hangs up."

Laura took one last look across the street then closed the front door. *I have to stop being so paranoid. It's Christmas Day, and that's the only thing I'll think about today.* Plugging in the tree lights, she marveled at how many presents there were under the tree considering it was only the three of them. She smiled as she straightened the two tall packages she'd place behind the tree. She hoped her 'boys' enjoyed their new fishing rods.

Laura scanned the tree and saw ornaments from a lifetime: a hand-painted Santa from her childhood, three Baby's First Christmas ornaments, the baby booties John's grandmother had knitted, a lobster from Cape Cod, a seashell from a family trip to Hawaii, all the sports-related ones, the Eiffel Tower that Steven had sent this week, and a hundred others that had sentimental meaning.

An ornament caught her eye—the one her father had given her the year before he died: 'From heaven above, the light of love, shines into our hearts at Christmas.' *I love you too, Daddy, Mom, Arthur, and everyone else looking down on us today.*

Christmas invites us to stop and remember all the beautiful memories. We appreciate the people who are in our lives today and those who will always be with us in our hearts. The traditions are like a bridge from year to year and remind us what we're most grateful for.

Laura looked down at her feet and noticed a large, flat, square box and saw that it was a gift for her from Jack.

"Open it, Mom," said Jack as he came into the room. "I think it'll bring back memories."

"I've just been thinking about all the memories that fill our minds this time of year. What can this be?"

Carefully slipping her finger under the tape, she slid the wrapping paper off the box. Opening the lid she saw a multicolored dream catcher with seven white feathers dangling from leather cords. "Jack, this is wonderful. Where did you find it?"

"On the Internet, of course. I ordered it after you saw the orb in your bedroom and talked about the one you had in high school."

"I love it, honey, thank you. Maybe it will help me dream of how I can solve the mystery of how Native Americans tie into the Conti case."

"Okay, let's get this show on the road," said John. "I see you started without me. You know you're supposed to open your stockings first."

The Beck family spent the rest of the morning opening gifts. John suggested that they get dressed and take a stroll on the beach to make this an official Florida Christmas. Laura slipped her hand through John's arm as they walked along the shore and passed the scorched remains of Conti's house. "And now there's a second offspring in the picture." She'd told her husband about Amy's conversation with the detective.

"I can't imagine either of the sons setting the fire when they stand to inherit the estate. And I'm sure Paolo didn't harm his father, but the other boy sounds like a nutcase. His alibi is questionable at best."

"No kidding, Laura. But the police have other suspects. What about his partner from New Jersey or those military guys?"

"Or some ticked-off husband?" added Jack. Laura had brought her son up-to-date about all aspects of the case.

"I wish we could do more to solve this," said Laura. "Every little thing out of the ordinary frightens me—including those threatening phone calls. The voice was disguised, but now that I think about it, there was something familiar in the man's tone that I can't put my finger on."

CHAPTER 52

CRACKERS

A my slept in late on Christmas morning, and when she opened her eyes, the room surprised her once again. She'd settled into the Ferguson's home fairly well, but some days she was disoriented when she awoke.

Alone. I should have made plans for today so I wouldn't feel this emptiness. Why didn't I think ahead? If I was in Atlanta, I'd be volunteering at the women's shelter today and at least feel I was making a contribution. She slowly got out of bed and went to turn on the coffee maker. Her neighbors' kitchens would be buzzing with activity, but hers was silent. They would be busy with their families, and although she was invited to dinner at Faith's tonight, the rest of her day was open.

'Why am I such a misfit? I am not just a nitwit.' The song from the classic *Rudolph the Red Nose Reindeer* animated movie popped into her mind. With a deep sigh, Amy walked into the living room, turned on the lights of the small artificial tree, and sat in the recliner. *Childless, no husband, and far away from any family I have left. I'm a medium in a society that mocks my abilities or can be downright hostile. I've been called evil and insane and other things I don't even want to think about. And yet I've helped so many people. Why did I choose*

this life before I came to earth again? There are so many other ways I could be of service without the stigma attached to my work.

Rising out of the chair, her eyes fell on the dining room table. The sight of 24 roses in a cheerful vase made something click inside. *Can I open my heart to a man one more time? I've survived the pain of failed relationships before, and who knows, maybe this time it will be different.* Her mood was lighter as she went to the kitchen to pour a cup of coffee and was surprised by the ringing of her cell phone. *Maybe Nate is thinking about me too!*

"Merry Christmas, Amy. We've just come back from a walk on the beach, and John's making omelets. Would you like to join us?" asked Laura.

With a split second of disappointment, she said, "Yes, that sounds wonderful. I'll shower and be over in 30 minutes, if that's okay."

"Perfect, see you then. And you don't need to bring anything."

Amy sang *Have Yourself a Merry Little Christmas* as she showered. Last Christmas had been the beginning of the end of her relationship with Doug. What should have been a joyful time was extremely difficult, and she had pushed down the painful memories. She still felt there were things she needed to say to him, but she would wait until they could speak face to face when all this craziness was over.

Her phone rang as she opened the front door to leave, and this time her heart leapt when she heard Nate's deep, mellow voice. "Merry Christmas, Amy. So glad you liked the flowers. My son's fiancée, Isabella, helped me pick them out."

"I can't tell you how much the roses have brightened my day. I can thank Isabella in person next month when I meet her and Will. And Merry Christmas to you too."

Amy and Nate chatted for the several more minutes until she remembered that her friends were waiting to start brunch until she arrived. "I'll call you tonight when I get home from dinner. And thank you again for the roses and . . . everything."

Ringing the doorbell at the Beck home, Amy was once again reminded of arriving at Faith's Atlanta home the day after Thanksgiving, when so many lives changed forever. Charles was gone; she had moved to Florida and had become embroiled in a murder mystery; she had new friends—and possibly a new romance.

"Hi, Ms. Temple. Mom and Dad are in the kitchen."

Amy followed Jack and noticed the piles of wrapping paper and presents under the tree as they passed the living room.

"It looks like Santa came last night, Jack. Did he bring you anything special?"

"A new smart phone and a whole lot of beach stuff. But the best gift of all was airplane tickets for Kate and me to go to Paris in March. We all get to visit Steve, and I can't wait!"

"Merry Christmas, Amy. What would you like in your omelet?" John asked. "We have two types of cheese, bacon, ham, peppers, mushrooms, and chopped tomatoes."

This is what I want—a traditional family and a husband that cooks. "A little bit of everything would be great, John. Thanks so much for inviting me over. I was feeling a bit lonely."

"Nate will be back soon," Laura said. "I'm sure he'll make you feel better."

The color rose in Amy's cheeks. "I hope you're right. I was shocked when he invited me to meet his son in Brooklyn next month. And he's comfortable with my work."

"You've made a positive impact in so many people's lives, Amy. But you're right, I'm glad he's open to your abilities. It makes your relationship so much easier when the person you share your life with accepts all aspects of who you are. Now, how about some of Jack's famous home fries with your omelet?"

"You have a son that cooks too? I'm impressed."

"Our son Steven is a foodie too. I'm certain he's learning a lot about French cooking in Paris. I'm so glad the four of us are going in March, but we'll miss having Jenny there."

"Before we know it," John added, "we'll all be together again."

"Amy, you're going to Faith's for dinner, aren't you?" asked Laura as she added potatoes to her friend's plate and carried it to the table.

"Yes, at 6:00."

"I bought Christmas crackers, and there were a dozen in the box. Since we only need three this year, would you please take four with you tonight?"

"Crackers?"

"The traditional British favors. Here I'll show you one. They're cardboard tubes wrapped in heavy paper and cinched at each end. There are two strips of paper inside and when you hold on to them and pull the ends they make a popping sound like a firecracker." Laura placed her fingers inside the ends of the tube, and there was a *POP* as the cracker flew open and the contents spilled across the table.

"Inside there's a paper hat, a silly joke, and a prize like in a Cracker Jack box. This one has a string of 'pearls' and a purple hat shaped like a crown. We always wear the hat during dinner."

"That's too funny," said Amy. "Of course I'll take them tonight. Anything to lighten Faith's day will be good." She looked up and noticed something hanging on the wall. "That's a beautiful dream catcher."

"Thanks, Jack gave it to me this morning because of the experience I told you about with the orb in my bedroom. He thought it might spur my intuition to solve the case."

"I'm having trouble figuring it out too. Maybe I should get one as well. We'll do it, Laura, we'll help solve the crimes," Amy said. "This omelet is delicious, John. The potatoes are great too, Jack. You'll have to teach me how you make these."

"Anytime, Ms. Temple. Maybe you can teach me how to connect with the spirit world," Jack answered. "I really want to understand how the universe works."

Amy smiled. "I'll do my best to tell you all I know. I enjoy sharing my gift."

CHAPTER 53

MOON DOGGIE

A llison rushed into the living room and headed for the packages under the Christmas tree. She was looking for one in particular—a gift she'd asked for but wasn't sure her mother would buy. There it was, hiding behind the tree.

"Merry Christmas, Allie. Are you looking for something special?" said Cassie.

Allison giggled, ran over, and hugged her mother. "I didn't think you wanted me to learn how to surf. Can I see the board now?"

"Go ahead, love. Open it up."

Allison squealed with delight when she ripped the wrapping paper off the surfboard and saw the unusual design painted on the front. "It's wicked cool, Mom. I haven't seen one like this before."

"I had it custom made for you. Do you see the maps of Massachusetts and Florida in the design? And your name is disguised in the artwork, but it's there."

"This is awesome, Mom, thanks so much. I can't wait to try it out. I hope there are huge waves today. Wait till Clara sees this tomorrow!"

"It's a little chilly in the ocean this time of year. Why don't you open your other presents, and see if there's something that will help."

It was a frenzy of flying paper as Allison opened her gifts and found a wetsuit among other more traditional presents. She hugged the suit to her chest and danced around the living room. In her stocking, Allie discovered a gift certificate for surfing lessons.

"You're the best, Mom. This is sick!" wrapping her arms around her mother and squeezing her tight.

"I'm going to make some coffee. Would you like a hot chocolate?"

"Yeah, thanks," she said moving away. "Can I call Clara? I'm sure she's up by now."

"Okay, I'll start breakfast."

I got Allie the right presents this year, and it's so important after all I've put her through. Guilt can make parents do strange things. I'm not crazy about Allison learning how to surf, but it's what she wants and she'll be well trained. I wish I'd never seen movies where surfers are attacked by sharks—especially the one where the young girl loses her arm.

Cassie was filling the kettle with water for the hot chocolate when she noticed a figure rushing by the far side of Betsy's house. It looked like someone in a black hoody, but the person never reappeared.

"What's the matter, Mom?" Allison said as she joined her mother at the sink.

"Oh, nothing. I just thought I saw someone at Mrs. Biddle's house, and I know she's out of town. Maybe it was someone who's going to sell the house. Mrs. Beck told me it's going on the market soon. Now, let's get breakfast on the table."

An uneasy feeling followed Cassie the rest of the morning. She knew it wasn't someone from the real-estate office at the house next door, but she didn't want to scare Allison. The threatening phone calls Laura had received made her anxious, and she was worried they'd be next. She would do anything to protect her daughter and regretted getting involved with Eduardo.

"Mom, Clara can't wait to get here. I'm so glad she's coming. Her mom said she'll call you tomorrow when the plane leaves Boston."

"We'll have to think of fun things to do while she's here. Any ideas?"

"I want to show her the whole island, like, everything. And maybe we can rent a board for her so we can try to surf together. And we can go shopping at St. John's Town Center and . . ."

Cassie smiled as she listened to the light-hearted sound of her daughter's voice. *Allie is so resilient and forgiving, much more so than I was at her age. I'm glad that Clara's parents allowed her to come. An old friend is just what Allison needs and surprisingly I have an old high-school friend to help me through this difficult time too. At some point I'll have to thank Robert for his shocking kindness. I never imagined he'd respond so generously.*

Allison paraded around the house in her wetsuit and stood her surfboard against the dining room hutch. "Is the board your guest for dinner, Allie?"

"He's part of the family now. He's better than a puppy because you don't have to clean up after him or take him for walks. And when we're in the ocean he does all the work."

"Have you thought of a name for your new friend?"

"Moon Doggie, like in that old beach movie we saw. You know, Gidget's boyfriend."

Cassie laughed and thanked her lucky stars that Allison was in her life. "You never fail to amaze me, Allie. You have such a great imagination."

"And someday I'll use my wild imagination to write TV shows. Just you wait and see."

"I have no doubt you'll be a huge success. So becoming a lawyer isn't in your future?"

"Not a chance, too boring. I want to live in New York or Hollywood and write comedies and dramas and even funny commercials."

I wonder if her birth parents are writers. Sometimes it's a little unnerving not knowing Allison's genetic background. The information I received from the adoption agency was minimal. I dread the day she wants to find out about her birth family. I'll do anything I can to help, but there will always be that worry that I'll be replaced in her heart.

At that moment, Allison walked over and hugged her mother. *It's almost like she can feel my anxiety,* Cassandra thought. *I need to show her how much I love her each day, and everything will be fine.*

CHAPTER 54

HAVE FAITH

Miles and Austin crept into the living room on Christmas morning like they were small boys. They peeked in their stockings, then counted the presents for each of them and were assured, as usual, that they had the same number of gifts.

A smile crossed her face, as Faith watched them from hallway. *They haven't changed, Charles, not one little bit. They're still children at heart.* Faith caught her reflection in the mirror beside the fireplace. *Am I going to talk to a man who isn't here for the rest of my life?*

"Merry Christmas. Still counting presents I see."

"Hey, Mom, Merry Christmas," Miles and Austin said in unison as they got up to embrace their mother.

"Thank you, my wonderful boys. Now, is it time to see what Santa brought?"

"Just a minute, Mom. I have something for you."

Faith looked at Austin who smiled and shrugged his shoulders. Miles returned with a small box wrapped in gold paper with a red bow on the top.

"I found this on the top shelf of my closet at home when I was hiding my gifts for you and Austin. Dad must have put it there before . . . before Thanksgiving."

"Your dad was always full of surprises," Faith said as her son handed her the box. Her legs felt heavy as she walked to the sofa and sat down. Carefully she unwrapped the present and opened the silver box. Inside there were large diamond stud earrings and a note folded in half. Tears escaped her eyes as she put the diamonds in her ears. She read the final note she would ever receive from her husband.

"Your father wrote that he wanted to give me two diamonds to symbolize the two incredible sons I gave to him. Never doubt how much he loved you both."

"You look beautiful, Mom," said Austin as he choked back tears.

"Well, my darling boys, it's time to open the rest of the presents."

Although unspoken, all three felt Charles' spirit with them as wrapping paper was flying. After gifts were piled around the tree and they finished breakfast, the Proctors went to the Christmas service at a small Baptist Church on South 14th Street.

"Why don't we drive into town?" Austin asked as they left the church. "There's still lots of time before Miss Amy is coming over for dinner."

Centre Street in Fernandina Beach was almost empty of the usual locals and tourists. They drove down the lovely, winding street to the end, crossed the railroad tracks, and parked in the lot adjacent to the wharf.

"Your father loved watching the sail boats slip into the harbor. He was looking forward to retiring on Amelia Island and maybe buying a boat of his own," said Faith as they walked down the boardwalk.

Two boisterous couples came up behind the Proctors and walked passed them. The men were calling to others standing on a large yacht moored on the southwest side of the harbor.

"They're having a good time," said Miles. "Mom, look at the name of the yacht."

"Oh mercy. It's called Have Faith. What a coincidence."

"Or Dad directed us here today. I didn't know what made me want to come into town but now I do," added Austin. "Let's go home. We got the message, Dad."

Faith was cheerful after she spoke with her parents and her sister, Amanda, and told them of Charles' final gift. *Thank you, my love, for the earrings and leading us into town. You'll always be a part of our lives, and someday we'll be together again. Until then I'll take good care of our boys.* Holiday memories ran through her mind as she started dinner.

Amy waked into the kitchen and was pleased to see her friend smiling as she prepared a salad. "I didn't hear the doorbell. Merry Christmas, Amy."

"I was just about to push the button when Austin opened the door. Maybe he's developing his sixth sense. Those are beautiful earrings. Are they new?"

"A final surprise that Charles left in Miles' closet. Now, tell me about your day. Did you talk to your brother? Oh, and of course, did you talk to Nate?"

"Yes, I just got off the phone with Nate. I was sure I wouldn't get involved with another man for a very long time after Doug. But this whole year has been full of surprises. The horrible kind and the marvelous."

Faith placed the paring knife on the counter, walked around the island, and placed her arms around Amy. "It's fine, we'll all be okay in time. I know I have to go on with my life, for the boys and for myself. Time will make it easier to bear."

"You are tower of strength, Faith. I admire your fortitude and resolve."

Resolve to dissolve, thought Faith as she returned to the dinner preparations. "Resolve to dissolve. Weren't those the words on the paper in Cassie's music box? What could they possibly mean?"

"I still don't know. Now, what can I do to help make this yuletide feast?"

"The potatoes need to be mashed, and the cream needs to be whipped for dessert."

Amy chuckled, "The last time I tried to make whipped cream, it turned into a curdled mess. I think I'll stick with the potatoes. Oh, I brought some Christmas crackers from Laura, the kind with the paper hats and gifts inside. I put them beside the plates in the dining room."

"Wonderful. It can be a new tradition to add to the old."

"Didn't you go to college in Charleston?"

Amy saw a shadow cross her friend's face. "Yes, for my first two years, then I transferred to the University of Georgia. Why do you ask?"

Amy told Faith about her astral adventure in South Carolina and the ghost on Legare Street. "It was quite a journey. There's still so much about the spirit world and how we can interact with it that we don't understand. I'm not sure I'll have another spontaneous OBE again. Have you been back to Charleston lately?"

"No, no, I never went back. Would you please ask the boys to come and help us carry the dishes to the dining room?"

Amy could tell that Faith was upset and decided not to mention South Carolina again.

CHAPTER 55

THE MUSICIAN

"Clara!" yelled Allie as she ran to her friend exiting security at Jacksonville airport on December 26. "I'm so happy you're here."

"It was snowing when I left Boston. It's cool here but so much better than at home," Clara said they walked across the road to the parking garage. "I can't wait to see the beach!"

Cassandra gave Clara a driving tour of the Island before heading to the house. As they pulled into the subdivision, Cassie saw Laura talking to Janice beside the For Sale sign on the Biddle front lawn. "Allie, why don't you take Clara inside to unpack? I want to say hello to Mrs. Beck."

The girls rushed inside, "Clara, I can't wait to show you Moon Doggie."

"Hello, Ms. Harcourt," said Janice. "Do you know anyone who'd be interested in moving to the neighborhood?"

"No, but I'll let you know if someone comes to mind. Did Betsy say why she decided to move right now?"

"Not really. She didn't seem quite herself when I last spoke to her. Betsy is always so talkative but not this time."

"The bionic busybody, Betsy Biddle," Amy said as she walked over to the group of women. "I wonder if she found out something she shouldn't have."

"That crossed my mind too,' Laura added. "Here's the Thanksgiving case journal, Amy. Maybe you'll have more luck figuring things out than I've had," she said as she handed the book to Amy. "By the way, Janice, have you talked to your cousin who works at the police department lately?"

"No, Sheila spent Christmas with her in-laws in St. Pete Beach on the gulf side of the state. Cassandra, did your husband already return to Boston?"

"Uh, um, Robert and I have gone our separate ways. It's just Allison and me living here now." *I'll bet Janice already heard about my affair with Eduardo, and she knew Robert and I were getting a divorce. That was just mean,* Cassie thought. *There's no way I'd ever recommend her as a real-estate agent.*

"Is Betsy coming back to pack up the house?" Laura asked.

"No, her son-in-law is flying out next week to make the arrangements for the move. Oh, did you hear that it was arson?" asked Janice. "That the Conti house was deliberately set on fire?"

"Yes," said Amy. "I spoke to Detective Davis about it. The whole thing is unnerving."

"Our police force is excellent, and I'm certain they'll find out who committed all these crimes," said Janice. "It's unusual for anything exciting to happen on Amelia Island."

A car pulled up beside Betsy's house, and the driver-side window was rolled down. "Hey, Mrs. Blackwell, is now a good time for Shirley to clean Mrs. Biddle's?" asked Ronnie Gordon.

"Yes, go ahead. The front door is unlocked," said Janice. "I'll be back in a few hours when Shirley is finished. Just send me a text when she's done."

Ronnie popped the car trunk and retrieved the cleaning supplies for his sister. The young woman smiled at the ladies and was humming a tune as she walked up to the front door.

"She's such a sweet girl. It's too bad she's a little slow. Well, I'll see y'all later," said Janice as she got into her car.

A massive, grey cloud covered the sun, instantly chilling the air. "Looks like a storm is on the way. I guess Allie won't be riding Moon Doggie today." Seeing the quizzical look on her friends' faces, Cassie explained about Allison's new surfboard. "As Janice would say, I'll see y'all later."

Laura and Amy walked across the cul de sac under the threatening sky. "It's too bad the weather isn't cooperating. John and Jack wanted to go fishing today because they're leaving tomorrow. But there'll be time later. It's still amazes me that we own a house in Florida."

A crack of thunder sent the women running to their homes. "Laura, call me in the morning after you drop off John and Jack at the airport."

Amy walked through the silent house, and a heavy sensation filled her heart. *Now what? Why am I feeling so blocked about what's happening on the Island? My intuition is erratic, and it's difficult to focus. Maybe I'll try and get more information about Marilyn's situation.*

Nestling into Mr. Ferguson's recliner, Amy took several deep breaths and began to clear her mind of all chatter. After several minutes of meditation, she began to feel a shaking sensation as her astral body separated from her physical body, and this time 'she' instantly traveled to South Carolina. Arriving at Marilyn's house, she floated through the front door and immediately ascended the stairs. On the landing, the spirit of Violet Ashford, her chestnut hair flowing down her shoulders over her long, ivory chiffon dress, was peering out the window. Slowly, she turned as Amy approached.

"*I do not want that woman in my house.*" The words entered Amy's mind, but there seemed to be less anger in the ghost's voice.

"Did Marilyn invite you to the party?"

"*Yes, but I abhor the changes she's making to MY house.*"

"Violet, isn't there a way you can co-exist with the new owner? Marilyn is only trying to improve the house, and it appears that you're not ready to move into the Light."

"*Perhaps, but she is changing so many things. The color she chose for the kitchen is appalling. It has to be yellow. My favorite color is yellow, and she cannot paint it that awful green.*"

"What if I tell her to keep the same color, and she invites you to any other festivities she has in the house?"

"*Well, all right, for now.*"

With a blast of cold air, Violet disappeared. Amy expected to return to Hopeful Court, but instead her energy body traveled across town to the College of Charleston, one of the oldest universities in the country. Looking around the lovely campus, she saw two students in maroon-colored Cougar sweatshirts strolling across the historic section of the grounds. She followed them to a coffee shop near the school.

Amy was drawn to a small stage at the back of Carly's Coffee House where a handsome, young black man, with short-cropped hair, was playing an acoustic guitar and singing softly. He was wearing a navy blue T-shirt, jeans, and work boots. It took her a moment to understand that she was the only one who could see or hear him, and she realized he was a spirit. Amy could hear his melancholy song, *"Faith is in my heart, now and forever."* Slowly he raised his sorrowful eyes and stared directly at her. *"ASHLEY."* The word echoed in Amy's mind as she was instantly propelled into her physical body, which jolted backward in the Lazy Boy.

Wow! That was astounding. Who was that musician? Who is Ashley? I wonder if Faith will be able to help me understand why I was drawn to the College of Charleston, but I'm not sure how she'll react to being questioned. Yet I feel I need to talk to my friend about it.

CHAPTER 56

COUSINS

Laura drove John and Jack to the airport the following morning and hugged them for several minutes before they walked into the terminal. John was going to St. Louis, and Jack was flying to Seattle for the remainder of the Christmas break. She would miss her men and was glad that John would be returning for New Year's Eve. She couldn't imagine starting the year without her husband by her side. *Brave, I must be brave now that I'm on my own again. How long will we have to live with this anxiety? I pray the crimes*

are solved soon, and I don't get any more threatening phone calls. It's December 27th–the day that Conti's note said something was going to happen. What's next?

Driving over the Amelia River Bridge and through the town, Laura tried to imagine what else could possibly happen on this peaceful island. At every corner, she anticipated seeing black sedans filled with military-looking men armed to the hilt. Eventually, she took a deep breath and decided that whatever was going to happen was probably not going to take place in the city. And now it couldn't take place at Conti's house since it was a smoldering pile of rubble.

Laura felt compelled to drive into Old Town Fernandina Beach at the northwest end of the Island. She drove past Bosque Bello Cemetery and turned left at White Street. She parked near the Plaza San Carlos historical marker and stepped out of the car. Turning around, she thought she saw movement in the upper-most window in the house that was featured in the 1988 movie *The New Adventures of Pippi Longstocking*.

Is that a person or a ghost? Amy would probably be able to tell and even communicate with the spirit. Oh, yeah, I was supposed to call her this morning. My memory is not what it used to be. I'll talk to her when I get home.

An elderly African-American woman, dressed in a tailored navy suit and matching pillbox hat, walked up, and followed Laura's gaze. "You see her don't you? The lady in the window."

"I was trying to decide if it was a live person or one that had died but isn't resting in peace."

The woman chuckled, "Well, it could be either, don't you think? Someday soon, I may be the one haunting a house in the area. So many of our cousins have passed recently."

"Hi, I'm Laura Beck, and I recently moved to the Island part-time. I'm hoping to write a novel set on Amelia, and I'm interested in the history. So, you have a lot of family members living in Old Town—a lot of cousins?"

"Oh, no, the people born and bred in Old Town call each other 'cousin' whether we're black or white. There's a strong sense of community in this part of town. I'm Eloise Shelton."

"It's a pleasure to meet you, Eloise. If you're not too busy, could you tell me about the history of this area?"

Eloise told the story of the Native Americans who lived on this land for over 3000 years. Her tales of the French, Spanish, and British who occupied the area followed. She described how the Embargo of 1807 closed the US ports to the trade of European luxury goods and slaves from Africa. But since Florida was still under Spanish control, Amelia Island became a haven for pirates and smugglers, who transported contraband and slaves into Georgia across the St. Mary's River.

Her next story was about David Levy Yulee, one of the first senators from Florida who championed Florida's entrance into the Union then sided with the Confederates during the Civil War. Yulee was responsible for convincing the townspeople of Fernandina, in the early 1850s, to relocate their town a mile south so his new railroad would not have to cross the salt marshes at the edge of town. The original town became Old Town Fernandina.

"There were a lot of bad things happening when the pirates came. But that was a very long time ago. It's remarkable that several violent events have occurred in the past month. What's happening to the tranquility of this Island?" asked Eloise.

Laura wasn't certain how to respond. *Should I tell her how I'm involved?* "My husband and I found Mr. Conti's body on the beach Thanksgiving night, and I've been drawn into the case for other reasons as well."

"Oh my Lord, sorry I mentioned it."

"Don't worry about it. I feel I have a connection with the case, and my three neighbors and I have been working with the police. But it's unsettling sometimes, especially when my husband isn't here—like now."

"I believe in destiny," said Eloise. "Didn't you say you were a writer? Perhaps you're involved with the crimes because you're meant to write about the murder once it's solved."

Laura laughed. "I'm having a hard time wrapping my mind around the notion that I'm any kind of writer. Well, maybe after I finish my novel, I can think about writing a non-fiction based on the events this past month. I certainly hope the end is near and the police and FBI bring everyone involved to justice."

Eloise placed her arthritic hand on Laura's arm. "Good luck, my dear. I'll look forward to reading your books—both of them." Slowly, she walked toward Lady's Street, which once housed dozens of brothels frequented by the sailors in the heyday of Fernandina. Calling to Laura over her shoulder, Eloise said, "It wasn't a coincidence that we met today."

Was she reading my mind? I was just thinking that it's a coincidence or synchronicity that I decided to come to Old Town. What will happen next on this strange journey that has become my life? Laura thought as she drove toward Main Beach at the east end of Atlantic Avenue. She parked beside the shorefront restaurant and retrieved her notebook and a book about the history of the Island. She sent a text to Amy saying she'd be home in an hour.

Planting herself on a bench, Laura leafed through the book looking for inspiration for her novel. A manuscript about the Conti murder and aftermath would have to wait until the crimes were solved, and even then such a book might expose Cassie's involvement. Laura wasn't certain she wanted to do that to her friend.

CHAPTER 57

DANNY B

While Laura was learning about the history of Old Town from Eloise, Amy and Faith were sitting in the Proctors' kitchen. They listened as Miles and Austin teased each other while they packed their bags for the trip back to Atlanta.

"Today's the day something is supposed to happen, according to Conti's note," Amy said. "And I still have no idea what it is. I left a message for Detective Davis, but she hasn't returned my call."

"I'm glad the boys are driving back to Buckhead this morning. If something terrible is going to occur, I don't want them here. I even thought about leaving with them, but in the end decided not to. I told them about the note, but I don't want them to needlessly worry."

"I understand your concern and the fine line between informing our loved ones about possible danger and creating unnecessary panic."

"Okay, Mom, we're ready to go," said Miles as the boys came into the kitchen with their suitcases.

"Have a safe trip, my wonderful boys. And don't worry about me—Amy will be right next door if I need her."

Faith hugged and kissed her sons several times before they finally drove away in Miles' black VW Jetta. She watched until the car was out of sight, then joined Amy in the living room.

"I don't mean to upset you, Faith, but I need to tell you about my second journey to Charleston. I believe I'm having these experiences for a reason, and they're tied to you."

Faith slowly lowered herself on the sofa. "Go ahead, tell me what happened."

Amy explained about her second trip to Marilyn's house, her subsequent visit to the College of Charleston, and the coffee shop near the campus. "When the young musician mentioned Faith, I immediately thought of you. Do you have any idea about who this young man could be?"

"I promised my father I would never tell a living soul, but I suppose I should start the New Year with a clear conscience. If it's who I think it is, his name was Daniel Benjamin Washington, and everyone called him Danny B. He was a local boy who worked at the coffee house, and he was a remarkable singer and songwriter. I was sure he'd be famous someday. He had the most amazing voice—like velvet—and a smile that could melt your heart.

"I met him when I was a freshman, and we began dating in the fall of my sophomore year. I didn't tell my parents about him because he wasn't a college student and he was black. They wouldn't have approved."

"I can see why you were concerned," said Amy. "What happened to your relationship?"

"Everything was wonderful until the weekend before my final exams the next spring. Unfortunately, Danny and I bumped into my great uncle. He was an influential businessman in Charleston. I'll never forget the look on Uncle Lawrence's face when he saw us holding hands as we walked down Broad Street. After the semester ended, I returned to Atlanta and called Danny whenever I could. Then one day he didn't answer his phone, and when I called his cousin to find out where he was, no one knew. Danny had disappeared off the face of the earth."

Amy sat quietly listening to her friend's story, knowing full well that it wasn't going to have a happy ending.

"I drove to Charleston shortly after he vanished. Sorry I lied to you about never returning to the city. I contacted the police, but they said they knew nothing of Danny's whereabouts and told me that he'd probably gotten into trouble and skipped town. Danny was an only child, and his parents had died several years earlier. He'd been living with his aunt and cousin, but they had no idea what happened to him.

"One night, he simply didn't return home or show up for work the next day. It was unlike him not to tell his cousin where he was going. I was devastated but didn't believe he had run away like the police said. I knew he wouldn't leave without telling me. He was in love with me, and I was falling in love with him too."

"Did you ever find out what happened to him?"

Faith was silent for a long while, and Amy could see the slight shaking of her friend's hands. "It was Thanksgiving, several years after I left Charleston and the second year of Charles' and my marriage. My Uncle Lawrence was visiting for the weekend, and one night I overheard him arguing with my father in the library. Father was shouting about the terrible mistake, and Uncle Lawrence insisted that what happened to the boy was an accident. My uncle's henchmen were only supposed to frighten him."

"Oh my gosh, Faith. Did your uncle admit to having Danny killed?"

"Not in so many words, but I knew what they were talking about. My father said he hadn't asked his uncle to do anything violent—he was just supposed to keep an eye on me. I don't believe my dad had anything to do with Danny's death. My uncle was prejudiced and took matters into his own hands after he saw Danny and me together."

"Wow, no wonder Danny's spirit is still in Charleston. But who is Ashley?"

"I have no idea. I don't remember anyone by that name in college. Let me think about it."

"Did you ever confront your uncle?"

"I never had the chance. He died of a massive heart attack the following year. And there was no point in pursuing Danny's killers and damaging the family name. I swore to my father that I wouldn't talk about it to anyone, and until now I never did. Even Charles didn't know why I was an emotional mess during that time."

"Keeping secrets is harmful to the spirit," said Amy. "I'm glad you've let me share your burden. That's what friends are for. Look how much harm Cassie's secrets caused her and Laura and probably everyone else in her life."

"It's like Danny has forced me to reveal our relationship. Do you think he knows that Charles has crossed over and I'm alone?"

"I'm not sure, because he seems stuck in that coffee house. Maybe my visit to Charleston opened a portal because of our close connection. Could what happened to Danny give us a clue about Conti's murder?"

"I don't see any similarities, but one never knows."

They sat quietly for several minutes. "Now that the boys are gone, I have too much time on my hands," Faith continued. "Do you want to take a drive around the Island to see if we can notice anything suspicious? What if we could stop whatever is supposed to happen today?"

"That idea crossed my mind too, Faith. Let's start with lunch then meet up with Laura later."

CHAPTER 58

SURF'S UP

Cassie lay in bed on the morning of December 27th and listened to Allison and Clara giggling in the next room. *The most beautiful sound in the world is the laughter of children—even those who will be young adults soon. It makes me realize how important friends are to our well-being. I've walled myself off from other people way too much. Like Allie, I need to embrace the people I can trust.*

With her robe tightly wrapped around her, Cassie stood outside her daughter's bedroom door and listened to the girls' light-hearted conversation. She wasn't expecting the change of subject matter.

"Did you know your mom had an abortion when she was a teen? That was all anyone at school could talk about after the YouTube video of Pastor Stanton went viral. Someone who was in the chapel and knew her name posted it on Facebook, talking about the video."

"No, I didn't know about her relationship with Stanton, and I didn't want to see the video even though my mom wasn't in it. What a horrible thing he made her do when she was still so young. Only a year older than we are now."

"I'm so not ready to have sex or even think about what I'd do if I got pregnant."

"Me neither," said Allie. "I can wait."

"Too bad your mom's getting another divorce. Is this her second?"

"No, her third," Allie said. "But in some ways, I'm glad I don't have to deal with my stepfather anymore. He could be such a jerk sometimes and had a wicked temper."

"What happened this time?"

Cassie drew in her breath as she listened for Allie's reply. A long silence followed.

"She slept with another guy. He was murdered, and it all came out. He lived in a huge house on the beach, and people say he was a criminal. Please don't tell anyone at school."

"Your secret's safe with me," said Clara. "My dad had an affair a few years ago, and it almost ripped our family apart. My parents are getting along okay now, but there's a piece of me that can't trust my dad again. I'm always looking to catch him in a lie. I didn't even tell you about it, and you're my best friend."

"Clara, I knew something was up, but I didn't want to hurt your feelings so I didn't ask. I kinda guessed something like that was going on because you seemed so mad at your dad all the time."

"Yeah, I wanted to tell you, but I promised my mom I wouldn't say anything. She was humiliated because he was sleeping with another mom from my dance class."

"How did your mom find out about it?"

"A neighbor saw my dad and the woman at a hotel on Cape Cod when he was supposed to be at a conference in New York."

"Why do grownups do such stupid things?"

Not wanting to eavesdrop any longer, Cassie went to her bathroom and turned on the shower. The running water would wash away the tears that were streaming down her face. *Will Allison ever completely trust me again? Have I done irreparable harm to my child? What kind of an example have I set?*

After drying her hair, Cassie calmed herself and started breakfast. *Honesty is what I should strive for with Allie from now on. And not make any more stupid mistakes.*

The aroma of cooking bacon brought the girls rushing into the kitchen. "Are we having pancakes?" asked Allie.

"Of course, love. Pancakes, scrambled eggs, and bacon. I know they're Clara's favorites too. It looks like a warm day. Do you want to take Moon Doggie to the beach later?"

"Can we get a board for Clara?"

"Of course. We can rent one at the store on Sadler Road. Let's pack a lunch and spend the day by the ocean. Tomorrow we can go shopping at St. John's Town Center and stop at the Huguenot Park and take a photo of the sign for your project." *And I want to keep Allison's mind off the fact that this is the day Eduardo wrote on the slip of paper that something would happen. If we stay at the beach all day, hopefully we'll avoid any danger.*

Allison slid her surfboard into the back of Cassie's SUV and threw the wetsuit in beside it. After renting a board and wetsuit for Clara, they drove to the north end of Amelia Island where most of the surfers hung out. Parking on the sand-covered road, the girls carried their boards across the boardwalk over the dunes to the ocean. Several surfers were already riding the large waves that were rolling to the shore. In the distance was the half-mile fishing pier located in the Fort Clinch State Park.

Allie and Clara slipped on the wetsuits as two boys, with long, damp hair and their wetsuits half off, sauntered over and started a conversation with the girls. Allison obviously knew the boys from school and introduced Clara. Cassie watched as the teens did the equivalent of a mating dance, and she realized that human nature is consistent over time. She thought back to her first year of high school and how she'd introduced Laura to her male classmates.

Cassie set up her chair and opened the book Allison had given her for Christmas. It was a political thriller set in Washington, DC, and Boston. She still loved the experience of opening a hardcover book for the first time and starting a journey with the author. She had a tablet where she often downloaded novels, but it couldn't replace the feel of a book in her hands and the smell of new paper.

Allison and Clara paddled their boards behind the boys, who gave them surfing instructions. One boy, with sandy blond hair continually looked at Allison in a way that made Cassie sure he was interested in her daughter. After several tries kneeling, both girls managed to stand on the boards for several seconds before tumbling into the water. Cassie frequently looked up from her book to make certain there were no dark fins near the surfers.

Maybe I didn't need to buy surfing lessons for Allie. It looks like these young men will teach her and Clara the basics. I'm glad I brought extra food for the picnic. They'll all be hungry after a morning of surfing.

CHAPTER 59

BOOK COVER

"**M**om, I have a surprise for you. I forwarded an email that you have to see." Jack said as Laura answered her cell phone after lunch. She rushed into the living room and turned on her computer. With her less than perfect vision, it was much easier to read things on the larger screen rather than on her cell phone.

"Okay, Jack. Just a minute, the connection is slow today. Oh my God, where did this come from?" Laura asked as she saw a beautiful photo of Kate standing by the ocean with the words 'Dreams of Amelia, A Novel; Laura Beck' on the picture.

"I told my friend, Travis, about your novel, and he said he had the perfect picture for the cover. He took the photo last year when we went to Hilton Head for spring break. He's a computer wiz and really creative. What do you think?"

"It's amazing! It makes me believe this novel can actually exist. Thank Travis and tell him I'll pay him for his work. I can't get over how beautiful Kate looks and how perfect the cover design is for the book. Incredible!"

"You can do it, Mom, I know you can write a bestseller. And it will make a great movie someday. Did you see how the photo wrapped around the spine and back?"

"Yes, it's perfect. I'm glad I have remarkable children with talented friends. Thanks so much, Jack. I know I'll turn my dream into a reality. Say hello to Kate and her family for me."

Laura stared at the mock-up of her book cover for 10 minutes trying to imagine holding the published novel in her hands at The Left Bank indie bookstore in St. Louis. *So many people talk about wanting to write a book, but how many actually complete a manuscript and have it published? I know I have a great love story to tell and an important message, but can I tell it well enough? Will anyone other than my family and friends buy the book?*

I've gone from 'what am I going to do with my life?' to 'how am I going to manifest my vision?' What incredible progress in such a short time. I have a plan for the future for the first time in years.

An incoming text message interrupted her thoughts. 'Can you meet Faith and me at the harbor in half an hour?' Laura texted, 'See you then, Amy.'

Driving into town, Laura turned left on Ash Street around the massive live oak in the middle of the road. Kate Bailey's Tree, as the locals called it, was over a hundred years old in the late 1800s, when the town decided to pave the road and cut down the tree that obstructed the way. Legend has it that the house next to tree was owned by Effingham and Kate Bailey, and the young woman was so passionate about saving the beautiful oak that she armed herself with a shotgun and threatened to shoot anyone who tried to chop it down. She was successful, since the tree was still standing in the 21st century.

Sometimes one person can make a difference. Maybe I can make a difference too.

Laura parked in the south lot near the wharf and saw her friends standing outside Brett's Restaurant. "We've decided to treat ourselves to an afternoon cocktail," Faith said opening the door for the ladies. "Our menfolk have departed for the time being, and we need to take care of each other. And what we need today is to bond over a martini."

Lemon drop martinis were ordered, and the ladies took the drinks to the outside patio where the afternoon sun was warm and welcoming. "Look, there's a ship in the Fernandina port, but it's not a ro-ro," said Laura. "I drove around the Island this morning and even went to Old Town. I didn't see anything suspicious. Have the police been in touch with you today, Amy? This is D-day."

"Not a word. Faith and I did our own tour before we drove here. We went to the gated entrance of the Fernandina port, and there was nothing unusual. My intuition tells me that all is quiet here today."

"Let's pray that whatever Conti was involved in has moved elsewhere. We need our peaceful Island to return to normal," Faith said.

"Oh, wow. I forgot to tell you. A friend of Jack's designed a book cover for me. Here, I'll show you on my phone."

"That's beautiful, Laura. He did a wonderful mock-up. Is that Kate in the photo?" Faith asked.

"Yes, Jack and a group of his friends were on vacation in Hilton Head last year, and the photo was taken one evening before they went out for dinner. Kate loves vintage clothing, and she'd found the dress in an antique store in Seattle. Doesn't she look great?"

"It's wonderful. How can your novel not be a success with such a great book cover? How's the writing going?" said Amy.

"I started reading the book you gave me about reincarnation, and it's really inspired me. The author describes Cayce's readings for young people that provides advice for their careers. He talked about tapping into the knowledge and skills that were developed in a past life. Now during my meditations, I try and connect with the part of my soul that lived a lifetime as a writer."

"That's extraordinary," Faith added. "So many of the things you and Amy talk about are foreign to me. Can you actually use the abilities from one lifetime in another?"

"I believe that child prodigies do exactly that. The young singer, Jackie Evanco, comes to mind. At ten years old, she had the voice of a world-class opera singer. She honed her skills in past lives and chose parents who would give her the physical abilities to realize them."

"I agree," said Amy. "There are so many examples of brilliant, talented children who achieve amazing things at a young age. Many of the children born today also have highly developed psychic skills and are called Crystalline or Rainbow Children. They're here to lead the world to a better place. I'm glad the book helped."

"It's interesting that the Cayce book's author, Noel Langley, was a cowriter of the screenplay for *The Wizard of Oz*. I Googled him, and he also wrote children's books. His most famous one was a story about Aladdin's son. Didn't you find the book and the Aladdin-style lamp on the same day?" asked Laura.

"Yes, and that's synchronicity at work," answered Amy. "It's the belief that we're all connected on an energetic level, and we can learn to access the power of the universe to help us in our lives."

"One passage in Langley's book stuck in my mind. He describes how when we take responsibility for choosing our lives, 'it destroys the convenient sugar-coated alibi that you are a victim of an angry, vengeful and palpably half-witted Jehovah, who controls you with invisible strings from the flies of a most naively ill-conceived marionette-master's Hereafter.' He wrote what I've always believed, that it's our souls who have chosen when and where to be born—and when to leave. We aren't victims of God's will."

"It's funny that you and I were just talking about the same thing on our trip to Jekyll Island. It's like confirmation that we're on the right track and you should talk about these concepts in your book," said Amy.

The women sipped their martinis and watched a sailboat glide past the dock. The afternoon sun danced on the water, and the serene landscape had a calming effect.

"It truly feels like whatever was supposed to happen today has moved someplace else," said Laura. "I feel like I can relax for the first time since Thanksgiving."

"Andy, wait up," a tiny girl called as she ran after a tow-headed little boy on the wooden dock beside the restaurant.

"Andrew, Ashley, get back here," said a harried mother as she jogged after her children.

"Memories of chasing after my babes," said Laura, "and now I'm looking forward to grandchildren someday."

The women watched the young mother swoop the children into her arms as they giggled with delight. "Time to go, Daddy's waiting for us."

"Faith, did you figure out who Ashley is?" asked Amy, her memory triggered by the little girl's name.

Taking another sip of her drink, Faith made a decision. "I've come to the conclusion that secrets are not healthy for the heart or the soul. Laura, I want to tell you about a part of my past that I've kept hidden for decades." Faith briefly recounted the events that led to Amy's encounter with Danny B's spirit in Carly's Coffee House. "But I don't remember anyone named Ashley."

"I'm glad you shared the story, Faith, and I understand why you'd want to protect your family. Charleston looks beautiful and is on my list of places to visit. Aren't there some interesting islands near the city?" asked Laura.

"Yes, if you go across the Cooper River, you'll reach Sullivan's Island and Isle of Palms. And James Island and Folly Island are in the opposite direction when you cross the Ashley River."

"Faith! That's it. Ashley isn't a person it's a river. That must be where they took Danny. Does that make sense?"

"Perfect sense. But what can I do at this point? The wild life would have claimed his body long ago."

"Maybe you should go to the river with flowers as a tribute. Honoring Danny's life may help his spirit move on. We can make plans to drive there soon."

"You are very wise, my friend. Let's plan on going soon, Amy. This may be the closure both Danny and I need."

"Closure and the revealing of secrets is always good for the soul," Amy said.

CHAPTER 60

HUGUENOT MEMORIAL PARK

"Let's go shopping, Mom," Allie said as she and Clara bounded into the kitchen. "Can we leave after breakfast?"

"Sounds good. Now what are you ladies in the mood for this morning? French toast?"

"French Huguenot toast since we're going to drive by the park today."

"You are very clever, Allison. We'll stop at the park on the way so you can take the photo you need for your project."

As she made breakfast, Cassie was thinking about her conversation with Laura the previous evening. She'd called to say that she would be able to go to the Becks' on New Year's Eve, but Allison and Clara would be spending the night at Madison's house. Laura talked about her uneventful tour of the Island, meeting Faith and Amy for a drink by the harbor, and their feeling that whatever was supposed to happen based on Conti's note was going to take place somewhere else or not at all.

Cassie wasn't as confident as her neighbors that the danger had moved elsewhere. She couldn't shake the feeling that the drama was not complete, and Cassie was glad she was taking the girls into Jacksonville today.

Driving south on Highway A1A and across the bridge to Big Talbot Island, Cassie enjoyed listening to the conversation in the back seat.

"Wasn't it great learning to surf yesterday?" Allison said to Clara. "Maybe we can go again later today when we get home from shopping."

"It was amazing, Allie. I can't believe you live in a place where you can surf all the time! And those guys were wicked cute."

"Look, Clara. There's a creek named after you—Simpson Creek."

"You're lucky you live here, Allie. It's so cool."

Cassie drove past the sign for Kayak Amelia and kept her eye out for the sign for the Huguenot Park on the east side of the road. She knew it was before the Mayport ferry, which took cars across the river to the continuation of A1A, but she was unsure of the exact location.

At the last second, Cassie saw the sign and slammed on the brakes as she made a quick turn into the entrance. The girls were tossed around in the backseat and squealed as they were thrown about.

"Nice driving, Mom. I'm glad we didn't smack our heads on the doors."

"Sorry about that. Are you two okay?"

"We're fine, Ms. Harcourt. You should be a stunt driver. That was awesome."

Cassie parked by the side of the road as Allie and Clara got out to take pictures of the Huguenot Memorial Park sign. After several photos using Cassie's camera, where each girl took turns posing, they hopped back into the car. As they were about to pull out into the southbound lane, a large transport truck carrying numerous vehicles drove past. Before Cassie was able to move, two black SUVs sped by.

Instinctively, Cassie followed the cars driving north instead of heading toward Jacksonville. She kept a safe distance but was still able to see the black cars as they crossed over the bridge on the Fort George River Inlet to

Little Talbot Island. The girls were reviewing the photos they'd just taken and didn't notice they were going in the wrong direction.

Before long, the first SUV sped around the transport truck as the passenger side window rolled down. A man's arm appeared holding a large gun. The barrel of the weapon was aimed at the driver. Cassie watched in horror and started to brake. The truck driver swerved to the side of the road and skidded to a stop on the grass-covered shoulder as the second SUV stopped behind him. Cassie slammed on her brakes and pulled off the road.

Armed men exited both cars. Dressed in black with ski masks covering their faces, two men jumped on the running boards of both sides of the cab and held guns to the driver's head. Four others began climbing the on the back of the transport truck toward the last vehicle that had been loaded.

"Girls, get down!"

With a quick look in the rearview mirror to make sure the road was clear, Cassie made a U-turn with squealing tires, throwing up grass and mud from the shoulder. She began driving away from the scene at 80 miles per hour. The girls were thrown around in the back seat, but neither one said a word. Before ducking their heads, they had seen enough of the action to know they were in a dangerous situation. Thirty seconds later, Cassie said with as much calm as she could muster, "Allie, get out your phone and dial 911, then hand the phone to me."

Cassie relayed to the police dispatcher what she had witnessed, but before she could finish, wailing sirens came toward them, and half a dozen police and unmarked vehicles went speeding past. The dispatcher told her to continue to move away from the area, that the police had been notified. Cassandra pulled over to the side of the road and turned off the engine. Her adrenaline was still rushing through her veins, and her hands were shaking as she lowered her head to the steering wheel.

"Mom, Mom. Are you okay? What was that? Who were those guys with the guns?"

"I don't know, I . . ."

"They wanted something on that truck didn't they?"

"I'm not sure, Allie."

"They didn't shoot the driver. They just wanted him to stop. Then they climbed toward the ambulance that was strapped on the back of the truck."

CHAPTER 61

RESOLVE TO DISSOLVE

" The police have everything under control. Do you want to go home or go shopping?"

Allie and Clara were busy tweeting about what had just occurred and said together, "Shopping."

"That was crazy," Clara said. "It was just like being in a movie."

"Scary but definitely cool," Allison answered.

Cassie turned on the engine and drove south over the huge expansion bridge on Highway 295 to the St. John's Town Center exit. Her heart rate and blood pressure returned to normal as she parked and followed the girls into several upscale stores. Her mind was focused on making sense of what she had witnessed and how the action fit into what she knew about Eduardo's activities.

While the girls wandered around the Forever 21 store, Cassie called Laura and described everything that had happened. "Please call Amy and see if she can get in touch with Detective Davis and find out what went on today. It would be great if this whole chapter was closed."

"How are the girls?"

"They seem fine. Shopping has taken their minds off the situation. I pray this is the end of it."

"Me too," said Laura. "I'll ask Amy if someone from the police department can meet with all of us at one time. We need to have this mystery solved. Talk to you later."

Cassie followed the girls around several other stores while trying to figure things out. *Allison is right that those men were interested in the ambulance. Is that the medical connection Amy told us about? But what does it have to do with ammunition? And where does Eduardo fit in all this?*

* * *

Laura called Faith to tell her of Cassie's frightening experience. Then she called Amy and asked if she would contact the Fernandina Beach police department. Arrangements were made for the women to go the station on Monday afternoon when the interviews with the suspects would be complete.

The drive to the police station on Monday seemed to take longer than usual, and the four women were quiet as Laura turned down Lime Street. Entering the station, they were greeted by Detective Davis, who ushered them into a conference room. Bottled water was available on the table, and each of them declined the offer of coffee.

"First of all, I'd like to thank you for your help. The information you provided was invaluable. Now, I'm sure you have many questions, so let me bring you up to date," said the detective.

"Thank you," said Amy. "We're anxious to have this situation over with."

"The men who attacked the truck driver were European mercenaries hired by a company based in Atlanta called Southern Sentinel Security."

Amy gasped. "That's Doug's company!"

"Yes, Ms. Temple. Your husband's firm attempted to intercept a vehicle that was carrying contraband from the port on Blount Island, in Jacksonville, to the Fernandina port. From there the vehicle was to be shipped to Bermuda. The senior executives of the Southern Sentinel have been questioned by the FBI."

"What contraband?" asked Laura.

"It's state-of-the-art ammunition that dissolves after hitting a target. The outer layers of the bullets dissolve so the weapon used can't be traced."

"Resolve to dissolve," said Faith.

"Was it hidden in an ambulance?" Cassie added.

"Yes. The ambulance was loaded onto a vehicle transport ship in Miami, and we're still investigating how that was allowed to happen. The ambulance arrived at the port on Blount Island on December 27th—the date that was indicated in Mr. Conti's note. The last set of numbers and letters identified the ship, and the middle numbers were license plate of the ambulance."

"When did you figure this out?"

"We were following the clues you provided about the date and type of ship when a concerned citizen gave us a solid lead. The owner of Ciao Italian Bistro overheard patrons in his restaurant speaking French. The owner is Italian, but he was raised in Nice, France, and is fluent in the language. He heard the men talking about forcing a truck off the road on Little Talbot Island on its journey from Jacksonville to Fernandina."

"We were at the restaurant that night too, and I overheard them speaking French. They said something about sisters," added Laura.

"That was the information we needed. Sisters Creek is just north of the Blount Island port, and the FBI had agents staked out there for several days. And on Friday it paid off, when two SUVs arrived and waited for the truck to pass by. The agents let them commandeer the truck before moving in. Local and port authorities aided the FBI, converged on the scene from the north and south."

"And I got myself caught in the middle of it," said Cassie.

"You were fortunate, Ms. Harcourt, that you and your daughter weren't hurt. What made you decide to follow the SUVs?"

"A nose for trouble, I guess. Or I've been hanging around Amy and Laura too much, and my intuition kicked in. But how did Eduardo fit into the picture?"

"Mr. Conti purchased the ammunition from a contact in Miami and initially was planning on selling it to the private security company, Southern Sentinel. He was offered a higher price from a military security company and changed his plans. The first company pushed back, and that's what led the car bomb at Mr. Conti's funeral. It was a warning to back off. This was more than a single deal—it was a test case for the movement of contraband from the US to Bermuda and then on boats to other ports."

"Have you arrested anyone from Southern Sentinel?" Amy asked.

"We're letting the FBI handle that part of the case, so I'm not sure if Mr. Masterson will be indicted or not."

"That's why I couldn't get a clear picture of what was going on—because Doug's company was involved. I knew there had to be a good reason," Amy continued. "But who killed Conti and why? And who set his house on fire?"

They were the questions on everyone's mind. The detective took a deep breath, stretched her arms, and linked her fingers behind her head. "That we still don't know. We've interviewed everyone involved in the ammunition deal, and no one is admitting to the crimes. According to the neighbor, Ricky Thompson, the man Mr. Conti argued with the night of his murder was someone he probably knew. We're still investigating the mercenaries and Conti's other acquaintances."

"But how did Doug and Conti get involved in the business deal in the first place?" Amy asked.

Detective Davis slowly put down her arms and placed her hands on the table. She looked around the room until her eyes rested on Faith. "That's where Mr. Proctor comes into the picture."

CHAPTER 62

CONNECTIONS

Faith gasped and turned white as a ghost. "Oh my gosh! How on earth could Charles be a part of this?"

"We learned from Mr. Masterson that he and Mr. Proctor met Conti when they were paired up while playing golf on an Amelia Island course last year."

"Faith, do you remember when they came to Amelia for a long weekend in the fall? You were busy with your charity work, and I was helping with the missing child case, so the guys came alone."

"Yes, but how did they end up becoming involved with Mr. Conti?"

"Mr. Conti was looking for a buyer for his ammunition and a company that would have use for his other commodities. Smuggling firearms was to be his next venture. He'd heard of Southern Sentinel Security and suggested a deal when he met Mr. Masterson but hadn't figured out a workable plan at that point. When he mentioned that shipping the contraband to Bermuda from the Fernandina port was an option, Mr. Proctor said he had an acquaintance in Bermuda that might be interested in participating."

"But why would Charles do such a thing?"

"We believe it was for the money, Mrs. Proctor. We understand the company he worked for has been floundering for years, and he may have seen this as a way to secure additional income."

Faith lowered her head as tears pooled in her eyes.

"We think this was going to be an ongoing arrangement, but for some reason Mr. Conti double-crossed Southern Sentinel and decided to go with a private military company instead. Perhaps he thought he could do more business with them in the long term."

"Paolo Conti said something about a 'triple-cross.' Could Conti have betrayed the second company, and that's what got him killed?" Laura asked.

"The authorities in Bermuda are questioning the owner of the company that was to receive the ambulance. It appears that he double-crossed Southern Sentinel too and agreed to be the contact for the military company. But there isn't any evidence of an additional player. We've ruled out Conti's connections from New York and New Jersey."

"Does Jeremy Baxter have anything to do with all this? I had a feeling he didn't come to Faith's Christmas Eve party for the eggnog." Amy said. "And he told two different stories about where he was spending the holidays."

"Yes, Ivan Whitman was concerned that Mr. Proctor's car crash wasn't an accident. He recruited Mr. Baxter to speak to the Proctor boys to see if there was any discussion about what happened to their father—whether it was quietly being investigated as a homicide or suicide."

"He used my boys!" Faith cried. "How dare he."

"But why would Charles be in danger?" asked Cassie.

"Mr. Proctor contacted the FBI the week before he passed away, but the scheduled meeting never took place. We're surmising that he was going to reveal the plan. He may have regretted his involvement with illegal activities."

"How could I not have known Doug was involved with this?" said Amy. "I have to be the world's worst psychic."

Laura reached across the table and took Amy's hand. "This is not your fault. Your marriage was breaking up, and you said yourself that Doug's a chameleon. You were just too close to the situation for your intuition to be on point."

"But the police said it was an accident. Charles was speeding and not wearing his seatbelt."

"We agree, Mrs. Proctor. The Atlanta police found no evidence of foul play or deliberate action on your husband's part. From what we can tell, he was speeding and hydroplaned on the wet road. It was an unfortunate accident. But I guess Southern Sentinel was concerned. Even though they were technically out of the deal, they planned to 'rescue' the vehicle before it was shipped out of the country."

Silence enveloped the room as the women tried to digest all they had been told. The serious actions of their loved ones weighed heavily on Faith and Amy.

"But who killed Eduardo Conti?" Laura asked. "We still don't know."

"It's still under investigation," said Davis.

"My gut tells me that the person is close by, and I'm still afraid," said Cassie.

"Speaking of intuition, is there any connection to Native Americans in this situation?" Laura asked the detective. "I had the feeling that all the signs and symbols about Indians I've encountered were tied to Conti and that John and I found his body for a reason."

"If there's a link, I'm not aware of it," said Davis. "But I'll let you know if we uncover anything new. I have another meeting scheduled. Thank you all for your help. I'll be in touch."

"I'm still in shock," Faith said as they exited the police station. "Not in my wildest imagination did I think my husband would be involved in something illegal."

"Let's go home," Amy said. "We all need time to work through what we just heard."

CHAPTER 63

THE LULLABY

L aura awoke to the sound of rain on Tuesday morning after a restless night. She was glad that the mystery of the music box was solved, but she had a haunting suspicion that all was not right with the world. She'd called John the night before and recounted what the police had told them.

"Thank God it's over," John had said. "Even though they're not confessing, it was probably one of those mercenary guys that killed Conti and set his house on fire. That's the only thing that makes sense."

"I hope you're right and this case is over," Laura replied. "Why do I drive myself crazy worrying about things that might not happen? It's time to let it go and move forward. I'm glad you're coming here tomorrow, John."

"Me too. Talk to you later."

Grateful that she'd gone grocery shopping on Monday before they went to the police station, Laura began preparing for the New Year's Eve party the next day. Along with her famous coconut shrimp and chili, she was making an Oreo cheesecake with a cookie crust. She was taking the cake out of the oven and jumped when her cell phone sitting on the kitchen table rang.

"How are you today, Laura?" Cassie asked.

"A little tired and still in shock over everything that's happened."

"I am too. The whole thing is so unbelievable, and I regret ever getting involved with Eduardo. I think I'm through with men for a very long time."

"There are still some good guys out there. Look at Amy—she seems to have found a good one in an antique store."

"The girls and I are going to a movie this afternoon, and I was wondering if you'd like Shirley to come to your house instead of mine since you're having the party tomorrow."

"That's a great idea. I don't mind cooking, but cleaning is definitely not on my list of fun things to do."

"Perfect. I'll call her and tell her to go to your place around 2:00. Talk to you later."

Serving dishes were arranged on the dining room table, labeled with the appetizer or dessert they were to hold. Laura, satisfied that she was in good shape for the party, decided to work on her novel. A blank page on her computer was all she had after 30 minutes, and she got up to roam around the house looking for inspiration. The doorbell interrupted her unsuccessful search for creative ideas.

"Shirley, come in. I'm glad you could come today. You can start in the kitchen. It really needs a good cleaning with all the cooking and baking for the holidays."

"Okay, Mrs. Beck. I'll get right to it."

There's something different about Shirley. She still has her beautiful, long braid, so it's not her hairstyle that's changed. Laura went back to her computer and clicked onto her Facebook page instead of going back to her novel. Turning to local news site online, she read an article about the hijacked transport truck on A1A that stated a source in the Fernandina Police Department was confident that the men they arrested were also responsible for the murder of Mr. Conti.

If that's true, then why do I feel they're mistaken? I have no proof anyone else was involved and yet . . .

After returning several emails, Laura shut down her computer and wandered down the hall toward her bedroom. She could hear Shirley humming in the master bathroom. An idea began to swirl in Laura's mind as she listened to the song that Shirley was humming—*Rock-a-bye Baby*. Shirley walked into to the bedroom, and it was obvious to Laura that the young woman's face and figure were fuller. Shirley was pregnant.

Laura stared for a long moment.

"Mrs. Beck, are you okay?"

"Oh, ah, yes Shirley, I'm fine. Um, there are Christmas cookies in the Santa jar when you're finished. You can take some home with you."

"Thanks, Mrs. Beck. I'll take some for my brother too, if that's okay."

Laura walked into the kitchen, overpowered by her thoughts about Shirley. *There's no doubt in my mind that she's pregnant, but who could the father be? Ronnie doesn't seem to let her out of his sight. Will the baby have dark hair like her mother?* Looking around the room Laura's eyes fell on the dream-catcher hanging on the wall. *Oh my God! The Gordons are Native American. Shirley's long braid should have made me think of that.* Just then the doorbell rang. Ronnie Gordon was standing under the porch light with a black hoodie pulled over his head to protect him from the rain.

"Mrs. Beck, is Shirley done?"

Laura sucked in her breath and stared at the young man. "Uh, yes, she'll be right here." Their eyes locked for a long moment. Panic washed over Laura like a tidal wave as she saw a dark energy cross his face. Quickly she spun around and walked back into the kitchen. Placing her hands on the counter for support, Laura's heart pounded, and her breathing became labored. Finally, she composed herself and went to the pantry for a storage bag for the cookies. After several deep breaths, she handed them to Shirley along with a check.

Shirley slipped into her coat and opened the front door. "See you next time, and Happy New Year."

Laura avoided looking at Ronnie as she locked the door behind the Gordons. Fear raced through every cell in her body. She plugged in the Christmas tree lights to chase away the dread and poured a glass of pinot noir to calm her nerves. She called John, but his phone went to voicemail. She grabbed a blanket and curled up on the sofa.

Does Ronnie suspect that I know about the baby and who the father might be? Is that why he looked at me that way? Was it him who was snooping around Betsy's house on Christmas morning? His hoodie looked just like the one I saw. And what could he have been looking for?

I don't have any proof that Shirley is pregnant or that Conti may be the father, but should I call the detective with my suspicions? I don't want to accuse anyone without some proof. I need to talk to the ladies first, so I'll wait until tomorrow.

A short time later, John sent a text saying he was having dinner with coworkers and wanted to know if Laura needed him to call. She texted that she was fine and would see him tomorrow. She checked the windows and doors to make certain they were locked and set the alarm. Laura went to bed at midnight after watching a *Castle* marathon on TV.

CHAPTER 64

WAKE UP!

Silence. Laura awoke with a start. Something had interrupted her sleep, but now there was only silence. She looked at the clock on her nightstand, but it was dark. Reaching for the lamp, she heard a sound in the hallway. She tried to turn on the lamp, but the click of the switch still left her in the dark. She reached for her phone cord, but it was empty—she'd left her phone on the coffee table in the family room. Slowly she opened the nightstand drawer.

Her eyes adjusted to the darkness, and she gasped as a dark figure loomed in the bedroom doorway.

"Get out! I'm warning you—I have a gun," she yelled at the approaching intruder.

In a split second, the intruder was standing over her, and a gloved hand covered her mouth, forcing her head backward. A pillow came over her face muffling her scream. She continued to search the nightstand drawer until her hand gripped the canister. Working quickly to find the nozzle with her right hand, she tried to break free with the left. Gasping for air, she sprayed her assailant with the can of wasp killer, hoping her aim was true and the poisonous liquid hit his eyes.

An unearthly sound came from the man, and Laura knew she'd hit her mark.

* * *

"*Wake up! Wake up! Your friend is in danger.*"

Amy bolted upright in bed and looked around her empty bedroom in the dim glow from the nightlight.

"*She's in danger. Go, now.*"

Without hesitation, Amy jumped out of bed and slid into her slippers. Grabbing her coat she ran toward the front door. Unlocking the deadbolt she hesitated, then rushed to the kitchen drawer for the loaded handgun Doug had given her. Amy sprinted outside and looked around the deserted, darkened street. *Which friend is in danger, Grandma?* Amy's eyes darted from house to house, and she hoped that she was in time.

A man's scream came from Laura's house, and Amy rushed to the front door and shook the locked handle. Racing around the house to the lanai, she pushed opened the glass door.

"Laura, where are you?"

A muffled sound came from the master bedroom, and Amy ran through the pitch-black house, tripping over an end table then scrambling to her feet, as pain seared through her leg. Arriving at the bedroom door, she was knocked backward, and her head slammed against the wall. A dark figure moved past her and stumbled down the hall. Amy lunged forward and grabbed hold of the man's pant leg and held on with all her might.

The intruder fell forward and landed with a thud. With a quick motion, he used his free leg to kick Amy in the chest. She flew backward as Laura stumbled out of the bedroom, gasping for air. The man got up once more and started to run but toppled over the same end table that had tripped up Amy.

Laura rushed past Amy and once again sprayed the wasp killer in the man's eyes before he could get to his feet. Screaming in pain, the attacker released a torrent of profanity and wiped his eyes with the sleeve of his hoodie. Amy staggered forward and stood over the man writhing on the ground.

"You move one inch, and I'll shoot."

With the illumination from the cell phone she retrieved from the table, Laura ran into the kitchen and located a roll of duct tape. "Put your hands behind your back," Laura yelled as she wrapped the silver tape around the intruder's wrists while Amy held the gun to the back of Ronnie Gordon's head.

CHAPTER 65

THE VELVET PURSE

Wailing sirens filled the night air as police vehicles drove down Amelia Island Parkway and approached Hopeful Court. After dialing 911, Laura had called Faith and Cassie to inform them of the intruder in her home, so they wouldn't be frightened by sound of the sirens. The four women and two girls huddled beside the Beck's front door as Ronnie Gordon was handcuffed and placed in the back seat of police vehicle.

"Are you okay? Would you like to make a statement or wait until the morning?" asked Detective Davis as she looked at Laura and Amy.

"We're fine," answered Laura. "Let's get this over with. Wait, my power is off. He must have cut the lines."

"Let's go to my house," said Cassie. "I'll make some coffee and get the girls hot chocolate. None of us are going back to bed for a while."

"I'll be right there," said Laura. "I want to throw on some clothes and call John."

The aroma of coffee filled the kitchen, as all eyes turned to Laura as she entered and took a seat at the table.

"Mrs. Beck, do have any idea why Mr. Gordon attacked you? Detective Majors is questioning him at the station, but I want to get your side of the events."

"Shirley Gordon was at my house today to clean," Laura began. "I knew there was something different about her, and when I heard her humming a lullaby I realized that she was pregnant. Then it dawned on me, because of Shirley's long, black hair and her dark complexion, that one of the Gordons' parents was Native American. I related the signs and symbols about Indians I've been receiving to Conti's murder, and now there was a connection with the Gordons."

"I'm not following."

"I believe that Mr. Conti is the father of Shirley's baby. She worked for him as well."

Gasps came from Allie and Clara, who were perched on stools by the kitchen counter. Everyone was quiet as they integrated this idea.

"I had that message from Conti to 'protect his girls.' Maybe he was talking about Shirley and his unborn daughter," added Amy. "He was worried that Ronnie would do something to harm them."

"Did you suspect that Ronnie shot Eduardo?" Cassie asked the detective.

"We investigated him since he worked for Conti but without a motive, there was no reason to suspect him. Now there seems to be a very good motive, if indeed Shirley is pregnant with Conti's child. There must have been a confrontation on Thanksgiving night, perhaps about child support."

"Ms. Temple, how did you know your friend was in trouble?"

"My grandmother contacted me from the other side and forced me out of bed. Sometimes this psychic thing is a blessing. Laura did a pretty good job of defending herself without my help."

"Heavens, Laura, whatever made you think of wasp killer as a weapon?" asked Faith.

"Some TV show that I can't recall mentioned it because the spray can shoot twenty feet. It seemed like a good alternative to a 3baseball bat for protection."

"Very clever," said Cassie.

"Now it makes sense," Detective Davis said quietly. "Mrs. Beck, remember when I told you there was something strange found on Conti's body?"

"Yes, but you didn't tell me what it was."

"In his pants pocket, there was a small velvet purse, and inside were a white feather, an arrowhead, and a note. The handwriting on the note looked childlike, so we assumed it was from one of his son's when they were younger."

"What did the note say?"

"It said, 'We are a family forever and ever.' That's why we thought it was from one of his boys."

"And if the Gordons are Native American, Conti or someone else on the other side was trying to bring that fact into my consciousness," said Laura. "I couldn't see the forest for the trees."

"Do you think Betsy realized the same thing too, and Ronnie poisoned Millie to scare her?" asked Faith.

"That's very likely," said the detective. "I'll call her tomorrow and question her again in light of this new information."

"We still don't know why Eduardo and Ronnie were on the beach that night and if the shooting was intentional or accidental," Cassie said. "I guess we'll have to wait until he's interrogated. I pray this is the end of the Thanksgiving mystery."

"Thank you all for your help with this case. Mrs. Beck, my neighbor is an electrician, and I'll have him come first thing in the morning to repair your wires," said Detective Davis.

"That reminds me, I have all that food for New Year's Eve in my fridge and no electricity."

"We can have the party at my place tomorrow—actually later today. Let's go to Laura's and get the food for the celebration," added Cassie.

CHAPTER 66

HAPPY NEW YEAR

John's flight was on time, and Laura rushed into his arms when he exited security at Jacksonville airport. Unexpected tears flowed down her cheeks as she held on to her husband.

"Are you sure you're all right?"

"I'm fine, John. I'm so relieved that it's over. Let's go home, and I'll fill you in on the details about last night. I emailed Steven, Jenny, and Jack and told them of the break-in and the resolution of the case. They all sent texts with their love."

"Did the electrician start to repair the damage?"

"Yes, he should be finished by tomorrow. Faith has said we can stay with her for the night, and Cassie is having the party. And we get to meet Amy's new friend, Nate tonight. It's incredible that this whole affair is over, and we can start the New Year without any fear that a killer is loose on the Island."

"I wish I could move here full-time and work out of the house, but I don't think it's an option right now. We'll give it a year to see if we want to keep the house or it's just too much trouble and decide to sell."

"Becoming a splitter has changed our lives in so many ways. And I think you're right, we should give it a year before deciding what to do."

The Becks arrived at Faith's house just as she got off the phone with the police.

"Come in, come in. You're welcome to stay as long as you need. I made up the queen-size bed in Austin's room. Now, let me fill you in on what the police found out from Ronnie Gordon."

Faith explained, "Ronnie admitted shooting Conti but insisted he hadn't intended on firing the weapon. He'd stolen the gun from Conti's home on an earlier date and just meant to scare him when he confronted Eduardo about his sister. Shirley was convinced that she was going to marry Conti and they would be a family. That's when she wrote the note and gave him her most prized possession—the arrowhead her mother had given her as a little girl."

"Poor Shirley, she had no idea what kind of man he was," said Laura. "But what were Conti and Ronnie doing on the beach?"

"Mr. Gordon had replaced the privacy gate on the boardwalk, but Mr. Conti wasn't happy with the workmanship. It was there that Ronnie got up the nerve to confront Conti about Shirley and the fact that she expected to marry the father of her child. Because of his religion, Ronnie didn't want the child to be illegitimate. Eduardo laughed in his face."

"As I said, Ronnie told the police he'd brought the gun with him to intimidate Conti. But all the rage Ronnie felt toward the arrogant, rich newcomers to the Island he's dealt with over the years made him snap. He fired a single shot."

"How terrible. After losing his parents then having his sister violated, I can understand his rage. But what about the fire, and why was he snooping around Betsy's house on Christmas morning?" asked Laura.

"Shirley eventually told her brother about the velvet purse with the arrowhead and note. He worried it may lead the police to Shirley and decided to set the fire to get rid of the evidence. He didn't know Conti had it in his pocket that night."

"And the Biddle house?"

"Ronnie knew that Betsy figured out Shirley's secret and wanted to threaten her to keep quiet. He'd lost a Swiss army knife, and the last time he remembered having it was the day he poisoned Millie. He was searching the yard for the knife, thinking no one would see him on Christmas morning. He didn't count on you and Cassie observing him and connecting him to the crimes."

"Why didn't he bring the gun when he attacked Laura?" John asked.

"He told the police that he panicked and had thrown it off the fishing bridge on the south end of the Island into the Amelia River."

"Thank goodness he didn't have a gun and I was able to stop him from smothering me and Amy arrived in time!" said Laura. "Faith, do you know what's going to happen to Shirley?"

"Her aunt and uncle from Tampa are going to take her in and help raise the baby. And you were right about the Gordons' Native American heritage—their mother was a Seminole."

"The whole picture. Incredible."

***

The New Year's Eve party was well under way at Cassie's house. Nate Jones was introduced to everyone, and Amy was glowing with joy. When the doorbell rang, all the women stopped talking and stared at each other as Cassie went to open the door.

"Happy New Year, everyone," Janice Blackwell said as she walked into the family room. "I have a small gift for Laura and John. I always give my clients a little something on the last day of the year to thank them for choosing me as their agent. My cousin, Sheila, filled me in on what happened last night, so I drove into the neighborhood to see which house was lit up."

"Thank you, Janice. Do you have time for a cocktail?" asked Laura.

"No, my husband is waiting for me, but thanks anyway. And Betsy Biddle sends her regards. I spoke with her today, and she told me to wish the Fearsome Foursome a Happy New Year. I assume she means you four ladies."

"We really are fearsome, aren't we? And good sleuths," Amy said. "Cheers to us."

Cassie, Faith, Laura, John, Amy, and Nate raised their glasses. "Here's to a new year and a new beginning," Laura said as they clinked glasses.

"Oh by the way, did y'all hear about what happened in the Plantation?" Janice asked. "They found a woman floating in her swimming pool. Sheila said she was wearing a full-length satin gown, stilettos, and a black sable coat. The police think she was murdered!"

ABOUT THE AUTHOR

Originally from Toronto, Canada, Louise Jaques and her husband Mike divide their time between their homes in St. Louis, MO, and Amelia Island, FL. The part-time move to the Island inspired Louise to write her first novel, *Dreams of Amelia*. The journey and challenges of becoming a 50-something, first-time author are included in *Splitters, An Amelia Island Mystery*. This coming-of-middle-age story involves changing life circumstances, forging new friendships, and how past secrets can be revealed in unexpected ways—and a murder mystery!

Trained as a hypnotherapist, Louise has conducted past-life readings and regressions for more than 25 years and has incorporated her beliefs and experiences in her novels. She continues to expand her knowledge and is working on her next project, *What If I Loved You Before? Relationships and Soul Memories*.

Please visit her at elouisejaques.com, or email your questions or comments to elouisejaques@gmail.com.

COMING SOON

What If I Loved You Before?
Relationships and Soul Memories

May 14, 11:11 am. Three women experience dramatic past-life memories at the same moment.

Fifteen-year-old Olivia, slips into a light trance as her history teacher drones on about the Salem witch trials. Suddenly, Olivia's consciousness is in Salem, witnessing the horror of the historic trials.

Nearby, Olivia's aunt, Samantha, drifts into a fitful sleep as she sits in her daughter's hospital room after a sleepless night. She dreams she is a woman in ancient Greece, and her child is critically ill.

A thousand miles away, Lily—Samantha's friend and mentor—cradles her dying neighbor, Charlotte, in her arms and has a vision of a past life with Charlotte, in the 1860s.

The profound impact that past-life memories can have on the present, are incorporated in the fictional stories in Part One of the book. Part Two provides techniques for readers to access past memories of their souls, including relaxation exercises; a regression script which is recorded on an enclosed CD; suggested ways to integrate this information into their daily lives; and how to use the knowledge to improve important relationships in this lifetime.